# More Than A Kiss

Saxon Bennett and

Layce Gardner

Copyright © 2014 Saxon Bennett, Layce Gardner

All rights reserved.

ISBN:1496001745
ISBN-13:978-1496001740

This is a work of fiction.

Published by Square Pegs Ink

Editor: Kate Michael Gibson

Katemichaelgibson.com

# DEDICATION

For Emma

## ACKNOWLEDGMENTS

Thank you to Judy Baker and Kate Michael Gibson. Also, we wish to thank all our loyal readers. You guys are the best!

## Jordan Falls Out a Window

This story takes place in the lovely state of Oregon in a city of green, politically enlightened hipsters who love coffee, trees, and have the most amazing system of bike trails. I am describing Portland, of course. There's music and museums and a humongous bookstore and the ocean is nearby. It is April, the star of spring, the season of love. Very little of this has anything to do with the story, but I wanted to let you know that it is a good travel destination especially in the spring. The people in this story like Portland and liking where you live makes for happy people. However, the people in this story are not too happy because they are still looking for love and their errant search for love is the point of this tale.

*Disclaimer: No trees were harmed during the making of this book.*

**Meet Jordan March.** Jordan lived in the Piedmont Historic District in an old Victorian house four stories tall that had belonged to her grandmother. Jordan was an artist at heart. Unfortunately, her heart couldn't pay the electric bill or buy groceries, so she labored as a writer and illustrator of children's books. She had three children's books available to buy on Amazon. These books had mostly good reviews. However, her sales numbers did not reflect the mostly four and five-star ratings. Her books kept getting edged-out by her competitors, Jamie Leigh Curtis and John Lithgow. She had a tendency to get upset over that, so it was best not to mention it.

Jordan was a sapphist. She was also lonely. She hadn't had a girlfriend for a year. And she had talked herself into thinking she liked it that way. You see, Jordan didn't know she was lonely. She thought she was in a slump. Two slumps actually - a creative slump and a sexual slump. Jordan had a theory that stated that creative juices and sexual juices flowed from the same fount. If one dried up, so did the other. She hadn't written or drawn anything decent in 276 days. She hadn't been laid in 277 days. You can see how she came up with her theory.

Jordan's greatest fear was that she wasn't a great artist. That the bright flame of artistic passion she felt burning in her breast was actually heartburn from all the coffee she drank.

At the beginning of this story, Jordan was sitting in her attic studio, bent over her drawing easel with chalk smudged across her forehead and oil paint spattered on her arms. She was surrounded by paint cans, piles of raw lumber and stacks of drywall because her crumbling Victorian house was in the throes of remodeling.

Jordan was drawing and muttering to herself about Jamie Leigh Curtis and Activia commercials when a remote control car careened around a corner, balancing on only two wheels. It flipped over twice and miraculously ended up on all four wheels. It sped off again, hitting maximum speed within a few feet and popped a wheelie without slowing down. It hit a bump, skyrocketed in the air, performed a slow-motion somersault and landed upright in just enough time to crash into a wall.

Mr. Pip jumped to his feet and shrieked. He arched his back. His tail went rigid. He bared his fangs and hissed. The little remote control car backed up, slowly turned to face Mr. Pip, and accelerated. The cat screeched and leapt onto the drawing table, knocking over a glass of iced tea.

Jordan jumped to her feet as the tea splashed all over her lap. "Dammit!" She grabbed the nearest book, a dog-eared, yellowed paperback copy of *Moby Dick*, and threw it at the speeding car. She had not been reading *Moby Dick*. But she had tried to read it several times over the years. She had even gotten so far as the Chapter Ten, *A*

*Bosom Friend*, but couldn't make it any further. Not one to give up though, Jordan kept the book on her to-read pile right next to her easel on top of the copy of *Catch-22* that she couldn't get through either.

So, Jordan threw *Moby Dick* at the car but only succeeded in taking out another hunk of crumbling drywall. In the space of three seconds, the car had attacked the cat and the cat had attacked the tea and the tea had attacked Jordan's lap and now Jordan was attacking the car.

Jordan yelled, "Edison! I'm trying to work up here!"

Sorry!" Edison yelled to Jordan. "I'm trying to fix it!"

**Meet Edison Burnett.** Edison was short and rather plain looking, but not without her charms. As the French are wont to say, she had a certain *je ne sais quoi*. Edison tried to overshadow her plainness by dressing and behaving oddly. She was under the mistaken impression that the stranger she was, the more people would love her – like how people with lousy comic timing think that the louder they say the punch line the funnier it is.

Edison was Jordan's ex-lover and still-roommate. Actually, classifying her as an ex-lover would be overstating the case. Edison and Jordan had only had sex once and Jordan didn't remember much about it as they had spent the evening sampling what was left in her grandmother's abundant wine cellar. Despite the wine and the drunken sex, Jordan and Edison remained best friends.

At this point in the story, Edison was sitting in her bedroom/laboratory, two floors below Jordan's attic studio. She sat in a rolling office chair in the middle of the room wearing a pair of sunglasses that weren't really sunglasses. They only looked like the type of mirrored sunglasses that cops always wore in the movies. They were actually monitor screens. Edison held a remote control in her hands and was moving the little joystick in tiny circles with her thumb.  Edison had invented a remote control that you could control from a distance of up to one mile.  By installing a teeny tiny camera on the front of the remote control car, she could see from the car's point of view on the monitor in her sunglasses.

Edison had invented dozens of things.  All of which were abject failures with the exception of sex toys.  Edison was quite well known in lesbian circles as the mother of sex toys.  She thought this invention might be her best one to date.  And if she could just fix the glitch that made the camera see things in reverse – left was right, right was left, and sometimes up was down and vice versa – then she could patent her invention.  Edison was ironing out the bugs on the long-distance remote on the car.  If she could master the car, then she was going to up the ante and use it on a vibrator by connecting the glasses to the fiber optic network to the gadget itself.  She could then market the item to long-distance couples.  That way a lesbian could sit in her hotel in Paris and make love to her partner in Omaha.

Though, as Jordan so eloquently pointed out, "Why the hell would a lesbian in Paris want to hole up in a hotel room to have weird long-distance sex through a camera when there's all those sexy French girls who are notoriously bisexual?"

Edison believed in her idea, though.  She thought it was a breakthrough in the adult toys market and one that would put her on the map right next to Steve Jobs.  That is, if Steve Jobs didn't work with computers and instead worked with women's personal massagers shaped like the male organ.

While Jordan was upstairs with a tea-sodden lap, Edison was frantically working the remote control and seeing things on the sunglasses monitor upside down.  She didn't know if the car was upside down or if something had happened to the camera in the car and it was upside down.  Then again it could be another glitch in the glasses.  She pushed the little joystick on the remote control to the forward position. Nothing happened. Maybe the car's wheels were stuck.

Edison jumped when she saw the face of Mr. Pip in a gigantic close-up in her glasses. She yelped. His face appeared gargantuan this close-up. It was like sitting in the front row of a 3-D movie. Mr. Pip bared his teeth and hissed, spraying feline spittle all over the camera. A giant cat paw swiped at her. Edison screamed, toppled over backwards in her chair and the remote control skidded across the wooden floor and under the bed. The force of the throw wedged it between the bedpost and the wall with the joystick stuck in the 'Go' position.

Meanwhile, upstairs in the studio attic, Jordan was mopping up the tea spill with a crusty paint rag when she heard a loud crash from downstairs that rattled the paint cans and shook the already crumbling plaster.

"I'm okay!" Edison yelled.

The little car was turned upside down on the carpet, its wheels spinning crazily. Mr. Pip crouched in his attack position, eyeing the car from the safety of beneath the drawing table.

Jordan was angry enough to kick Edison in the butt. But since she couldn't kick her friend, she did the next best thing. She threw down the rag, marched across the room and kicked the little car. It flew across the room, smashed into the wall, bounced, rolled over twice and landed on all four wheels. The wheels spun for a second, then dug into the carpet and the car popped a wheelie and took off.

That wouldn't have been so bad except the car was aimed right at Mr. Pip. Mr. Pip's eyes widened in horror and he turned tail and ran.

The car gained on him.

Mr. Pip ran in a circle and jumped over the table.

The car went under the table.

Mr. Pip jumped over the sofa.

The car went under the sofa.

Jordan ran across the room to head the car off.

The car caught up to Mr. Pip and ran over his tail. Mr. Pip howled.

"Run, Mr. Pip, run!" Jordan yelled.

Mr. Pip screeched, dug his claws into the carpet and sprung forward.

The car followed.

Jordan jumped in front of the car. It crashed into her leg. She yelped in pain, grabbed her shin and hopped on one leg in a circle.

Mr. Pip jumped up on the drawing table safely out of reach of the car. The car rammed into the table's legs. Mr. Pip squalled and jumped, shredding Jordan's artwork with his claws. Confetti flew in every direction.

"Edison! I'm going to kill you!" Jordan screamed.

A streak of gray fur that was Mr. Pip ran by Jordan with the car in hot pursuit.

"My joystick is stuck!" Edison yelled back. "I'm not responsible!"

Jordan chased the car in circles around the room, cussing with each breath. Every time she almost caught the car, it would either change direction or disappear under the sofa.

Like in an old Tom and Jerry cartoon, Jordan chased the car; the car chased Mr. Pip; the car chased Jordan; Jordan chased Mr. Pip; and Mr. Pip got confused and chased his tail.

Edison ran in circles in her bedroom. She was seeing what the car camera saw: Cat butt; Jordan butt, shredded paper flying, more cat butt, under the sofa, over the rug, Jordan's foot; cat face. She worked frantically to un-stick the joystick as she spun herself in circles chasing the car in her monitor. Then she got dizzy and toppled face-first onto her bed.

Back in the attic studio, the melee continued until

Jordan officially put an end to it. She hadn't played soccer on her high school team for three years for nothing. She brought her leg back and as the car raced by, and let loose with a kick that Mia Hamm would have admired.

The car sailed out the open window.

Goal! Jordan celebrated with fists pumping the air and a dance that involved several exaggerated pelvic thrusts.

She stopped dancing when she heard a whirring noise behind her. She turned around and the car bashed into her toes.

How could that be? She had kicked the car out the window. Hadn't she? If it wasn't the car she kicked, then what was it?

"Mr. Pip!" she screamed. She ran to the open window and leaned out. "Mr. Pip!"

"Meow!"

Jordan looked up. Mr. Pip was dangling from a tree branch right outside the window. He looked like that inspirational poster from the 1970's. The one with the kitten hanging from a tree limb with the caption "Hang in there, baby."

Jordan cupped her hands around her mouth and yelled, "Hang in there, baby! I mean, hang in there Mr. Pip! I'll be right there!"

Edison ran into the studio to find Jordan leaning out the window and talking to Mr. Pip. Jordan reached out the window, stretched her arm as far as she could, but her fingertips were about a foot too shy.

Edison took off her sunglasses. She blinked her eyes and shook her head and the dizziness subsided. "What're you doing?" she asked.

Jordan leaned further out the window. "Mr. Pip is dangling from the tree branch. He's going to fall if I don't grab him first."

"How'd he get out there? Why is he out there?"

Edison said.

"I kicked him. It was an accident," Jordan said defensively. "This is all your fault."

"It's my fault you kicked the cat out the window?"

Jordan threw a leg up on the windowsill and reached out again. She still needed another four inches. She held on to the windowsill with one hand and leaned out further.

Edison dashed across the room and grabbed Jordan by waistband of her shorts. "What're you doing?"

"I'm going to rescue him. What does it look like?" Jordan said.

"You're three stories up! It's too dangerous!"

Jordan looked over her shoulder at Edison. "You want to do it?"

"No."

"Okay then, shut up and let me go."

"Meow!"

"Okay, okay, but be careful." Edison turned loose of Jordan's shorts. She stood back, watching fearfully, and making whimpering noises.

Jordan turned until she was sitting on the windowsill with her legs outside. Very carefully, she pushed herself to her feet, balanced on the sill, grabbed the lattice on the outside of the house with one hand and reached toward the tree branch with the other.

"Meow!"

"I'm almost there, Mr. Pip," Jordan said.

Edison bit her fingernails as Jordan leaned further and further. She breathed out a sigh of relief as Jordan's hand grabbed Mr. Pip by his scruff.

"Thank God," Edison muttered.

*Crack!*

"Oh no," Edison amended.

Jordan was slowly moving further and further away from the window – the lattice was peeling off the house.

Edison ran for the window. But she was too late. Jordan and Mr. Pip plunged three stories. Edison covered her eyes and screamed.

"For God's sake, stop screaming," Jordan yelled from below.

Edison un-peeked her eyes and looked out the window. "You're alive!" she said.

Jordan lay spread-eagle on her back in the dumpster they had rented for the construction project they called home. Luckily, she'd landed on carpet padding that they'd removed from the den. Mr. Pip sat regally on Jordan's chest. Without so much as a thank you, Mr. Pip leapt out of the dumpster, leaving Jordan covered in dust.

"You're welcome," Jordan said. Then she noticed her bloody hand. As is the way with injured body parts, she didn't notice the pain until she saw the blood. Then she screamed. She surveyed the area and saw the piece of glass from the broken shower door. After she finished screaming she called up to Edison. "Will you please bring me a towel?"

"Why? Did you pee your pants?"

"No, I'm bleeding," Jordan yelled back up at her.

Edison turned and ran out of the room, panting, "ohmygodohmygodohmygod!"

## Amy Meets Jordan

"What do we have here?" Amy asked.

Jordan looked down at her bloody shirt and answered, "A ruined shirt and a really bad home first-aid job."

**Meet Dr. Amy Stewart.** Amy was too short, too brown, too fat and too smart. That's what she thought anyway. She still pictured herself the way she looked as a sophomore in high school. Since that time, Amy had shed twenty pounds, gotten contacts, highlighted her hair and made good use of her brains. But when she looked in a mirror, she still saw her old self. It was like reverse alchemy. Her mirror turned gold into lead.

The first time Amy laid eyes on Jordan was in the emergency room at University Hospital. Amy sat on the rolling stool in a curtained-off cubicle and surveyed her patient. To say that Jordan was good-looking was an understatement. Amy thought Jordan was perfection personified – speaking purely from an anatomical viewpoint. Not that Amy was much of a judge of anything other than medicine, but to her this woman, with the sculpted body and long dishwater-blond hair, looked like one of those Olympic volleyball players everyone went gaga over. In short, she was the type of woman Amy despised.

Well, maybe despised was too strong a word. Loathed? No, she didn't loathe Jordan just because she was the type of woman that stared out at her from magazine covers, made a sports bra look sexy, and made her feel inadequate and homely and invisible. Hate? No, she didn't hate Jordan either, not exactly. She hated the *idea* of Jordan. Amy hated that there were women out there who looked like Jordan and made women like her feel like something you had to scrape off the bottom of your shoe.

Jordan asked, "You look like you're going to be sick. You're not going to throw up over a little cut and some blood, are you?"

"Of course not," Amy said, lifting her chin defiantly. "I'm a doctor."

"Yeah, but that was an 'I'm going to puke' face if I ever saw one."

Amy took a deep breath and assumed her professional look. Her professional look consisted of knitted eyebrows, a squinted right eye and pursed lips. If she wanted to be super professional she tapped her fingertip on her chin. She had perfected this look in front of her mirror in the bathroom at home. She thought it made her look smart, knowledgeable, caring and in control all at the same time.

"You're not pooping, are you?" Jordan asked.

Amy laughed.

"Because that face you're making looks like you might have I.B.S. or something."

Amy decided she was going to have to cultivate another professional look, perhaps one without the eye squint. "Who's the doctor here, you or me?" Amy joked.

"You are," Jordan answered. "Unless..." she said with widening eyes, "you stole a lab coat and scrubs and are impersonating a doctor."

"A doctor with I.B.S.," Amy corrected. She pointed to Jordan's overly bandaged hand, saying, "So, that's some first-aid job. If I didn't know better, I'd say that's an oven mitt under all that gauze. An oven mitt covered in gauze and attached securely by duct tape."

"It *is* an oven mitt attached securely by duct tape. This is what happens when you let a handyman slash inventor slash horror movie fanatic slash best friend play nurse."

Amy gently turned Jordan's hand over. "Well, it looks like the oven mitt did its job. Though I think it was due more to the tourniquet quality of the duct tape."

"Don't tell Edison that. That's my friend who did this first-aid job. She's already a huge fan of the stuff. Edison always says if you ever have to make a run for it, be sure to pack a hundred dollars in quarters, duct tape, and Vaseline."

Amy agreed on the first two counts, but wasn't sure if she wanted to know about the Vaseline. "So, tell me what happened." She held Jordan's hand in an upright position and gently prodded at the rest of her arm, checking for contusions or broken bones.

"I fell out of a window. I was rescuing Mr. Pip. He was hanging from a tree branch."

"Who is Mr. Pip?"

"He's the old man who lives next door."

Amy's eyes widened. Jordan laughed. "I'm kidding. He's my cat."

Amy almost laughed out loud. If she wasn't careful this woman was going to make her stoic doctor personae crumble. "Okay, you fell, but how did the cut happen?"

"There was a broken piece of shower door in the dumpster."

"You fell into a dumpster?"

Jordan nodded. "Dumpster diving. Literally."

"So, what happened to Mr. Pip?"

"He's fine, although he didn't say thank you."

"Cats," Amy said, shaking her head in mock disgust.

"When I came to he was sitting on my chest licking his butt."

Amy chuckled. "Why don't you get out of that bloody shirt?" She peeled off her latex gloves and tossed them into a white can sitting on the floor. "Throw it in there."

Jordan looked at the symbol on top of the trashcan. "Because I'm a biohazard?"

"Pretty much. I'll find you another shirt to wear and be right back." She swished aside the curtain, drawing it closed behind her and went in search of the supplies she needed.

## The Mole

Amy rounded a corner of the hospital hallway just as Jeremy did and he crashed into her.

**Meet Dr. Jeremy Blevins.** Jeremy was tall and skinny and had his hair pulled back in a ponytail. He looked like he had never outgrown the garage band look of his teen years. Jeremy was Amy's roommate and whenever she needed a last minute date to chaperone her somewhere, he was always available. As long as there was free food. It was a give-and-take system that had worked well for them for several years.

"I heard you had a hottie come in," Jeremy said. "Wanna trade patients?"

Amy sighed. If Jeremy wanted to trade patients it meant he had somebody really bad. "Who do you have?"

"Mrs. Markus," he said. "She thinks her mole is changing colors again."

Amy grimaced. "No thanks."

"No, you should really see it this time. It *is* a different color, I swear. It's green today. Last week it was magenta."

"Maybe it's a mood mole," Amy said. She looked closer at Jeremy. His eyes were bloodshot and glassy. "How long have you been on?"

He squinted at his watch and moved his lips in silent calculation. "Sixteen hours and counting. Why, you need some help?"

"Go home," Amy said. "You look like homemade poop."

"I believe the metaphor is homemade soap," he corrected.

"It's not a metaphor it's a simile."

Jeremy wagged his finger in her face. "I know what you're doing. You're trying to distract me from the hottie."

Amy answered, "I hate the term hottie."

"No, you don't," Jeremy said. "You only hate it that I didn't call you a hottie."

Jeremy dodged Amy's playful swat. He laughed and walked backwards down the hallway saying with an ominous vampire accent, "Don't be late for supper. Isabel is preparing dinner."

Isabel was their other roommate. You will meet her later in the story. Isabel was a budding chef. She liked to try out exotic recipes and Amy and Jeremy were her human guinea pigs.

Amy wrinkled her nose in disgust. "You go home first. Text me if she's boiling organ meat again, and I'll smuggle in some fast food."

"You're looking pretty perky for pulling a double shift in the emergency room," he said. "If I didn't know better, it almost seems like you're, oh, what's the word?" He snapped his fingers. "Happy."

"It's just a figment of your addled and sleep-deprived brain. Go make Mrs. Markus happy and see if her mole turns blue."

## Low Blood Sugar

Back in the E.R. cubicle, Amy watched in amusement as Jordan tried to put on the green scrub top with only one hand. So far, she had her injured hand through one of the shirt's armholes and her head sticking out the other. She was attempting to worm her way out of the mess, but wasn't having much success. Unless she was trying for a straightjacket effect in which case she was having terrific success.

"Alittlehelphere?" Jordan mumbled with her mouth full of shirt.

Amy gently pulled the scrub top over Jordan's head and then not-so-gently pushed her head back through the proper hole.

"Thanks, Doc," Jordan said. "Usually people are trying to get me out of my clothes, not put me in them."

There was a split-second where Amy was shocked. Then she quickly covered her expression and smiled in an overly polite way. The blood pounded in her ears. She knew if she were to take her own pulse right now it would be racing.

"Whoops," Jordan said, "TMI. Maybe you can test me for Asperger's while I'm here. I'm not good in social situations. That's what my Pre-K teacher wrote on my first report card. That and 'if she doesn't stop licking the other students she will be expelled.'"

Amy's mouth literally dropped open. "Did you say licking?"

"I liked to pretend I was a puppy," Jordan explained. "I got over it by second grade when I finally realized licking friends was not socially acceptable."

Amy laughed and looked away. She found it hard to hold Jordan's gaze for any longer than three seconds. She didn't know why except that it was so... intense. She gathered her surgical implements on a tray and pulled out a pair of latex gloves from the cardboard box. "Are you wearing a wedding ring?" She snapped the gloves about five times too many.

"Wedding ring?" Jordan asked.

"Any rings? Any kind of jewelry?"

Jordan smiled coyly. "Are you trying to find out if I'm available?"

Amy blushed. She could feel Jordan scrutinizing her. It was pleasant and unpleasant at the same time. Which was kind of like eating ice cream when you had a sore throat. It felt both good (ice cream) and bad (sore throat).

Amy squirmed in her chair and said, "I'm going to have to cut close and I don't want the scissors to get caught on your ring." She added, "If you had one."

"I don't. So, Doc, are you married?"

Amy slipped the scissors under the first layer of duct tape. "No, I'm not married."

"Haven't found the right person?"

"Something like that." Amy noticed that she had said 'person' not 'man.' If she wasn't mistaken, Jordan was flirting with her. But maybe she was wrong. She didn't get flirted with often and never had a woman flirted with her, so she was no expert. The only flirting she'd ever witnessed between two women was in that movie about the fried green tomatoes, and even that had to be pointed out to her. (By her mother of all people.)

She began to cut at the duct tape. "This may pinch a little."

Jordan winced.

Amy asked, "What about you? Does someone like you have a sweetheart?" She could kick herself. Sweetheart? What kind of word was that? What was she, raised in the 1950s? What was next? She was going to talk about sock hops and poodle skirts?

"What do you mean, someone like me?" Jordan asked. "Am I that un-presentable? I knew I should have brushed my hair before I came to the emergency room. My mother always used to tell me to wear clean underwear all the time in case I got in an accident. I never understood that line of logic. I mean, if I was in an accident I'd probably mess my pants so what would the underwear have mattered in the first place?"

Amy had a sudden flash of what Jordan would look like in underwear. What kind of underwear were they? Red and lacy? White and cotton? You could tell a lot about a person by their underwear. What was wrong with her brain today? It kept taking these weird erotic turns. Must be a lack of caffeine. Or maybe too much caffeine.

Amy said, "I just meant someone like you who is so… attractive. I meant you must have a lot of admirers." Admirers? Did she really just say that? My God, she was turning into her grandmother who always asked her about 'gentleman callers.'"

"Well, thanks for the compliment. But you see that's the problem. I seem, through no fault of my own I guarantee you, to bring out the worst in my girlfriends."

Girlfriends, Amy thought. So she was gay. Her blood pressure spiked and her heart picked up in tempo. The only bothersome part was that she had used the word 'girlfriends', as in the plural sense. Of course, Jordan was so beautiful she had her pick of women. She could have oodles of women on the line. God, did she really just think the word 'oodles'?

Amy finally managed to unwrap the hand. "In what way do you bring out the worst?" She got up and put together a sterile bath for the hand.

"Most of them turn into a combination of Medusa and a green-eyed monster."

Amy looked puzzled.

"Jealous. And if I'm with someone I don't cheat.

Sometimes I think I must be the only lesbian left on the planet who believes in monogamy."

Amy nodded. She knew exactly how Jordan felt. Her love life hadn't exactly been a stunning success. She'd had Nick who couldn't keep his dick in his pants, and Joe who had been overbearing and jealous, and now she had Chad who played the egotistical ass. Yup, her love life definitely sucked as well.

Jordan asked, "Can I ask you a question?"

God, here it comes, Amy thought. She's going to ask if I'm a lesbian and I'll have to say no and then she'll stop flirting or whatever it is she's doing just when I was beginning to enjoy it.

"Sure," Amy said, sounding not so sure.

"Why'd you become a doctor?"

Okay, so she was wrong about the question. While she formulated her answer, she turned to Jordan and flicked the needle of painkiller. Jordan looked at the needle and paled.

"Needles?"

Jordan nodded.

Then Amy did something she'd never done before. Something she had never even thought of before. Something that this time yesterday she would never ever have done. She pushed her coat and her scrub top off her shoulder and showed Jordan her tattoo. "I don't like needles either. But I sucked it up long enough to get this tattoo. It's my one claim to adventure."

"Beautiful," Jordan said. And when Amy looked up Jordan wasn't looking at the tattoo.

Amy blushed and turned her back to her. She held Jordan's hand under her arm and began to inject the painkiller into the wound but where Jordan couldn't see what was happening. "You just keep your eyes on my tattoo. I'll be done with this before you even know it."

Jordan's eyes lingered on Amy's shoulder. The

tattoo was a solid blue. Not green like old school tats, but a deep almost purple blue. It was the caduceus, the medical symbol, complete with snakes climbing the pole. It was an artist's version, though, and as Jordan stared at it, it seemed to be almost three-D. It was eerie and mesmerizing at the same time.

Jordan reached out and lightly touched the tattoo with her finger. "I wouldn't think someone like you would have a tattoo."

"Someone like me?"

"Someone so smart and beautiful."

Amy was silent. She was stunned that she had actually been called beautiful. She finished with the needle, but kept her back to Jordan. She didn't want to see those eyes looking at her. She needed to regain her composure. Finally, she took three deep breaths, stood and tossed the needle into the biohazard can.

When she turned around, Jordan was staring at her. Her eyes roamed over Amy's face and lingered on her exposed shoulder.

Embarrassed (and a little thrilled) to be looked at with such daring, Amy pulled her top and coat back into place. "Where's your friend?" Amy asked. "The one who did this amazing first-aid job?"

"She's in the waiting room."

"I'm going to go tell her that you're all right, but it's going to take a while to do all the sutures. What does she look like?"

"Short, curly black hair, red cat-eye glasses, camo pants and a big black hoodie. Just call for Edison and she'll pop up."

"Edison? Okay."

And Amy left. As she walked the hall, she tried to collect her emotions. This is what she said to herself in her head as she walked: *Amy, what are you doing? That is a real-live gorgeous woman in there and you are here only to stitch up her hand. You date men, you've never really considered a relationship with a woman and just because this beautiful, sexy, smart woman is flirting with you does not mean you're going to change your entire life perception of how the world operates. Jordan probably flirts with everyone. It's what gorgeous people do – they play with the rest of us because they can. Still Jordan didn't seem like that...the way she looked at me was so disarming.*

Her heart raced at the thought of Jordan's finger on her skin. She might not ever wash there again.

It wasn't working. Amy's pep talk with herself was having no effect on lowering her heart rate. So she did the next best thing. She stopped at a vending machine and bought a candy bar. She hurriedly unwrapped the candy and stuffed it into her mouth. She chewed, swallowed, and sighed with relief.

"See there?" she said to herself inside her own head. "I'm not a lesbian. I just was having a low blood sugar moment."

## Mustaches and Mistakes

Completely unaware that she had chocolate smeared above her upper lip, Amy opened the door to the waiting room, looked out over the huddled masses and called out, "Ms. Edison? Is there a Ms. Edison here?"

Edison waved her hand in the air *a la* Arnold Horshack, saying, "Ooh, ooh, ooh! Tell me she'll live."

Jordan's description had been right on target except she wasn't wearing glasses.

"She'll live," Amy said, shaking Edison's hand. "Thanks to that superior taping job of yours. It was extremely difficult to remove."

Edison stared at Amy's chocolate mustache and mistakenly thought it was a real mustache. After all, the chocolate matched Amy's hair color. Edison's mistake was understandable. She'd not worn her glasses. Edison thought Amy would be really pretty if she practiced hair removal.

Amy mistakenly thought Edison must be hard of hearing or maybe even deaf since she was obviously staring at her lips and trying to lip-read. So, Amy talked very, very loudly and made sure to enunciate crisply. "I. Am. Pleased. To. Meet. You. Edison."

Edison thought maybe Amy was not only hairy, but also deaf and that was why she so carefully said her words and had no volume control. Edison raised her volume to match Amy's, "It is so wonderful that you were able to become a doctor!"

"Thank you!" Amy shouted back.

Edison continued shouting, "I think it's wonderful to see people overcome their circumstances and fulfill their dreams!"

"I agree!"

"So are you going to be able to put Humpty Dumpty

together again?"

"Huh?"

"Jordan's cut hand?" Edison said, making elaborate cutting gestures with her own hand.

Amy added some sewing gestures to her next sentence so Edison could understand better. "Oh, yes, I can put it back together, but it will take a while. I did not want you to worry!"

"Can I watch? I find gore fascinating!" She stared intently at Amy's lips like a bird dog awaiting a signal.

Amy nodded enthusiastically. "I don't see why not! You can help to distract her while I sew her up!"

"If I know Jordan, you've already distracted her plenty!"

When Amy looked puzzled, Edison explained, "Jordan always notices the pretty ones!"

Amy led Edison down the hallway and since Edison was deaf and walking behind her, Amy didn't bother to keep her thoughts inside her head. "Wow. Here I am being called pretty again. Twice within five minutes. Must be some kind of record. Or maybe it's just a thing with lesbians. She said Jordan noticed pretty women. That means Jordan must be some kind of playgirl. And the way Edison said it was even more telling – like she was jealous. Is Edison her girlfriend? A better question is why am I even thinking about all this? I would have been safer and saner with Mrs. Markus' mood mole."

Edison said, "What's a mood mole?"

Amy froze. "You heard me say that?"

"Sure," Edison said, "You're the one who's deaf, not me."

"I'm not deaf," Amy said.

"You're not?"

Amy shook her head. "So if you're not deaf, why were you staring at my lips?"

Edison shuffled her feet. "I'm sorry, I know it's

rude, but I've never seen a woman with a mustache before." Afraid of offending Amy, she quickly amended her words. "I mean, I've seen mustaches on women before, but not a nice, thick mustache like yours."

Amy wiped her upper lip. "It's chocolate," Amy said. She licked her finger to prove her point.

"Oh," Edison said, relieved. "Thank God, 'cause that was really scary looking."

Amy licked her upper lip. "All gone?"

Edison nodded. "Yep. Oh, and Jordan's not a playgirl."

Amy pushed open the curtain to Jordan's cubicle, saying, "Good to know."

## The Sex Eye

Jordan had spent her interlude away from Amy giving some serious thought to the dilemma of asking Amy out. Using all her superhuman lesbian powers, she had deduced that Amy was straight, but interested. Jordan knew that she would have to tread carefully. She would have to entice Amy without being overbearing. She would have to be coy without being standoffish. The next few minutes would have to play out like a delicate surgery.

Jordan's thoughts were interrupted when Amy led Edison inside the cubicle. "What the hell are you doing here?" she asked.

"I'm your doctor," Amy said. "Don't you remember me?"

"Not you. Her," Jordan said, pointing with her good hand.

"I'm your distraction," Edison said, peering down at the cut hand. "Now that it's not bleeding it looks good in an awful kind of way."

"Has the medicine taken effect?" Amy asked.

"Well, I can't feel my hand anymore. It's like it's not even a part of me," Jordan said.

Amy sat in the rolling chair in front of her. "That means it's working."

Edison hovered over Amy's shoulder, fascinated with the procedure. Jordan whispered to Amy, "I can't believe you let her come in here."

Edison leaned over even further, sticking her nose between the injured hand and Amy. "The doc asked me to distract you," Edison said.

"Actually, right now, you're distracting *me*," Amy said.

"Oh, sorry. I'll wait over here. Tell me when you want me to distract." Edison moved to the far side of the room and leaned against the wall.

Jordan realized that Edison being in the room with them had changed the energy. What had been there before, if indeed it had been and wasn't just a figment of her imagination, was completely different now. The room felt deflated, flat and... solid. That was it. Before it was fluid and liquid and moving, now it was solid and heavy.

"You never answered my question," Jordan said to Amy.

"What question?"

"Why you became a doctor?"

"The usual reasons, I guess," Amy said. She put Jordan's hand on a small table. She moved the instrument tray closer and brought over a lamp. She studied her task under the bright light.

"What? You're not sure of her abilities? She looks pretty competent to me," Edison said.

"I have the utmost confidence in... what's your first name?" Jordan asked.

"Amy."

"Can I call you that?"

"Yes." Amy looked up at her. "You may not want to watch this part."

"I want to watch," Edison said.

"No," Jordan and Amy said in unison. They looked at each other and laughed.

"I promise I won't move and I won't throw up or anything," Edison whined.

"Okay," Amy relented, "but don't hover. And stand behind her, not me."

Edison gleefully took up position behind Jordan and watched over her shoulder.

"Story time, Amy," Jordan said. "Distract me with the tale of why you became a doctor."

As Amy stitched she gave her stock answer, "I became a doctor because the human body has always fascinated me."

"It fascinates me, too," Edison said.

"You're only interested in certain parts," Jordan said.

Edison giggled.

"So, Jordan, what do you do?" Amy asked.

"She's a writer. She writes children's books. And illustrates them, too," Edison answered for her. Edison leaned in closer. "Is that stringy white-looking thing the tendon? Amazing. You can sew it together like that? Wow."

"I can't listen to a play-by-play with color commentary," Jordan said.

"Will that black thread be in her hand forever?" Amy shook her head. "It'll dissolve over time."

"Amazing."

"You can help her with changing the dressing, I hope?" Amy asked Edison.

"I'd love to!" Edison said a bit too enthusiastically.

"You're putting her in charge of the nursing? It was all her fault this happened in the first place," Jordan said.

"Well, in that case," Amy said, "she has to work off that karmic debt. Or in her next life she'll have to do it all over again."

"Hmmm... I'm not sure I want a doctor who believes in reincarnation. Somehow it seems to go against the entire reason for making this life last," Jordan reasoned.

"I want to be your nurse! You know how much I love looking at wounds and stuff," Edison said. "Maybe I can get one of those sexy nurse outfits. With the little apron and feather duster."

"You're thinking of a French maid costume," Jordan said.

"Oh," Edison said. "You're right. What do nurses wear?"

"Scrubs," Amy said. "They're not very sexy either."

Turning her attention back to Jordan, she said, "I'll write you a script for Vicodin. Enough to get you through a week."

"Don't bother. She won't take them," Edison said.

"You know," Jordan said sarcastically to Edison, "it's truly amazing that I could conduct my life before you came along."

Amy had trouble keeping up with these two. They were like Ab Fab but without the accents. "You two sound like an old married couple."

"We're not married," Jordan said. "In fact, after this, we may not even be friends."

Edison laughed. "She doesn't really mean that."

Amy was still not sure what their relationship was, so she cast her fishing line out even further by asking, "So, you two aren't a couple?"

Edison answered, "Nope. We tried the girlfriend thing, but she said I was too bossy which is true, so now I'm her roommate. It really was for the best. We wouldn't have lasted. I would've punched every girl who gave her the sex eye and would probably be serving time right now."

"The sex eye?" Amy asked.

"You know," Edison explained, "when a girl looks at you like I-Really-Want-to-Get-Nasty-With-You without the preliminaries."

"Preliminaries?"

"Yeah," Edison said. "The part where you do dinner or drinks and show each other pictures of your fur kids and tell cute stories about your cat where you personify him with dialogue. You speak in a high voice like you imagine a cat would." Edison demonstrated in a squeaky voice, "My name is Mittens and my owners torture me. They dine on fresh kill whilst they make me eat dried tasteless cereal. They dangle things in front of me and yank it away." She continues in her own voice, "Then you make sure that you each have a frequent mover card for U-

Haul." Edison paused dramatically. "Then you get nasty."

Jordan chuckled. "Not necessarily in that order."

"Oh," Amy said. "What if you don't have a cat?"

Edison's eyes widened. She put her hands on the sides of her face like the kid in the *Home Alone* posters. "Surely, you jest!"

Jordan said, "Every lesbian has a cat."

"Really?" Amy asked. "Is that like an unwritten rule?"

"No, it's written down," Edison said. "It's in the rule book."

Amy laughed as she dressed Jordan's hand. "Okay, now about the Vicodin. Sure you won't change your mind? It's going to hurt plenty when the shots wear off."

Jordan said, "No drugs for me. I prefer a nice glass of Pinot Gris and a couple of Aleve."

"She's got a wine cellar in her house," Edison explained. "The place is enormous. An old four-story Victorian or three-story with an attic, which makes it a four-story. We're restoring it to its original grandeur only better."

"Tell me you didn't fall out of the fourth story window," Amy said.

"I didn't fall out of the fourth story window," Jordan said with a straight face.

"She did, too," Edison said.

Amy shook her head. "Unbelievable. It's a miracle you don't have any broken bones."

Jordan said, "I know how to fall. You ever hear of those stories about babies falling from ten story buildings and not getting anything but a couple of bruises? It's because they go limp. That's the secret. Just go limp and bounce."

Amy smiled.
Jordan smiled.
Edison frowned.

Amy turned her back to the two and scooped extra gauze and tape into a baggie. Jordan quickly motioned for Edison to leave. Edison opened the door, but before she could walk away, Amy stopped her by saying, "Edison?"

Edison turned. Amy handed her the bandage supplies. "That's enough for a couple of days. You should go by a drugstore and stock up on more."

Edison nodded. "Thanks, Doc." Edison looked at Jordan and spoke stiffly like a really bad soap opera actor, "I'll just go get the car and bring it around to the entrance, Jordan. You shouldn't be walking on that... hand." She left.

"So," Jordan said, standing. "I guess that's it then."

Amy said, "I'd like to see you again."

"I'd like to see you again, too," Jordan said.

"What I meant was I'd like to see your hand. In two weeks. I can take the stitches out then."

"Oh." Jordan blushed. "Of course that's what you meant. But, you know, wherever my hand goes, so do I. So you'll probably see me again, too."

Amy smiled. "That would be expected. Here's my card. You can call during work hours to make an appointment, okay? Or call anytime. It doesn't have to be during work hours. For the appointment."

"Okay then, it's a date. I mean it's not really a date. I know that. But it is a date. Of sorts."

Amy laughed. "I know what you meant."

"Okay. I'll call then. I mean tomorrow. Whenever. I'll call." Jordan headed for the door before she embarrassed herself further. She was halfway out the door before she turned back around. "So, you never said... Do you have a cat?"

"Not yet," Amy smiled, "But I'm thinking about getting one."

Jordan grinned and turned to go, but at that moment, Jeremy rounded the corner and they smacked into each other.

He took his time looking Jordan up and down before muttering, "Excuse me."

Jordan smiled awkwardly at him, waved goodbye to Amy with her bandaged hand – which looked more like she was erasing a chalkboard than waving – and headed down the hallway.

Jeremy turned to Amy, waggled his eyebrows *a la* Groucho Marx and said, "I think she likes me, don't you?"

"What're you still doing here? I thought you were leaving."

He pooched out his lower lip in a bad imitation of a pouty child. "If I didn't know better I'd think you didn't want me around."

Amy felt the electrical charge that Jordan had infused her with draining away. "Sorry," she said. "I'm tired. How was Mrs. Markus' mole?"

"You were right about the diagnosis. I intentionally made her angry and it turned red."

Amy laughed.

Jeremy continued, "And then I intentionally stopped by hoping to help you out with the hottie."

"Hottie. That's so derogatory. I don't understand why women like you."

"Touchy touchy. You're the only woman I know who doesn't throw herself at my feet."

Amy looked at him smugly. "Yeah, well, I didn't see Miss Hottie throwing herself anywhere in your direction."

He feigned hurt by clasping his hand over his chest as if he'd been shot in the heart. Then he laughed. "She's probably a lesbian."

"As a matter of fact she is," Amy said. "And she was flirting with me."

Jeremy eyes widened. "Really?" He clasped his hands in front of his chest, begging, "If you two go on a date can I come too? I promise to be real quiet and just watch."

Amy rolled her eyes and stalked out the door. She was halfway down the hallway when Jeremy poked his head out the doorway and called after her, "Just kidding!" He added under his breath, "But not really."

## Conversion Version

"You like her," Edison said as she opened the door of her ancient Volkswagen bug.

"Maybe," Jordan said, climbing into the passenger seat.

"But we don't even know if she's family," Edison said. She started the car, ground the gears until she found reverse and backed out of the parking space without looking behind her. A car slammed on its brakes and honked angrily at her. Edison ignored it.

"Does it matter?" Jordan asked.

"Only if you want to date her." Edison steered the car out of the hospital parking lot and toward the exit.

"Maybe I can finally get that toaster oven I've always wanted," Jordan said.

"She's a little on the short side for you."

"You're going out a one-way," Jordan said.

"So?"

"The wrong way."

Another car honked at them and the driver shook her fist. Edison waved brightly at the angry woman.

Jordan said, "I don't think she's waving."

"What makes you say that?"

"The pinched red face and the spittle spraying out of her mouth."

"Some people are so excitable," Edison said. She screeched tires onto the street and the angry driver laid on her horn and sped past. Edison shook her head and sighed. "You'd think one-way signs are written in stone or something."

"Well, they are kind of the law and all that."

They drove the next five minutes in silence. Jordan closed her eyes and held her breath each time Edison cornered the car without braking.

"How old do you think she is?" Edison asked.

"Who?"

"You know who."

Jordan shrugged. "Thirty."

"How do you know that?"

"I don't know that. You asked me how old I *thought* she was and I *think* she's thirty."

Edison frowned. "Kind of young for you."

"I'm thirty-two. It wouldn't be like I was robbing the cradle."

"Your last one was much older." Edison punched the gas to make it through a yellow light.

Jordan braced herself by pushing her undamaged hand against the dash. "Age is relative."

"I'm pretty sure she had a straight vibe," Edison said.

"Everyone's straight until proven guilty."

Edison took her eyes off the road and looked at Jordan for a long moment. "So, what's the verdict? Are you going to ask her out?"

"No. Please watch the road."

"No?"

"No. I don't do conversions." Jordan pointed out the windshield. "The road, please."

Edison looked out the window, saying, "You converted me."

"That's your version. My version is that it was an accident."

"You make it sound like you tripped and fell on top of me until I came," Edison said.

Jordan sighed. "Ed, I don't want to talk about us again. We're best friends. We're better off that way. And as for the doctor... I'm not going to try to convert her, that's all, end of story."

Edison looked doubtful. She said in an off-handed way that meant it wasn't really off-handed, "Some conversions do themselves."

It was true that Jordan had met Edison when she was straight. No, erase that. Jordan met Edison when she wasn't a *practicing* lesbian. She had hired Edison to hang some new cabinets in the kitchen. Only half the cabinets were hung before Jordan had introduced Edison to the world of practicing lesbianism and it had been kind of an accident.

Jordan didn't blame herself. She blamed her overactive vagination. If Edison didn't want to be seduced and taken on the kitchen floor she shouldn't have bent over like that with her butt crack showing.

Jordan sighed. She loved Ed. But she loved her like a best friend. The problem was that Ed loved her like a lover. Jordan wasn't sure how it had happened, but Edison had moved into her house kind-of-sort-of uninvited. Something about her apartment being flooded and being broke and she worked all day at Jordan's house anyway and she had more than enough room and her portion of the rent could be taken out of what Jordan was paying her to remodel. The problem was that the remodeling was going on forever. Jordan wondered if that was intentional.

Edison pulled her Bug into the driveway of their home. They looked at the old house and sighed. Once upon a time it had been a beautiful old Victorian but now the paint was peeling, the yard was overgrown and the windows looked like the cloudy cataracts of a senile old lady. If the house were a person it would be Mrs. Haversham from *Great Expectations*.

"I wish this conversion would do itself," Jordan said, pointing at the house and referring to the ongoing house renovations.

"Where would the fun be in that?" Edison said. "Isn't putting in elbow grease and sweat and hours upon hours of work worth having something of your very own, something special and worthwhile, something to give your life meaning?"

Jordan got out of the car. "Are we talking about the house or the doctor?"

"You tell me." Edison shut her car door and headed for the porch.

## Blue Amy

Jordan sat cross-legged on the floor in her drawing studio, in the middle of plastic tarps, paint buckets and half-painted walls, drinking Pinot Gris out of a coffee mug and contemplating her own conversion. There were three distinct stages of her conversion.

**Before she fell out the window:** Jordan did not believe in true love. She did not believe in romance and happily-ever-afters. She thought all that malarkey about love was brainwashing doled out by men to keep women barefoot and pregnant. It was so ingrained in the female mind that even lesbians had contracted it like it was a pandemic flu.

**During the fall:** The moment she slipped, the exact moment she reached for something to grab hold of and there was nothing there and she realized she was hurtling toward earth and imminent death, Jordan thought of how she was dying too young. She thought of all the things she hadn't done yet. She hadn't traveled to New Zealand. She hadn't been to the top of the Empire State building. She hadn't written the novel that would be her seminal masterpiece. She hadn't experienced true love. That was her last thought and it was the clencher. True love. She was going to die a virgin, metaphorically speaking, of the heart.

**After the fall:** Jordan saw Amy in the emergency room. Maybe it was too many endorphins caused by the fear coursing through her veins, maybe it was the loss of blood, maybe it was the full moon, maybe it was the chili peppers she ate for dinner last night, but whatever it was, Jordan was now pretty damn sure she was in love.

She shook her head, gulped her wine, and reminded herself sternly that she did not believe in true love. She did, however, believe in a second glass of wine. She lifted the bottle from between her legs and sloshed more into her cup.

She looked at the half-painted walls and wondered when Edison would ever get around to finishing them. It seemed like the whole house was always only halfway done. Edison had steadily worked on projects but was always sidetracked by her brainchildren – the inventions that she was forever tinkering with. As a result, the new dishwasher sat in the middle of the kitchen floor, the guest room toilet was in the hallway, sheets of drywall were stacked in the living room and not a single wall in the whole place was fully painted.

Jordan decided to be proactive. She jimmied open a can of paint with a screwdriver, stirred the paint, grabbed a brush, and dipped it into the blue paint. It was cerulean blue and her favorite color. Edison stored most of the paint up here in her studio so that when it came time to paint a room she'd know where, in the mess of remodeling, she had stored the paint.

Jordan slapped the paint on the wall with one hand and sipped her wine with the other. Well, she tried to sip her wine. She couldn't hold the mug in her left hand because of the stitches and bandages. And pain. She located a roll of duct tape, which wasn't too hard because Edison bought the stuff by the case and left it lying all over the house. Using her teeth, her knees and her good right hand, Jordan taped the mug of wine to her left hand. She gave it a trial run by raising it to her lips and drinking. It worked beautifully. Jordan thought that Edison should invent something like this - a paint holder that had a sippy cup attached to it. She could market it to the depressed artist. And weren't all artists depressed?

Jordan picked up the brush and smeared some of the blue paint on the wall. She drank. She painted. She let her mind wander.

Jordan thought about Amy. She thought about

Amy's face. She was beautiful in an unassuming, unpretentious way. Jordan thought about using Amy's face in one of her illustrations. She might be perfect for her book-in-progress. Jordan had been working on her children's book for the past year. She drew picture after picture but was never satisfied with the end result. Using Amy's face might give her the inspiration she needed.

Jordan had a photographic memory. She could recall in startling detail every face she'd ever seen. That talent came in quite handy in art school when she never finished a drawing class by the time the bell rang. She'd simply go home, finish from memory and hand it in the next day. This talent would also come in handy if she were ever mugged or kidnapped or a victim of a senseless crime. Which hadn't happened, thank God, but if it did she'd be able to draw her own police sketch.

While she painted the wall, she thought about Amy's eyes. They were beautiful, sure, but so were a million other eyes Jordan had seen. The thing that made Amy's eyes different was that what was behind them leaked out. Okay, leaking wasn't the best word choice. What she meant was Amy had eyes with a depth past the ordinary blue. They were a blue so deep that they seemed to get darker near the center and swallow her up.

And her lips. Perfect bow-shaped lips. Teeth that showed when she smiled. She had one tooth in the front that was a tiny bit crooked. Just enough to not be perfect. Cheeks with just a hint of color. A dimple in her right cheek. Not in her left. Just her right. Her hair wasn't long, wasn't short, wasn't straight, wasn't curly. It defied description. It was perfect.

Jordan's thoughts were interrupted by a whirring noise. She turned and saw the little remote control car roll into the room, travel across the floor and stop about a foot from her feet. There was a manila envelope duct-taped to the top of the car. Written on the envelope in Edison's scrawl were the words *Dossier of Dr. Amy Stewart*.

Jordan peeled the envelope off the car and opened it. Inside were several pages of paper.

"What's all this?" Jordan called out. She knew Edison had to be somewhere close by.

Edison leaned in the doorway with the monitor sunglasses perched on top of her head. She froze when she looked at the wall. "A better question is, what is that?" she said, jabbing a finger at the wall.

Jordan followed Edison's stare and gasped. She had painted Amy. A large blue portrait of Amy on the wall. She hadn't even realized what she'd been doing. She raised her left hand and took a gulp of wine. She choked. "It's an illustration I'm working on."

"Uh huh," Edison said. "It looks like a blue Amy if you ask me."

"I didn't ask you." Jordan waved the papers in the air. "You Googled her?"

"I found out a bunch of stuff."

"Oh?" Jordan tried to act only mildly interested while her heart pounded.

Edison looked at Jordan's mug taped to her hand. "Ingenious."

"I know, right?"

Edison took another coffee cup off Jordan's drawing table, poured the dregs of Jordan's early morning coffee into an old paint can and filled it to the brim with wine.

Unable to look at the dossier, Jordan put the envelope on her desk. "Are you going to tell me what you found out? She's a murderer? A black widow? An angel of death? A Lorena Bobbit?"

Edison took a drink then said, "About what you'd expect really. She's thirty years old – you were right on the nose. Grew up here. Got her medical degree in San Diego, interned in Phoenix, practiced two years back in San Diego and then came here. She graduated at the top of her class, has some awards of excellence – I couldn't understand what they were for, medical mumbo-jumbo of some sort. Get this - she volunteers at the free clinic downtown. She works for free. That's like sick and wrong."

"Wow."

"Yeah, wow. She sounds too good to be true, huh?"

Jordan drank. "What do you mean?"

Edison eyed the painting on the wall, walking from one side of the room to the other. "Spooky. It's like her eyes are following me everywhere I walk."

Jordan drank, nervously waiting for Edison to drop the bomb.

Edison took another drink. "A person can't be that good, you know. There has to be a skeleton or two in the closet."

"I suppose you've found out what these skeletons are?"

"I did find out that she's living with another doctor."

"Living with?"

"It's a guy. A damn good-looking guy, too." Edison extracted a printed photo from the dossier and showed it to Jordan, saying, "Here's a picture of them together. They went to some formal gala together a couple of months ago. His name is Dr. Jeremy Blevins."

Jordan recognized him right away. "I ran into him."

"When?"

"At the hospital as I was walking out the door. I literally ran into him as he was coming in."

"Well, I'm afraid your romance with the doc was short-lived. She's already taken." Edison did not look sorry or afraid. She looked gloating.

Jordan picked the brush back up. She had her back to Edison, but she could hear the smile in her voice as she said, "You'll have to Kilz that first or it'll bleed through."

Too bad I can't Kilz her face from my mind, Jordan thought. She took a drink and stared at Amy's blue face and didn't hear when Edison left the room. Jordan decided not to take Edison's advice about the Kilz to paint out Amy's face. Instead, she kilzed the bottle of wine and left the portrait on the wall. Blue Amy staring down at her would serve as a reminder. A reminder to never again allow herself to fall for the true love myth.

## Banana Peel

"Hey, sexy lady," a smarmy voice said.

Amy looked up from her desk and quickly closed her laptop. Her heart sank when she saw who was leaning in the doorway of her office.

**Meet Chad Dorring.** Ladies' man extraordinaire. Suave, sexy and single. Metro-sexual. He was the heartthrob of the hospital. If he hadn't chosen to be a doctor he would have made an excellent soap opera actor.

Chad stood in the doorway of Amy's office with a leer on his face. Or maybe it was a smile, not a leer, Amy thought. Maybe his smile only resembled a leer. Either way, it was creepy. Like how chimpanzees show you their teeth and you think they're smiling and so cute, then suddenly they're attacking you.

Chad raised one eyebrow in a suggestive manner and asked, "What're you doing later?"

Amy assumed the eyebrow raising was supposed to suggest that she was doing *him* later. The thought of it made her want to gag.

"Are you okay?" he asked. He walked uninvited into her office and plopped down in a chair. He stretched his long legs out in front of him. He looked like a cat toying with a mouse – like he could sit for hours in front of a cabinet waiting for the mouse to innocently poke its head out so he could rip it off. "You look a little sick."

"Hello, Chad, won't you come in? Have a seat, make yourself right at home," she said with ultimate sarcasm. "And, no, I'm not sick. You just surprised me is all." She drummed her fingers on the desk, hoping her gesture conveyed her impatience and he would excuse himself and walk away never to come anywhere near her again. Well, the never again part might require something more extreme than tapping her fingers.

It didn't happen. Chad smiled instead. He made sure to give her his toothiest smile - the one with the high-wattage bling factor. When he did that to the nurses, Amy swore she could smell sex pheromones emanating from every pair of panties in a two-block radius.

And then, as if to compound matters, there was that cleft chin. Amy abhorred that cleft in Chad's chin. All the nurses drooled over that cleft, but Amy thought it made his chin look like a tiny little butt on the end of his face. She must be the only woman in the world immune to his cleft and good looks. She'd seen all the nurses fan their faces and pat their hearts when he walked by. Amy wrinkled her nose like she smelled something stinky anytime he was near. To tell the truth, she was sick of Chad and tired of all good-looking male doctors. What she wouldn't give to work with a measly, shrimp-y, ugly doctor with a wart on his chin instead of a cleft.

Chad gestured to her closed laptop. "Did I catch you looking at porn?"

"What? No," she said quickly. Maybe too quickly. Saying it quickly like that made her look guilty.

Chad laughed. She hated his laugh. It wasn't genuine. It sounded like the canned laughter in a sit-com. She knew Chad had probably carefully cultivated the tenor and rhythm of his laugh. It was designed to charm a woman out of her panties. Well, it wasn't going to work on her. Not again.

Amy had been with Chad once before. *Once.* It was when she was new at the hospital, and didn't know any better. Chad had shown her lots of attention those first two weeks. He showered her with his cleft, his laugh, his toothsome bling. He asked her out for a drink and she tried to say no, but he made it impossible. And, maybe the truth was that she might have been a little bit lonely. Okay, a *lot* lonely. She met him for one drink that turned into four or five or who the hell's counting and next thing she knew she was too drunk to drive and they were sharing a cab and sharing his bed.

The sex was unremarkable – at least the parts she remembered. Not that she was all that well versed in this particular human diversion, but she didn't have an orgasm that was for sure. Why did she keep chasing that elusive orgasm? She knew it wasn't something physically wrong with her – she could give herself one. Was it a mental deficiency on her part? Or perhaps emotional? Maybe it was due to the poor performance of the man.

When Chad was *kaput*, he rolled off her. She jumped up and grabbed her clothes on the floor. She dashed for the bathroom, but it was dark, and she was still half-drunk and she didn't see the used condom he had thrown on the floor until it was too late and when she stepped on it, she slipped, fell and conked her head on the hard wood floors. While she was unconscious, Chad rushed her to the emergency room and when she came to she was wearing only a T-shirt and her undies. Why the hell didn't he dress her in proper clothing first?

The doctor, she didn't know him, thank God, asked her what happened and she told him the first thing that came to mind: She had slipped on a banana peel. Oh, she could kill herself for saying that. Who slipped on a banana peel outside of a Three Stooges movie? It didn't take long for the rumor to circulate around the hospital that she had hooked up with Chad and slipped on a "banana peel."

This all happened months ago but the rumor still hadn't died completely. Was it still called a rumor if it was mostly true? She had become a running joke of the hospital. She kept finding banana peels in the trashcan in her office and nurses giggled at her over the tables in the lunchroom while they exaggeratedly peeled a banana. Once in the cafeteria she had walked away from her table to get a Sweet'N Low and when she came back there was a banana peel on her tray.

Then Chad had suddenly appeared at her side. He pinched the peel between his thumb and forefinger, held it up like it was contaminated and said loudly, "Be careful, doctor. I've heard these can be very dangerous." The whole cafeteria busted a gut laughing.

And the worst thing about the whole banana debacle? Chad now thought it meant they were dating. He acted like he owned her or something. Like they were an item. She even heard him refer to them as "Chamy" as if they were a power couple like "Brangelina."

That was why she hated Dr. Butt-Chin Banana-Man Chad Dorring.

"I'm shopping for a birthday present for my nephew," she lied.

"And here I thought you weren't the maternal type," he said.

"Shows how much you know me," she retorted. She didn't know why she said that. She really wasn't all that maternal and she didn't have a nephew. But she didn't want Chad to know that.

Chad shrugged like it didn't matter either way. "I dropped by to give you a heads up. I'm having dinner with you tonight."

"Wrong," Amy said. "I'm having dinner with my roommates tonight." What Amy couldn't figure out about Chad was that the meaner she was to him, the more he liked it. Was he a masochist? And did that make her a sadist?

"So am I," he said. "Jeremy invited me."

He stood and stretched his arms over his head in a calculated move so she could admire his sculpted abs as his scrub top rose up. Gross. The last thing she wanted to see was his hairy belly.

She opened her laptop and looked at that instead. Chad placed both hands on the edge of her desk and leaned his face in close to hers. He said, "Just thought I'd warn you so you can be sure to get all gussied up for me." He winked and strode out the door.

Gussied up? What the hell kind of word was that? Women hadn't been getting gussied up since the turn of the century.

Amy looked back at her computer. Staring at her from the screen was a smiling picture of Jordan March. It was her author profile page on Amazon. Jordan had written three children's books and all of them had great reviews. She not only wrote the books, she illustrated them as well. She was beautiful *and* smart *and* talented and had a hairless belly. It didn't get any better than that. Maybe those drunken kisses with her college dorm mate were a precursor... like little seismic shakes right before the big earthquake.

Amy chose the boxed set of Jordan's books, clicked on the 'add to cart' button and selected expedited service. Maybe she could get Jordan to autograph them for her.

## Ch...Ch...Ch...Changes

Amy pulled her gray Nissan Sentra into the driveway and parked behind Jeremy's enormous gas-guzzling Buick. She turned off the car but didn't turn off the radio. She sat for a moment, listening to NPR. She looked at the house. She looked at her car. She looked at her clothes. She looked at her fingernails with the clear nail polish. She looked in the rear view mirror at her lightly applied make-up.

She didn't recognize this woman, the one she had become. When did she turn into this person? The Amy of old used to be daring – she'd gotten a tattoo after all. Admittedly, she was a weekend rebel – one didn't get through med school without a effort, but she went to Nirvana concerts, wore high heels, a leather bomber jacket and groovy sunglasses. When did she morph into this person who lived in the burbs, drove a sensible car, had a sensible job, wore sensible clothes and sensible make-up? She even listened to NPR! And now her exciting Friday night was coming home to a dinner cooked by her best friend and after dinner she would force herself to pretzel her body through a yoga video, then curl up in bed with a book.

And now she wasn't even going to get to do that because her boyfriend she didn't like was coming over to see her all gussied up. Was this how women ended up getting married? They settled or were bullied into the matrimonial state? If that was her future, Amy didn't want anything to do with it.

Amy opened the front door and was assaulted by smells coming from the kitchen. She didn't realize how hungry she was until her mouth began to water. Then so did her eyes.

**Meet Isabel Craig.** Amy's other roommate. Isabel

is the product of an upper middle class family. She is a middle child and used to being ignored – not in a bad way, but in the way of middle children who don't cause trouble. Her parents have no aspirations for her other than "being happy."

But happiness is elusive. It is especially elusive when the person seeking it isn't particularly good at any one thing. Isabel had, by her own count, held over seventy-three jobs in the last ten years. Right now, she was training to be an Extreme Chef.

Extreme chef-ing is a relatively new occupation. It involves creating absolutely never before seen or smelled recipes. There is a lot of trial and error and guinea pigs are necessary; not the cute furry rodent kind, but the human kind. This is the reason the independently wealthy Isabel has roommates when she could afford her own apartment.

Amy entered the kitchen. Isabel looked up from the stove and smiled. Isabel even looked like an aspiring chef. She was short, round, pleasant, and bubbly. She had dark hair cut in a no nonsense bob tucked behind her ears, glasses that were always fogged up from steam off the stove, and cheeks always red from the heat of the oven. Amy even thought of Isabel's body in terms of food: Her breasts were plump dinner rolls, her butt was pork tenderloin and her stomach was pudding.

Isabel and Amy had been best friends for three years. They had met when they showed up at the same time in answer to an ad Jeremy had placed in the paper for a roommate. They had all three hit it off immediately – in a Three's Company sort of way – and Jeremy had rented out a bedroom to them both.

Over time, they had each staked out their own personal space in the large house. Isabel was in charge of the kitchen and dining room, Jeremy was in charge of entertainment and the living room and Amy was in charge of... Well, she was in charge of staying out of their way.

Amy put the paper bag down on the counter and Isabel's eyes brightened. "Is that what I think it is?"

"Pinto Gris. Two bottles."

"Two? And I think you mean *Pinot* Gris."

"They had a two for one sale," Amy said.

"Start pouring, girlfriend, start pouring."

Amy pulled two wine glasses out of the cupboard.

Isabel did a double take on the second glass. "Since when do you drink wine?"

"I'm going to change," Amy said.

"I hope so," Isabel said. "It's hard to eat dinner when a doctor is sitting across the table from you in blood-splattered clothes."

"No." Amy laughed as she poured. "I'm not changing clothes. I mean, I am. But I'm going to change myself. I've decided that I'm boring and consistent and I need to put a stop to it before it's too late."

"Oh yeah?" Isabel raised an eyebrow.

"Yeah."

Amy handed over a glass of wine. They toasted to nothing and sipped.

Isabel went back to stirring the pot with a long-handled wooden spoon. Amy downed her entire glass, poured another and giggled.

"What's so funny?" Isabel asked.

"You look like one of those witches. You know in that Shakespeare play. Bubble, bubble, toil and trouble."

"That was Shakespeare?" Isabel asked. "I thought it was from a cartoon."

Amy laughed and poured herself more wine. Isabel put the lid back on the pot and turned to her. "Okay," she said, "what's all this about wanting to change? Are you having an early mid-life crisis?"

Any hoisted herself up onto the bar and swung her legs. "I'm too plain. I'm plain and planned and… pained." She was thinking of her heart. Her heart hurt. It wanted someone to love. It wanted to have a companion – not like an extra heart in her chest, but a heart lying next to her, one she could hear beating and know that it beat for her. She didn't think these thoughts in words, of course, but in feelings.

"So, you want to spice it up?"

"Exactly," Amy said. She drank down half her glass of wine.

"What're you thinking about changing into?"

"I don't know yet," Amy said. "Anything, I guess. It's got to be more exciting than what I am now."

"Well, you came to the right place. I'm the queen of changing your life. Look at all the different people I've been."

That was true. Just since Amy had known her, Isabel had been a stockbroker, a pizza delivery girl, a locksmith apprentice, a member of the Geek Squad (even though she didn't know squat about computers), and had even gone to clown school. She had botched the balloon-animals class and dropped out.

Isabel stirred, thinking hard. "You could be a gypsy."

"Gypsy? Where'd that come from?"

Isabel shrugged. "I just think you'd look good in flowing scarves and bangles."

"I'm not talking about dressing up for Halloween. I'm talking about my life." She drank the rest of her wine and poured another.

"You better go easy on that," Isabel said. "I don't think making important life decisions while you're drunk is a good idea."

"*Au contraire, ma frère*," Amy said with a giggle. "It might give me the boost I need to take action."

Isabel took the lid off the boiling pot, dipped up a spoon of the brownish pulp and held it out to Amy to taste. "Tell me what you think."

Amy blew on the spoon and tasted. It took everything she had not to spit it back out.

Isabel asked, "So? More salt? More cumin?"

"You know what it needs?"

"What?"

Amy dumped her glass of wine in the pot. "More wine."

"You ruined it!" Isabel said, madly stirring the pot like that was going to somehow help. "I can't believe you did that! My God, it's all ruined." She whined and whimpered and cursed and stirred.

"Isabel?" Amy whispered.

Isabel looked at her.

"It was really kind of bad."

"It was?"

Amy nodded.

"Real bad?" Isabel asked.

Amy nodded again. "Foul, in fact."

Isabel looked back at the pot. She turned off the burner and said mournfully, "I wanted to come up with a new recipe, something with zing and pep that would make a good gravy for those tiny Italian noodles."

"You will. It just won't be that recipe," Amy soothed.

"I'm a horrible cook," Isabel lamented. A giant tear slid down her cheek.

Amy pulled Isabel into her arms and squeezed her tight. "You are not a bad cook. You are creative and inspired. What's that adage about Babe Ruth?"

"Who's Babe Ruth? Is she on the cooking channel?"

Amy laughed. "Babe Ruth was a great baseball player. Famous for hitting home runs. But what most people don't know is that he struck out more than he hit."

"I thought he was a candy bar."

Amy held Isabel at arm's length. "Just promise me

you'll keep swinging. That you'll keep trying out recipes."

Isabel nodded unconvincingly.

"You'll hit those home runs, I promise."

"Maybe," Isabel said under her breath.

"Listen to me," Amy said, giving her a little shake. "Do you know how much I admire you?"

"Me? Why?"

"Because you have a dream. You're living it. You know what you want. And you keep going for it. I wish I had your enthusiasm."

"Thanks," Isabel said. "Thanks for being my friend."

"Now drink your wine. I'll make dinner." Amy threw open the fridge door, rummaged inside and brought out a block of cheddar cheese. She went to the cabinets and took down a box of saltine crackers. She grabbed the bottles of wine and announced with full arms, "Madame, dinner is served."

Isabel grabbed her wine glass and asked, "You're sure it couldn't be saved?"

Amy put on the sympathetic face she'd practiced in the mirror for the day she might have to inform a family member that the patient had expired, and said in a somber tone, "I'm sorry. We did all we could, but we could not resuscitate the patient."

Isabel grabbed her glass and swallowed a healthy drink of wine. "Okay," she said. "Let's go out back and watch the sunset."

An hour later the sunset was gone and so was most of the wine. Amy and Isabel were lounging on the far side of the yard in metal lawn chairs. Amy nibbled on a big block of cheese like a mouse and Isabel munched on saltines like a squirrel.

"You know what really pisses me off?" Isabel asked.

"Is this one of those rhetorical questions?"

"Yes."

"You didn't have to answer that," Amy said, "It was rhetorical."

"Oh."

They snacked in silence for a full minute. Finally, Amy asked, "What pisses you off?"

"Oh, yeah," Isabel said, remembering what she was going to say. "Hot dogs."

"Hot dogs like in wieners?"

"Yep. They're sold in packages of ten. And buns are sold in packages of eight. That's not right. It's this giant food conspiracy and we just lay back and take it. We let them do it to us."

"I wish you hadn't pointed that out," Amy said. "Now I'm pissed off."

"What's going on out here?" a male voice asked. Both women jerked their heads toward the house and saw Chad looking out the back door.

"Hey!" Isabel said cheerily because she was at the stage of drunkenness where everybody is your friend and everything is potential fun.

"Ugh," Amy said disgustedly because she was at the tipping-point of drunkenness where all it would take is one little thing to tip her from happy to belligerent. And that one little thing was striding across the lawn toward her.

Chad approached carefully because he had spotted the wine bottles nestled in the crotches of the women. "Have we decided to forego dinner in lieu of drinking?"

"Forego. Lieu," Amy mocked. "Listen to how smart I am. I can say forego and lieu in the same sentence."

Isabel laughed. Cracker crumbs sprayed out her mouth and into her lap.

Chad squinted at Amy. "You need to eat something."

"I am eating," Amy said, showing him the one-pound block of cheddar cheese that had nibble marks around its entire circumference.

"Yeah, we are eating," Isabel said through another mouthful of crackers.

Then, in an unspoken display of drunken simpatico, Amy tossed the block of cheese and Isabel tossed the box of saltines, each to the other. They caught the other's toss and began to munch happily.

"You are drunk," Chad said.

"You are sober," Amy retorted. She held the box of crackers up to him. "Cracker?"

He waved away the box. "Where's Jeremy?" he asked.

Isabel said, "He came home, mumbled something about women and PMS and locked himself in his bedroom with a bucket of left-over Kentucky Fried chicken that he scavenged from the back of the fridge."

"I'd offer you a chair," Amy said, "but I don't want you to stay."

Amy and Isabel giggled.

Chad put his hands on his hips and stared down his perfectly shaped nose at her. "I want you to know, Amy," he said, "that you aren't making a good impression on me right now."

"Oooh, don't say such things, Chad. You're making me sad," Amy said. She didn't so much drip sarcasm as she spewed it. She giggled. "Chad. Sad. I rhymed!"

"I'm serious. If you're going to be my number one girlfriend you can't go around getting drunk and eating with your bare hands in the back yard like a feral animal."

"Here's a solution," Amy said. "Demote me to number three girlfriend. Or maybe number ten. Or how about you take me off the list entirely. How do you like them crackers?"

Chad crossed his arms over his muscular pecs. "Is this about the banana peel?" he asked.

"Could you possibly get any more asshole-ish?" Amy said. "Of course it's about the damn banana peel. It's about the basic philosophy behind the banana peel. First, by throwing the condom on the floor where it would prove a safety hazard you demonstrated what an inconsiderate fucktard you are. Second, by telling everyone the story you proved that you're a gossip and will do anything for a cheap laugh, and third just because I made the mistake of sleeping with you once, much to my regret, does not mean I want to have anything further to do with you."

"Brava! Tell it to him straight, sister," Isabel said.

Chad stared at Amy. "You don't mean that. You're not thinking straight. I'm going to give you a pass on tonight."

"Ugh!" Amy said, and pelted him with a cracker. It bounced off the side of his perfectly shaped head.

He glared at her. "Now you're throwing food at me?"

"You're lucky I didn't have the block of cheese in my hands," she said.

Isabel guffawed. "I saw a gorilla do that once. At the zoo. He got tired of this guy making faces at him through the bars and he picked up his feces and threw it at the guy. Splat! Right in the kisser."

Amy grinned at Chad. "Be careful. I may throw my feces at you next."

Chad stomped on the cracker and glared at her. "I've had enough. I'm going home to wait for your apology." He stalked back across the yard.

"You'll be waiting a long time," Amy called out after him.

He disappeared through the door. Amy and Isabel grinned. Then they tossed the cheese and crackers to each other and went back to nibbling.

## **Mirror, Mirror**

"How do I look?" Jordan asked. She stood in the hallway, scrutinizing herself in the full-length mirror that leaned against the "wall." "Wall" deserved quotation marks because the "wall" wasn't really a wall. The old, crumbly drywall had been taken down and all that remained were two-by-four studs and bare electrical wiring. This was the motif for the entire second story of the house. Whenever Jordan complained to Edison about the "walls," Edison only said, "Sometimes it's necessary to tear something down before you can build it back up." That may be true, but when it was going to be built back up was the problem. So, the mirror was leaning against the "wall" and Jordan was checking her reflection. She asked again, "Tell me the truth, Ed, how do I look?"

Jordan did a complete 360 to give the full effect of her ensemble. Actually ensemble may have been too expansive a word. Outfit was more suitable for what she was wearing: khaki shorts, sandals and a white linen shirt.

"You look casually sexy," Edison replied. "Or sexily casual. Depending on who's doing the looking."

"Not too casual though, right?"

"Right."

"Too sexy?"

Edison shook her head. "I think you've found the perfect blend of casual sex."

Jordan stood with her back to the mirror and peered over her right shoulder. "I can't see my butt."

"It's there, don't worry."

"Does my butt make my pants look big?"

Edison laughed. "Your butt is perfect and you know it."

Jordan grabbed her butt cheeks and lifted them up higher. When she took away her hands they bounced back into place. She sighed and grabbed her cheeks again. This time she squeezed her cheeks together in an effort to make them look smaller.

"My butt's too big," Jordan moaned.

Edison's face lit up. She pulled a roll of duct tape out of her pocket and held it high. "I could tape it. I could tape anything you wanted. I could make your butt smaller and your boobs higher. Or I could make your boobs smaller and your butt higher. Your choice."

"Do you use it?" Jordan asked.

"I have. It works great. Hurts like hell taking it off, though."

"I'll pass."

"Whatever. It's here if you need it." Edison put the tape back in her pocket.

Jordan turned around and looked full on at her reflection. "I just don't want to look too planned. Looking planned is the equivalent to looking desperate. And looking desperate turns women off."

"I don't know about that," Edison said, "I kind of like a quiet air of desperation. It means they're easy targets."

Jordan whacked Edison in the arm with the back of her bandaged hand. "Ow!" she exclaimed. "Your arm hit my hand."

"Listen, Jordan, reality-check here. You're just going to see the Doc so she can take out the stitches. It isn't a date. She has a boyfriend, remember the guy in the photo."

"I know that. But I'm not competing with him. I would just be presenting another option so this could be the precursor to a date with a person who is offering another type of relationship. You have to remember most of us didn't start off gay. We eventually realized it. Maybe Amy hasn't realized it yet. That's all I'm saying."

"So you are going to ask her out."

"If it comes up organically."

"How does asking somebody out come up organically?"

"You know like if her stomach growls and I hear it. I could say, 'You must be hungry,' and she'd say 'I *am* hungry' and I could say 'let's go get something to eat' and then she'd say…"

Edison picked up, "And she would say 'I'm hungry for you, baby' and you'd say 'Here I am, come and get it.'"

They laughed, but stopped abruptly when the door across the hall opened a crack and one eye peeked out.

**Meet Irma Kalandarishvili.** Irma had black hair, black eyes, and an entire wardrobe of only black clothes. Or maybe she just had only one black outfit. Jordan wasn't sure. Irma was tall and thin like a ballerina and her hair was slicked back in a severely lacquered bun. She never blinked. Nobody had ever seen her blink. She could've been mistaken for a stick of licorice.

Jordan had gone out on a date with her two years ago. The date was horrible but the sex afterwards made up for it. Irma and Jordan fulfilled a hunger in each other that other people couldn't. It wasn't based on banter or intellect or common interests. It was purely animalistic. So, Jordan and Irma became friends with benefits except they weren't really friends. And when Irma showed up one day needing a place to stay, Jordan rented her a spare bedroom.

Irma moved in and paid her rent on time with cash. Nobody knew where Irma was from – Russia? Germany? Or one of those Slavickstan kind of countries? Nobody knew how she made her money or what she did behind the doors of her room.

Ever since Irma had moved in six months ago, Jordan had avoided her. She didn't want to have a physical relationship with somebody that lived under her own roof. It had been fine to be fuck-buddies when your buddy didn't live with you but now it was different. Jordan reasoned that it was too much like that old adage, "Don't shit on the hand that feeds you." Or something like that. She'd told Irma that but Irma wasn't giving up so easily.

Irma eyed Jordan up and down and said in her thick accent that sounded like Natasha from *The Rocky and Bullwinkle Show*, "You are dressing for big date?"

Jordan shrugged. "Just a maybe date."

Irma leered at her. "If maybe date is not what dreams are made, you come to Irma and Irma will *un-dress* you and show things you never experiment in wild dreams."

Edison said, "I think you mean *experience* in your wildest dreams."

Irma looked at her coldly. "No. Irma mean *experiment* in wild dreams." She looked back to Jordan and smiled wickedly before she ducked back inside and closed the door.

"Someday I'm going to scream in her face. Just to see if she blinks," Edison said.

Jordan laughed. "She won't. I think her hair is so tight in that bun she can't blink."

Edison laughed. "I don't get what you see in her."

"We had an arrangement, that's all. It worked in both our favors."

"What an arrangement," Edison said with a huge eye-roll. "If you two aren't doing somebody else then you do each other."

"Operative word here is *did*. We no longer *do*. But I'm sure you could find the same type of arrangement if you wanted."

Edison said in an imitation of Irma's accent, "Edison not want. Edison want love true not buddy fuck in experiment love."

"You don't really believe in true love, do you?"

"Sure. Don't you?" Edison said, brushing a stray hair off Jordan's shoulder. She straightened her collar.

"Nope," Jordan said.

"Nope?"

"No." Jordan looked at herself in the mirror again. "I believe the concept of true love is just an illusion."

Edison looked at Jordan's face, at her reflection in the mirror, then back to Jordan. She imitated Irma's accent, "Edison think one of you is big fat liar."

## Happy Birthday to Me

Jordan paced back and forth in the small room. There wasn't much to do or look at while she waited for Amy. The décor left a lot to be desired. One gurney-type rolling bed, one rolling stool, and a small desk holding some medical torture instruments. The desk was on wheels, too. What was it with doctors and rolling devices?

There were two doors. One was the door that she had come in and the other door led to another room identical to this one. Jordan knew because she had peeked earlier.

She stopped pacing long enough to study the poster that was taped to the wall. It depicted a cartoon boy holding his hands over a sink. There were bugs and worms crawling all over his hands. Cartoon germs. She moved to the next poster. It was a drawing of the male anatomy complete with Latin-esque labels. Jordan leaned in close and studied the side view of the phallus. It was a sliced open view so you could see what the inside of the penis looked like. It looked all spongy. She reached out and touched it with one finger. It just felt like a poster.

She wiped her un-bandaged hand on the side of her shorts. Her palm was sweaty. It was a cold sweat. Nerves. She didn't like to admit it, but Amy made her nervous. Not like she was scared of her, but like she was scared *of* her. That didn't make sense unless you were Jordan. And it made perfect sense to her. She was scared of Amy, all right. Not scared of the physical person of Amy. More like scared of how Amy made her feel.

The small room was giving her an acute case of claustrophobia. The walls were closing in, making her brain play tricks on itself. She swore the cartoon boy on the "Always wash your hands!" poster was talking to her. Which was markedly better than the penis one talking to her. The cartoon boy told her she should wash her hands. Sweaty hands were germy hands and sing the Happy Birthday song because that was the specified length for optimum germ removal. She didn't know whether she should believe him or not but she had an instant driving desire to rid her hands of sweat and potentially hazardous germs.

She went to the sink, and turned on the hot water. She didn't want to shake hands with Amy and have a clammy, sweaty palm. That would be the death knell of any budding relationship. Almost as bad as kissing and slobbering on her face. She held her hand under the stream of water and sang the Happy Birthday song all the way through just like the cartoon boy in the poster told her to do.

When she turned off the water, she heard a voice. No, two voices. They were coming from the room next door. One voice sounded like Amy's. Jordan pressed her ear to the door that led to the room next door, closed her eyes and listened. There was a man's voice, and Amy's voice.

Here is what she heard the voices say:
"No! Don't!" Amy said.
"Why not? You want it. You know you do," a man said.
"I do not want it. Especially while I'm working."
"C'mon, this is the perfect place. That way if it makes you sick you're already in a hospital."
"I don't have time," Amy said. "I have an appointment any minute now."
"I'll be quick. Here, open your mouth."
"No!" Amy screeched. "Put that back where it belongs. I don't want to even look at it."
"Aw. C'mon. Just put a little bit in your mouth."
Amy screamed. Metal clanged against metal and fell to the floor. There was a giant *thud*.

Jordan immediately morphed into white knight mode. She bashed open the door and crashed into the room, hands held high in a karate posture. She *hai-yai'ed* and did the whooping crane stance that *The Karate Kid* made famous.

The frozen tableau she saw before her was this: Amy was in a corner. Jeremy was holding a bowl in one hand and a spoon in the other. He held the spoon, which had some type of green sludge in it, only an inch from Amy's lips. A bedpan was on the floor, still spinning from its fall.

"Unhand her," Jordan said because she was still thinking like a knight and Amy was her damsel in distress.

Jeremy clanked the spoon into the bowl and said, "Hey, you're the lesbian hottie."

Jordan relaxed, deflating from the whooping crane stance to one of an embarrassed penguin. "And you're Amy's boyfriend. Who's trying to spoon feed her."

Amy laughed and slapped Jeremy's chest with the back of her hand. "He's not my boyfriend. He's my butthole roommate. Who's trying to make me eat my other roommate's experiment."

"Um, okay," Jordan said. "I'll just be right over there. In the next room. Waiting." She held up her injured hand. "Stitches, you know." She saluted them. "Carry on."

Jordan backed out the door, smiling so big her face hurt. She closed the door and banged her head against it, muttering, "Dumb, dumb, dumb." She went back to the sink, turned on the water and washed her face with her one good hand while humming *Happy Birthday.*

"Is it your birthday?"

Jordan gasped and turned. It was Amy. She turned off the faucet and looked around for a paper towel. "No, it's not my birthday. I was just singing it because the cartoon boy told me to."

"Cartoon boy?" Amy asked. She tilted her head to one side. She squinted like she was trying to figure out if Jordan had gone bonkers.

Jordan gestured at the poster.

Amy studied the poster. She looked worried. "That boy in the poster talked to you? You know he's not alive, right?" Amy handed her a paper towel.

"No!" Jordan said. "I mean, yes, I know that. I meant the bubble over his head said to sing…well you know." She took the paper towel and dried her hands.

Amy laughed. "I was just kidding."

Jordan breathed a sigh of relief. "Oh. That was funny. You had me going there for a minute." There was an awkward pause while she wiped her face with the paper towel. "Um, sorry about bursting in on you like that. It sounded like, you know…"

"Yeah, I know," Amy said, "But it wasn't what you think. And he's not what you think."

Jordan nodded. She nodded too much. It was like she couldn't stop nodding. She felt like one of those toy Chihuahua dogs people put on the dashboard of their car.

"You're nervous, huh?" Amy asked.

Jordan nodded quickly about three hundred more times.

"No need to be. Getting stitches taken out doesn't hurt at all. Have a seat." Amy looked over her paperwork on her clipboard and jotted down some notes.

Jordan sat on the gurney-bed. She could feel the coarse paper lying across the top of it sticking to the back of her sweaty thighs. Great. She was so nervous that she was sweating all over now. Amy was going to think she had some kind of sweating disease.

Jordan closed her eyes and took three deep breaths. She couldn't ask Amy out. There was no way this brilliant, busy, probably straight doctor would go out with her. Jordan was certain she would just make a fool of herself by asking, and Amy was so nice that she'd have to make up an excuse and then they'd both know she was lying and that would make everything really awkward and tense and then she'd have to tell Edison about how stupid she'd been and she'd feel embarrassed about it for months or maybe even years.

"One down," Amy said.

Jordan opened her eyes. Amy was smiling and holding one tiny little black piece of thread in some tweezers.

"That didn't hurt, did it?" Amy asked.

Jordan shook her head. She'd been so wrapped up in the conversation with herself that she hadn't known when Amy had unwrapped her hand and taken out a stitch.

God, this woman was delectable. If she asked Amy to kiss it and make it better, would she? That was a wicked thought. Wickedly delicious, that is. Wasn't that the jingle for Lucky Charms? No, that was *magically* delicious. Jordan closed her eyes again and thought of sex. She had learned this trick while going to the dentist. Thinking about sex made having people poke and prod in your mouth much more tolerable. Now, she had Amy to think of having sex with. She knew she shouldn't go there, but she went there anyway.

"Done," Amy pronounced.

Jordan opened her eyes again and gaped at Amy. She had taken all the stitches out in less time than she could sing the Lucky Charms jingle.

"Wow," Jordan said for lack of anything better to say.

"Your hand is healing nicely. Now let's see how it functions.

"You made it bionic, right? 'Cause I always wanted a bionic hand."

Amy laughed. "Let's just see if you can open and close it first."

Jordan slowly made a fist while making bionic sounds. A sudden shot of pain made her stop and gasp. "Ouch." She looked at Amy. "That hurt."

"It will for a while. You did sever a tendon, you know. Practice opening and closing, making a fist, squeezing." Amy demonstrated the motion with her own hand. She looked like she was milking a cow. "You'll have to do some physical therapy in order to regain full use of your hand."

Jordan's world brightened a little. "I get to come here and do therapy with you?"

"No, you can do it yourself. At home."

"Oh," Jordan said when what she really wanted to say was "Damn." She'd had a little ray of hope there for a minute. Hope that she'd get to come to Amy's office and practice squeezing things. Whoops, there were those magically delicious thoughts again.

Amy rolled her chair over to the desk, opened a drawer and rummaged around inside. When she rolled back over, she handed Jordan a little yellow rubber ball. "Squeeze on that ball. Carry it around with you and when you have a spare moment, squeeze it. In a few weeks, you'll have complete use of your hand again."

Jordan gave it a try. She could barely make a dent in the ball.

"Keep at it. You'll see."

She stowed the ball in the side pocket of her shorts. Amy rolled away to the desk.

I want one of those rolling stools, Jordan thought. I could get all around my house and never have to stand at all.

When Amy rolled back, she handed Jordan a stack of books. Jordan accepted them with her good hand and was shocked when she saw they were the books she'd written.

"These are mine," Jordan said. "I mean, they

belong to you, obviously, but I wrote them."

"I bought them the other day. I was wondering if you'd do me the honor of autographing them?"

"Yeah, sure. Of course I will," Jordan said. She was stunned. She'd never been asked for her autograph before.

Amy handed her a pen.

Jordan opened the first book to the title page and had a sudden thought. "Who should I make it out to?"

"Me," Amy said.

Jordan bent over the page and wrote: *Amy, will you go to lunch with me? Jordan March.*

Jordan nervously handed it over. She watched as Amy read it and looked up at her.

"I'd love to," Amy said. "When?"

"Now?"

"Right now?"

"Do you not want to?" Jordan asked, her heart racing. Thank God, Amy didn't have her stethoscope with her – she might admit her to the cardiac unit for observation.

"No, it's the suddenness of it that startled me."

"We could do it tomorrow. Or next week. Or some evening."

Amy shook her head, saying, "We can't do it in the evening."

"Um, okay, I understand. You already have plans and…"

Amy interrupted her, "No, I mean you wrote 'lunch' so we can't do lunch in the evening."

Jordan quickly wrote in the next book: *Or dinner?*

Amy read it and laughed. "What are you going to write in the third book?"

Jordan shrugged. "Depends on how well lunch goes. When would you like to go?"

"Now?"

"Right now?"

"Isn't that what you said? You wanted to do it right now?"

Jordan shook her head. "I'm confused. Are we still talking about lunch?"

Amy giggled. Jordan liked it when Amy giggled.

"How about if I meet you out front in five minutes?"

"That'd be great," Jordan said. "See you then!" She hurried into the hall and headed to the elevator. She felt like skipping. She felt like skipping and singing and laughing all at the same time.

## Three's Company

Jordan exited the sliding glass doors of the hospital and did a touchdown victory dance that looked a cross between clogging and disco.

"Does this mean the date is on?"

Jordan jumped. "My God! Don't sneak up behind me like that!"

"I didn't sneak. I walked like a normal person," Edison said. "If you weren't so busy spazzing out, you'd have seen me," Edison said.

Jordan went back to her jubilant state, hopping from foot to foot. "She said yes. She said yes. She said yes!"

"So when's the big day?"

"Today. Now."

"Right now?"

"Yes, right now. She's meeting me out here in a few minutes."

Edison looked at her watch. "Okay. I guess I can do lunch."

"Not you," Jordan said. "It's a date. That usually means only two people. You know, the whole 'three's a crowd' saying."

"I thought it was 'three's company.'"

"That was the TV show, not the saying."

"I liked that show. I had a crush on the brunette. What was her name?"

"Maryanne, I think."

"No, that was the brunette on *Gilligan's Island*."

"Aha! I know what you're trying to do. You're trying to divert my attention so you can go on my date with me. But it won't work because her name was Janet," Jordan said.

"I'll drive you, that's all. I won't sit at your table or anything."

"You're going to stare at us. I know you. You're going to sit and stare and eavesdrop. I won't be able to concentrate."

"I will not! Besides, it's my car. I drove you here. How will you get home if I don't go and take you home after? And you don't want her to see where you live until the house is finished. Your house will make you seem like you never finish a project. I read a book once that had this psychological test where people went into dorm rooms and did a personality profile on the person based on what they saw. It was spot on. That's why if you're checking out a person you should go to their place and see what it looks like, then you'll know if you want to date them."

Jordan was horrified. "The state of the house is your fault."

"Ah, but you let me do it," Edison said.

Amy appeared behind them. "I'm ready."

Edison and Jordan jumped. Edison said, "My God! Don't sneak up on us like that!"

Amy laughed. "Yep, that's me. Miss Sneaky Pants."

"Edison is going to be our chauffeur. She'll be driving us to lunch. If that's all right."

"Great!" Amy said. "I left my car at the dealer."

"Is something wrong with it?" Edison asked, her I-can-fix-it-myself proclivity quivering with anticipation.

Jordan was certain if Edison ever got hold of Amy's car it would end up being Chitty Chitty Bang Bang – except it wouldn't be able to float or fly. Or even drive.

"No, they're giving it the once over so I can pick up my new car after work."

"New car?" Jordan asked. "What kind?"

"It's a surprise."

"Are you going to show me the surprise sometime or will I always have to wonder?" Jordan asked.

"We'll see how lunch goes," Amy said, smiling

mischievously.

"I'll go get my car," Edison said, giving Jordan the evil eye as she walked to the parking lot.

Jordan watched her go, thinking having Edison as a best friend was like having a cold sore – she never went away and as long as she was around, Jordan would never get kissed.

## Date or Date-Date?

As Jordan sat scrunched in the back seat, listening to Edison and Amy chatter, she began to wonder if this was a real date in the conventional sense that the word "date" implied. Meaning: two people sharing a meal, a couple of hours together, with romantic intentions. Maybe Amy didn't know it was a date. Maybe she thought it was friends going to lunch together. Maybe she thought they were going to talk about girl things and tandem eat sandwiches. How could Jordan let Amy know that she considered their mutual sandwich eating a date-date and not just a date without scaring her off? Then again, if it did scare Amy off didn't that mean she didn't want to date-date? And wouldn't it be better to find that out on the date before it became a date-date?

Jordan was working herself into a headache. This was exactly why she didn't date-date. Irma was so much easier. She wished she had taken Amy up on that Vicodin offer. Then she could pop one right now and relax.

Edison scored a parking spot right in front of The Original Dinerant, which was a miracle in itself. Jordan even had enough change to plug the parking meter for two hours. Another miracle. They got a table right away, a window seat – yet another miracle.

"Wow. This place is really cool. It's like retro," Amy said. She pointed to the staircase. Where does that go?"

Jordan and Edison looked around as if seeing it for the first time. They always ate here so they no longer realized the grooviness of the place.

"There's a lounge upstairs with couches and a floating fireplace. It's pretty awesome," Edison said.

Edison led the way upstairs, giving a tour of the couches and floating fireplace like she was the owner of the place. Jordan sat at a table and studied the menu while Edison chatted up her date. She hoped Amy couldn't see her seething behind the menu.

Ten minutes later, Jordan and Amy had both ordered a turkey sandwich with baked chips and extra pickles. Jordan took their turkey symbiosis to be an omen of their compatibility. She was silently pleased that Edison ordered breakfast.

Jordan caught Edison's eye and made head motions away from the table. Finally, Edison figured out what Jordan was trying to communicate in charades. She stood and said, "Well, ladies, if you'll excuse me now."

"Where are you going?" Amy asked.

"Um..." Edison said. "Um..."

Jordan jumped in with: "She likes to eat alone."

"I do?" Edison said. She quickly changed her question to a statement, "Yes, I do."

"I'll tell our waitress to send your crème brulee French toast up to the lounge," Jordan said.

"Why?" Amy asked.

"She has an eating disorder. That's why she's having breakfast instead of lunch at lunchtime," Jordan said.

"Oh no, but lots of people order breakfast food for lunch," Amy said, concerned.

"Not an eating disorder per se," Edison said. "More like an eating... phobia."

"You're afraid to eat?" Amy asked.

"With other people," Jordan answered for her.

"It's called masticaphobia," Edison said.

"Never heard of it, but I'm not a psychologist," Amy said. "If it would make you more comfortable we can leave. I don't want you to feel like..."

Jordan interrupted, "Stay, Ed. Sit down and eat with us." She couldn't keep the disappointment out of her voice. "Please."

"Okay, I'll try to overcome my fear of sandwiches and people eating sandwiches." Edison smiled tightly and sat back down.

Jordan sighed. It was obvious Amy wanted Edison to stay. A horrible thought struck her. What if Amy discovered that she liked Edison better? Ed was cute and very approachable. Jordan tuned back in to their conversation just in time to hear Amy ask Edison, "So what do you do for a living?"

Edison put her chin in her hand, looked at Amy and asked, "Well... Do you like toys?"

Jordan cleared her throat and kicked Edison under the table. "Ow!" Edison said and promptly kicked Jordan back, but Amy dove into her answer without missing a beat.

"Well, depends on the toy, I guess. I loved Barbies when I was a kid. I had maybe twenty Barbies and a dream house and a pink convertible. Tons of clothes for them and a cute little pink suitcase to carry them in. The problem was I had this puppy, his name was Humphrey, and he liked to chew on my Barbies whenever I left them on the floor, which was most of the time. So all my Barbies ended up with chewed off hands, gnawed feet, missing hair, teeth marks all over them. That's when I got the idea to be a doctor. I know that sounds stupid, but I turned the dream house into an operating room and surgically removed the chewed parts of the Barbies with steak knives. I made prosthetic devices for their missing limbs out of bent paper clips."

"Then we have a lot in common," Edison said. "I make prosthetic devices, too."

Jordan coughed loudly. Amy looked at her quizzically then asked Edison, "What kind of prosthetics do you make?"

Edison smiled. "Well... Do you like *adult* toys?"
"You mean like chess?" Amy asked.

"I love chess!" Jordan said much too quickly and way too loudly.

Edison ignored her and continued, "I mean like sex toys."

"Oh," Amy said. She took a sip of water, and said "Oh," a second time.

Jordan interrupted, "Ed, that's not appropriate lunch conversation."

"She asked what I did for a living," Edison said. "I'm giving her an honest answer." She turned back to Amy and said bluntly, "I make sex toys."

"Oh," Amy said.

"I'm an inventor," Edison explained. "That's why they call me Edison."

Jordan explained further, "She invents sex toys. She has several patents on file."

Edison sat up straighter and said proudly, "Dildoes are my specialty. I've invented The Corndog, The Muffin Mucker, and The Plunger. Just to name a few."

"I see you've chosen very descriptive names," Amy said.

After a long silence during which they all looked at their menus even though they'd already placed their order, Amy said, "I need to go to the rest room. I'll be right back."

Jordan watched Amy walk into the ladies' room before she turned and whapped Edison on top of the head with her menu.

"Ow!"

## The Ice Queen Cometh

Jordan whispered harshly, "What's with the sex toys talk? Are you trying to scare her off?"

Edison crossed her arms. "Wouldn't you like to know right off the bat if she's squeamish about lesbians? That way you don't waste your time?"

"Sex toys are personal. Not all lesbians use them, you know."

"Oh yeah? Name five who don't."

Jordan's eyes flickered to the front of the diner. "Oh, shit," she mumbled.

"Sex toys are a way of life…"

Jordan interrupted, "Not that. Oh shit, Petronella's here."

Edison immediately went into bodyguard mode. "Quick, hide."

Jordan looked around. "Where?"

"Under the table."

Jordan slid out of her chair and onto her knees. The tablecloth hid her from view. She scrunched herself into a little ball, knees under her chin, and watched in horror as Petronella's white heels clacked toward their table.

**Meet Dr. Petronella Bleeker**, the Dutch lesbian poet. She had gained a modicum of success for publishing a thin volume of poetry ten years ago. She won a few awards, made little to no money, and now much to her chagrin and humiliation was a professor at Portland State University. Petronella felt she was working below her status. A poet of her caliber should be teaching at Yale or Harvard or not even teaching at all. She carried a chip on her shoulder everywhere she went and never missed a chance to beat people over the head with it.

Petronella was revered by the lesbian community because she was the only poet who had ever successfully

rhymed the word vagina. Petronella always dressed in all white. Even her hair was bleached white. It was her signature color because it was the absence of color. She was also fashionably thin – all gristle, no white meat.
    *To Be Continued...*

## Jordan and Petronella's Story

Jordan and Petronella had been lovers for one year, twenty-seven days and three hours. At the beginning Petronella was everything Jordan had ever fantasized about. Petronella was smart, educated, creative, attentive, an excellent lover. She was beautiful in a Queen Frostine kind of way. But like all ice sculptures, she had melted over time and left Jordan standing in a puddle of cold water that turned her toes blue.

Jordan should have known Petronella was too good to be true. But how can somebody know something like that? You don't really know somebody until you live with them. Then their façade cracks and you get glimpses of who they truly are. That's where Jordan went wrong. She ignored the glimpses of the real Petronella that she saw between the cracks. She wanted to be loved so badly that she pretended.

The first time she had crossed paths with Petronella had been on campus. Jordan had been hired to teach a semester seminar on girls as protagonists in children's lit. The class was the Dean's brainchild – a liaison between women's studies and the Education Department's Early Childhood Development. Jordan had been recruited and hired because she was famous and local. She was more the latter than the former. She also worked for peanuts.

Jordan had been invited to the Women's Studies bi-annual potluck. She had felt out of place. Her contribution had been a bag of nacho cheese flavored Doritos and a can of bean dip. She put the dip in the center of the table and realized that once again, she didn't fit in. Everyone else had brought typical lesbian dishes: tabouli, humus, salad, stinky cheeses made out of milk that wasn't cow's, and gluten-free desserts.

Jordan sat alone in a corner of the room munching

Doritos when Petronella approached. Petronella stared. Jordan looked into Petronella's glacial eyes and a shiver ran down her spine. At the time she thought it was lust that made her tremble. She didn't realize until much later it was actually fear.

She held out the bag of chips to Petronella. Petronella only smiled. It reminded Jordan of the wolf's smile in the story of *Little Red Riding Hood*.

"Come," Petronella ordered.

Jordan obediently followed Petronella out the door and to her car. "Where are we going?"

"You will see and you will like it," Petronella said with authority.

Petronella drove four blocks from campus and parked in front of a beautiful house. She showed Jordan into the foyer, up the marble staircase, through the immaculate white bedroom filled with mirrors and out onto a terrace.

"You wanted me to see your house?" Jordan asked.

Petronella laughed. "No," she said. "I want to show you the only thing of beauty that even begins to compare to you."

Jordan laughed nervously. Petronella gracefully lifted her palm above her head and gestured to the moon. "Behold, the moon," she said dramatically. Everything Petronella did was with great flair as if she knew she was going to shape it into a poem later.

Jordan beheld the moon. It was orange, round and full. When she looked back at Petronella, she was shocked to see that she was disrobing. Petronella let her silk blouse slide off her shoulders to the tile floor. Her breasts glistened in the moonlight. She had large nipples like eyes opened wide and staring.

Petronella stepped out of her white wedge shoes, unbuttoned her linen slacks and kicked them aside. She was ghostly pale in the moonlight. She had no pubic hair.

Her entire body was smooth and white like a marble statue.

"I want to make love to you," Petronella said. "From the moment I saw you, I wanted nothing more than to hold you in my hands, suck you into my mouth, to feel your heat against my tongue, to make you writhe in orgasmic ecstasy."

"Wow," Jordan said. "You don't beat around the bush." She thought, but didn't say, "If there were a bush, which there isn't."

Petronella slinked up to her and boldly kissed Jordan's neck. Her shoulders. Her cheeks. Her lips. She lightly brushed Jordan's nipples and stroked her butt. Jordan felt her insides tighten, then release. Her body was betraying her.

Petronella knelt before her, took her into her mouth, and devoured her greedily.

Jordan stared up at the moon. When she came, she opened her mouth and swallowed the moon. It filled her belly and lit her up from the inside as if she were a Jack O' Lantern. Jordan knew this happened because the next day Petronella detailed their sexual liaison in her newest poem, "The Woman Who Swallowed the Moon."

When Jordan looked back at the sky, the moon was gone and she was in love.

Petronella led her back through the sliding glass doors and into her bed where she made love to Jordan three more times.

"You are my muse," Petronella said while she cradled Jordan in her arms. "I shall write beautiful poems about you. I will never let you go. Never, ever let you go."

It wasn't until months later Jordan realized she meant *exactly* what she said.

Jordan had been living with Petronella a full month before she noticed the control issues. Petronella told her what to wear, what to eat, what to read, what kind of coffee she should drink. Jordan noticed as time went on that she didn't even have to talk. Petronella took it upon herself to single-handedly run Jordan's life.

One day Jordan woke up and discovered that she no longer had a life. And to make matters worse, Petronella became possessive to the point that no one could look at Jordan without Petronella going ballistic. She swore that Jordan encouraged these looks. According to Petronella, Jordan was a vixen that needed watching.

It exhausted Jordan. And when she complained and said maybe she would rather live in her own house, maybe they should break up, Petronella had responded by throwing the *Anthology of Feminist Poetry as It Concerns the Vulva* at her. Jordan had been too surprised to duck and ended up with a black eye. Petronella cried. She promised things would change. She wrote her a poem. And afterwards, she made passionate love to Jordan.

The second time she tried to leave, Jordan was sneaky. She packed her clothes when Petronella was at work. She was in the driveway, putting the clothes in her car's back seat when Petronella came home early and tried to run her over with her car. She took a sledgehammer to Jordan's car's lights, the engine and the windows and then ran into the back end twelve times. Jordan's insurance didn't cover crazy girlfriends demolishing her car. Petronella cried. She promised things would change. She wrote her a poem. And afterward, she made passionate love to Jordan.

The third time Jordan tried to end the relationship was when she caught Petronella on her moonlit balcony devouring one of her graduate students. Petronella managed to turn the tables and make the whole thing Jordan's fault. That had to be the master manipulation of the century. She accused Jordan of being frigid, unemotional and unresponsive to lovemaking, consequently Petronella was forced into cheating on Jordan. All these insults were hurled at her along with books, picture frames, frozen fish, chopsticks, bowls, and the microwave.

The graduate student had cowered in the corner until there was a lull in the fighting and then she ran out of the house. She called 911 and the police came and escorted Jordan home. Jordan didn't press charges. She was just happy to be away from Petronella.

That was a mere six months ago. And since that time, Petronella had a knack of showing up anywhere Jordan was. Jordan was beginning to think Petronella had secretly installed a lo-jack up her ass.

## The Ice Queen Cometh, Continued

From the safety of under the table, Jordan stared at the pointy toes of Petronella's high heels and listened to the conversation between her and Edison.

**Petronella**: Hello, Jordan's little friend.

**Edison**: Hello, Dr. Bleeker. You look like an ice sculpture today and I mean that in the nicest way possible.

**Petronella**: Where is Jordan?

**Edison**: I'm fine, thank you for asking. How are you?

Petronella's right toe tapped three times.

**Petronella**: I have no fooling-around time. Where is Jordan?

**Edison**: Okay, I give up, where is she?

**Petronella**: I need to speak with her. It is urgent. There is an upcoming event that I would like to invite her to attend.

(Petronella did not speak in contractions. As an admitted member of the bourgeois, she considered contractions too lower class.)

**Edison**: I'll be happy to give her the message. Will there be anything else?

**Petronella**: No.

Petronella's shoes walked away.

**Edison**: You have a nice day, too. And by 'have a nice day' I mean go fuck yourself.

Suddenly, Petronella stopped.

"Oh, shit, oh, no," Edison said in a whisper to Jordan. "The Ice Queen is talking to Amy."

Jordan peeked over the top of the table and watched helplessly as Petronella blocked Amy's path and said something to her. Amy tilted her head. Petronella spoke again and pointed at Amy's feet.

After Petronella walked away, Amy looked down at

her feet. She raised a shoe. There was toilet paper stuck to her heel. She tried to step it off with her other shoe. It got caught on that shoe. She tried to kick it off. Finally after several electric slide dance moves, Amy succeeded in ridding herself of both the toilet paper and her dignity.

Edison lifted the edge of the tablecloth and looked down at Jordan. "You can come out now."

Jordan shook her head. "Huh uh. It could be a trick. Go follow Petronella and make sure she got in her car and drove away."

Edison nodded. "Good idea."

"And make sure she isn't just driving around the block either."

Just as Edison was about to walk away, Amy's feet appeared. "Where's Jordan?"

"She's under the table. I'll be right back," Edison said.

Amy squatted down and looked at Jordan under the table. "Are you hiding?"

Jordan fake-laughed. "Hiding? Me hiding? Don't be ridiculous."

"Then what are you doing under the table?"

About a billion answers to that question flitted through Jordan's mind: She was looking for a lost contact. Retrieving a dropped fork. Checking the cleanliness of the floor. Looking for gum under the table. Doing a study on the shoes of people in Portland cafes. Jordan reached into her grab bag of answers and pulled one out at random, and it just so happened to be partly true. "I was, uh, scared."

Amy's face softened. She crawled on all fours under the table and sat next to Jordan. "What are you scared of?"

Jordan said in a tiny voice, "I'm scared you don't know this a date. You know a date-date. With me."

"I know it's a date-date," Amy said.

"Really?"

Amy nodded.

Jordan asked, "And you're not weirded out or anything? You know, being on a date-date with a real live lesbian?"

Amy shrugged. "I'd be more weirded out if you weren't real or alive."

Jordan smiled. "How do you think it's going so far? For a first date, I mean."

"I think…"Amy said, "I think I want you to kiss me."

Jordan held her breath, closed her eyes and leaned in to kiss her. Her lips were only a fraction from Amy's when a waitress holding a basket of sandwich, chips and pickles in each hand, peeked under the table. "Who had the extra mayo?"

Kissi interruptus.

## Edison's Story

Edison drove her VW Bug two times over the posted speed limit and careened around a corner. Jordan gripped the strap and pumped her foot against an imaginary brake pedal. Jordan ascertained that Edison was upset about the whole Amy thing and it was sending her over the deep end. Edison didn't want Jordan getting hurt. Jordan knew that. Although her affair with Edison had been brief, a matter of hours really, Jordan knew Edison was infatuated with her. Jordan sensed that Edison found unrequited love blissfully painful. However, it was easier to tolerate when Jordan was not dating. Even when Edison was suffering through Jordan's relationship with Petronella it was easier because she knew that Jordan didn't love Petronella, but this Amy thing was different and Jordan knew that Edison knew that.

"You know, I'm really sorry that your lunch date with Amy didn't work out," Edison said. Before Jordan could answer, she went on, "I had an unrequited love once, too."

That was news to Jordan. Edison had never talked about her past before. Even when Jordan tried to draw her out, Edison would clam up like a... well, like a clam.

"I pined after the minister's daughter," Edison said, wheeling the car around a sharp curve.

"Ooooh, this sounds like *Oranges Are Not the Only Fruit*."

"Except it was the Amish version," Edison said. She stared straight ahead. "I grew up Amish."

"Amish?" Jordan hit her head on the roof of the Bug. "As in bonnets and long dresses and no cell phones Amish?"

"Is there another kind?"

"Amish? You're Amish. Seriously?" Jordan was

on the verge of laughing until she saw the pain etched across Edison's face.

Edison covered her face with her hands. "I shouldn't have told you."

"I wish you wouldn't do that while you're driving," Jordan said, reaching over and grabbing the wheel. Maybe that's why Edison is such a horrible driver, Jordan thought. Driving a buggy must be a lot different from driving a car. "I didn't even know Portland had Amish communities," she said.

Edison took the wheel and miraculously even slowed down. "I'm not from here. I lived in Ohio. I came here after I was shunned."

"You were shunned? Like thrown out?"

"Yes."

Jordan was beginning to feel like Detective Joe Friday in Dragnet – she'd loved that show when she was growing up. (Of course, she had been watching ancient reruns not the originals.) Plumbing Edison was a "just the facts" kind of interview Joe Friday liked; only Jordan wanted the story and a lot more than just the facts. "Why were you shunned?"

"I was raised in Holmes County, Ohio. We were Swartzentruber, but mother insisted we have a flower garden and a paved driveway so we were already living dangerously on the edge."

Jordan was already lost. "What's Swartzentruber?"

"It's like the super-Amish. They think other Amish people are not strict enough. My people don't have running water or electricity. They take the buggy thing seriously. We couldn't even have one of those reflective triangles on the back of the buggy. Do you know how unsafe that it? We couldn't use anything reflective."

"What? You're being serious here?" Jordan honestly thought Edison was fucking with her and she'd burst out laughing saying something like "I really had you going," only that part of the script didn't appear to be showing up.

"Yes. It was the reflective triangle and the sidelong glances between Melly and me that got me shunned. Melly was the preacher's daughter," Edison said.

"One question," Jordan said. "Did kids make fun of her and call her Smelly Melly?"

"That's not funny. I'm being serious."

Jordan studied Edison. She did look serious. "Okay, sorry," Jordan said. "Please continue. The triangle was like a symbol of your love or something?"

"No. Even then I was known for my inventions. Being Amish and having limited contact with the outside world, I didn't know about modern technology. I didn't know about most ancient technology either. I used to spend my nights in secret in the barn, inventing things."

"What kind of things?"

"Oh, you know, the Chop-o-matic, Wart Remover, The Clap On-Clap Off, which was much harder to make with oil lanterns than its electrical cousin."

"I bet," Jordan muttered.

"I had no idea those things already existed. Anyway, I had noticed a need for a reflective paint. There had been too many buggy accidents. You can't see a black buggy on a dirt road at night, you know. One night, Melly and her mother were out helping one of the sick people and they got rear ended by a teenage couple who were out for a drive in their car. Actually, I think the girl was giving her boyfriend a blowjob while he drove. They smashed into Melly's buggy. They weren't going very fast – probably because of the blowjob – and well they crashed and she bit his penis off."

Jordan's mouth gaped open. "Like in *The World According to Garp* kind of bit off?"

Edison nodded. "The townspeople got a little uptight about it. The loss of the penis proved to be the proverbial straw and things got ugly."

That was when Jordan realized that the loss of the boy's penis and Edison's predilection for inventing fake penii might have an emotional connection. "Then what happened?"

"I tried to fix things. I experimented with fluorescents."

Jordan thought Edison said that in the same way most people say, "I experimented with drugs." Jordan pulled the rubber ball out of her pocket and squeezed it. She was now using it as a stress ball. "I'm getting lost. What do fluorescents have to do with Melly?"

Edison flattened out her lips and furrowed her brow. "Let me tell the story in chronological order. I was eighteen and I kissed Melly in the barn. We professed our love. The accident happened. I snuck into the hardware store and stole coated phosphorescent pigment and a gallon of green paint. It's the only thing I've ever stolen. With Melly's help I painted all the backs of the buggies so they would glow in the dark. This appeased the townspeople. They thought the Swartzentrubers had caved. I hadn't counted on that. I just wanted everyone to be safe. I could've lost Melly in that accident. Word got out and that was the end of everything. The elders found out who'd done it and I was finished. I claimed full responsibility but Melly got in trouble too. She was only seventeen so she couldn't go with me. Her parents sent her to live with relatives in Pennsylvania. I never saw her again." Edison wiped a tear. "I hitch-hiked here."

"Wow," Jordan said, shaking her head.

"Don't tell anybody, okay?"

"Okay. Your secret's safe with me."

"Anyway, I'm sorry your lunch date didn't work out," Edison said. "The whole dating game is overrated. Don't feel bad about it. Lots of people are dating-challenged. You're just one of those people. Me too.

That's why we have each other. As friends – I know what you're thinking – as friends. I totally agree with your assessment on that matter. But if you ask me, and I know you're not, but if you did ask me, I'd say that today's dating disaster was worth it. Now you know that you and Amy aren't compatible. You got it out of your system. You're free to move on."

"Actually," Jordan said, "we have another date tomorrow."

Edison punched the gas and swerved the car around another corner. Jordan hung on for dear life.

## Lesbians in the Mist

Amy was nervous. Everything in her mind told her not to go. However, everything in her body said, *"Go! Go!"* She was stuck somewhere in between, vacillating between bliss and fear. The middle ground was nerves. That's where she was now. After the almost-kiss yesterday under the table, Jordan had asked her to go to the art museum with her. Amy's mouth had said yes without even consulting her brain.

Her brain had kept her up most of the night, dredging up excuse after excuse after excuse as to why she should not go on a date, technically a second date, with a gorgeous, sexy lesbian. Here were the reasons in no particular order:

Dating a lesbian would mean she was a lesbian and if she was a lesbian then…

She couldn't wear her cute shoes anymore.

She would have to get her hair cut short and that meant it would curl into its natural Afro state. Not her best look.

She would have to carry her lipstick in her pocket because lesbians don't carry purses.

They also don't wear lipstick, so nix on the last reason.

She would have to learn to cook so she could attend lesbian potlucks.

She would have to learn to like hummus. And learn how to pronounce it.

She would have to get a cat.

Then, in an act of fairness, her brain came up with reasons to become a lesbian. Here were the reasons in no particular order:

She would save a lot of money by not buying…

Pantyhose

Dresses

Make-up

Curlers

Razors (She was uncertain whether lesbians shaved their legs and under their arms. She hoped so.)

She could share a wardrobe with Jordan.

Amy knew she was being a little silly. Not all lesbians were exactly alike. She had seen a couple of episodes of *The L Word*. She was pretty sure her career wouldn't suffer and her mother – her father was long gone – would eventually warm to the idea. Still… it was a pretty big step. Especially for someone as clumsy in bed as she was. *See prior banana peel story.* However, Jordan had woken up certain parts of her body that had been hibernating for the past ten years. And like a bear crawling out of her cave after a long winter's nap, Amy was ravenous.

She wished somebody would write a guidebook. *Lesbianism for Dummies.* It would make things a whole lot easier. Or maybe she should infiltrate the periphery of lesbians. Study their culture, their mating habits, their sense of humor (assuming they had one), their sense of style (assuming they had that also). She could acquaint and acclimate herself to lesbians after careful study. She could be the Diane Fossey of Lesbians.

Early in the a.m. hours after zilch sleep, Amy decided to quit thinking with her brain. She made a pledge with herself to leave her brain out of the equation and let her heart and body do all the thinking.

The next morning, her heart and body took a shower, bought a new, funky wardrobe, and picked up her new car.

## First Kiss

Amy parked her new Smart car right in front of the Portland Art Museum, marveling over how it could fit anywhere. It was bright yellow and cute to boot. She loved how it complimented her new Tardis-blue Converse high-top sneakers. She had also followed Isabel's gypsy advice and purchased a dozen do-rags to wear while at work. She felt they gave her flair.

Amy hurried up the museum steps, her mind blank, her heart pounding, her body tingly. She was so deliriously happy at the prospect of spending the afternoon with Jordan that she didn't even feel tired or sleepy; she felt exhilarated.

She was barely inside the lobby when Jordan appeared in front of her. She was wearing a pair of baggy plaid shorts (she had shaved legs, thank God) and a plain white T-shirt. She had on sandals and her toenails were painted red. She was adorable.

"I hope I'm not late," Amy said for want of anything more original to say.

"C'mon," Jordan said, taking her by the hand and pulling her toward the escalator.

"What's the rush?"

"No rush. I just want you to see what I found."

Jordan pulled her up the escalator, taking the steps two at a time, and down the wide hallway. She pulled Amy into a room and stepped directly in front of her. "Close your eyes."

"We're in a museum," Amy said, "I thought the whole idea was to see things."

"You will, you will, trust me. Close your eyes."

Amy did as told. Jordan took her hands and slowly walked her forward. Then Jordan's hands were on Amy's shoulders and pressing gently down. She whispered, "Sit."

Amy sat. She felt Jordan sit beside her.

"Okay, now you can open your eyes."

Amy opened her eyes. She saw a large painting, covering most of the wall. It was whirls upon swirls of bright, thick paint. Bold strokes of every color imaginable. A mass of writhing, curving, serpentine vividness.

"What do you see?" Jordan asked.

Amy looked at Jordan. "Is this a trick question?"

Jordan shook her head. "No, not at all. I'm just wondering what you see."

Amy looked back at the painting. She tilted her head to the right. "I don't know. It's interesting in a messy kind of way."

"Keep looking."

She looked at Jordan. Jordan was clearly enraptured with the painting.

Amy looked at it again, determined to see something. She tilted her head to the left. She still couldn't discern any shapes, any type of anything. She thought it looked like a colorful tornado. Or maybe a bunch of different paints being flushed down a toilet. Or a rainbow caught in a whirlpool.

She looked back at Jordan and studied her profile as she gazed at the painting. Amy asked, "What do *you* see?"

Jordan took her time answering, "Ecstasy. Surprise. Gratitude. Joy. Elation. Happiness."

"All that?"

"And more. So much more."

"Hunh," Amy said. Clearly she wasn't up to snuff on modern art. She looked back to the painting and tried to see what Jordan had described. "But those are feelings."

"True."

"So, you're telling me that you're seeing emotions when you look at this painting?" Amy asked.

Jordan looked at Amy and smiled. "That's what art does. It *shows* you emotions."

"Oh."

"Close your eyes again," Jordan said.

Amy closed her eyes, wondering where Jordan was going to take her this time. But instead of taking her by the hand, Jordan kissed her.

Amy savored the feel of Jordan's lips on hers – the tingling, ecstatic, joyful sensation of a simple kiss.

"You can open your eyes now," Jordan said.

Amy did. She followed Jordan's gaze back to the painting. And this time, the colors swelled to life. They danced and twirled across the canvas. And she felt it. The feeling was tiny at first, no more than a pinprick. It centered in her chest then grew larger and larger. It was warm. Was she glowing? She felt as if she were lit from the inside like one of those paper Chinese lanterns.

Amy didn't know how to describe it. She had no words for this feeling. It was more. *More.* So much more than a kiss.

"Maybe I do see a little something," Amy whispered with her eyes still glued to the painting.

## Car, Duct Tape, Art

Jordan and Amy stood on the museum steps, each wanting to spend more time with the other, each unwilling to let the afternoon go.

Amy said, "I can't believe I've never visited here before."

"I come here all the time. At least once a week. I find it very inspiring. Especially the children's art. They have such freedom." Jordan led the way down the steps and to the bicycle rack where she had locked up her bike.

Amy said, "So, when you're painting, which comes first, the color or the emotion behind it?"

"It's hard to explain. Colors can make me feel, but feelings make me see colors. It's a matter of translating the feeling into color and onto the canvas. You've heard of the expression 'seeing red?'"

"Sure, when somebody's angry," Amy said.

Suddenly, Jordan's face turned a bright crimson. She clenched her fists and spun in a circle, punching the air, stomping her feet, and saying, "Damndamndamn! I can't believe it!"

Amy laughed at Jordan's antics. "I know what anger looks like," she said. "You don't have to show me."

"I'm not showing you. I *am* angry!" Jordan said. "Look!" She pointed at her lime green Trek bicycle. Both tires were flat.

"Oh my God," Amy gasped. She moved in for a closer look. "The tires have been slashed. Who would've done such a thing?"

"I have a good idea." Jordan fumed and paced away from the bike. Petronella had obviously followed her again. When she saw her kissing Amy, she'd taken out her revenge on the bike.

Jordan wiped her hand over her face, took a shaky

breath and collected herself. "Sorry I lost it like that." Now, she was embarrassed. She didn't want Amy to think she needed anger management classes, but this clandestine vandalism was getting old. Petronella had demolished her car, now her bike. What was next? She'd be reduced to roller blades?

"I'll give you a ride home," Amy said.

"Okay," Jordan said. "Thank you."

Jordan carried the bike, following Amy to her car. Jordan scrunched her face up when she stared at the car. "This is it?"

"Yes."

"I like it," Jordan said, leaning her bike up against the parking meter. She walked around the car. "It's adorable."

"It doesn't have a trunk exactly."

"Oh, that's all right. We'll just duct tape the bike to the roof," Jordan said.

"Really?"

"Sure. I'll line the part that touches the roof so it won't get sticky."

"But I don't have any duct tape," Amy said.

"I do," Jordan said, pulling a roll of hot pink tape from a small leather bag that hung behind her bicycle seat.

"Wow," Amy said. "Maybe I should buy stock in duct tape."

In a matter of minutes, Jordan had her bike secured to the top of the car. Amy backed away from the car and studied it. "It looks like art. Like some kind of modern art sculpture."

"It really does, doesn't it?" Jordan said.

A Japanese man stopped by the car, whipped out a camera and took a picture. Several other pedestrians stopped and gazed at the car. "Amazing," one man said. "It's a very interesting juxtaposition on the evolutionary drama between humans and their various modes of transportation."

Amy giggled.

Jordan shrugged. "You can turn anything into art."

Soon, there was a large crowd of people gathered around the car. Cameras flashed, people talked excitedly, throwing around phrases like *social commentary* and *melding of reality and art*. A pencil-thin woman wearing glasses emerged from the crowd, ran up the museum steps, stopped, turned, and flashed off several photos of the car and bike. Then she pulled a steno pad out of her purse and called out, "Who is the artist? Does anybody know the artist?"

Jordan stepped forward and pointed an accusing finger at Amy. "She is the artist."

Amy playfully slugged Jordan's arm. Jordan whispered, "Just go along with it."

The woman hurried over to Amy. "How wonderful to meet you. Do you mind giving me an interview? I write for *The Oregonian*. I would love to feature you in our paper as an up-and-coming artist. What's your name?"

The crowd of people surrounded Jordan and Amy, cutting off any easy escape route.

Amy eyes widened. She looked to Jordan for help. Jordan stepped up to the plate and told the reporter, "Sorry, but she's quite shy. You know artists and their peculiarities. Her name is Amy Stewart. This installation piece is entitled *First Kiss*.

"What an unusual title," the reporter said. "Is there a meaning behind it?"

Jordan raised an eyebrow at Amy, openly daring her to continue the charade. Amy accepted the dare and spoke up, "It's the melding of... it's about... Well, look it's a car, right? A tiny car that is as much like a bike as it is a car. And you have a bike. A wounded bike. Its tires are slashed and it may never... transport... again. Until it meets the car. Then through the power of duct tape it is carried by the car. So, it's like kindred spirits. Meeting."

"Huh," the reporter said. She turned and studied the car and bike for a moment. She popped off another couple of pictures with her camera. Finally, she said, "I get it. It's like they're kissing, right?"

When she turned back around, Jordan and Amy were kissing. She got a picture of that, too.

## Aunt Jemima

"You look like a sexy Aunt Jemima," Chad said, standing in Amy's office doorway.

Amy had been hoping her do-rag would turn him off. Instead, here he was remarking on it. Not only remarking on it but flirting with it. "It's the new me," she said.

This morning, Amy had chosen a black do-rag bandana with a yellow day-glow Ms. Pac-Man on it. She felt it embraced her burgeoning sense of feminism.

"I heard rumors about your new wardrobe." Chad came around the desk and peeked under it. "They *are* Dr. Who shoes."

Amy whacked him in the head as she opened the desk drawer.

"Ouch!" He rubbed his forehead that now had the imprint of a tiny keyhole. "Is this still about the cheese?"

"Cheese?" Amy said. She had no idea what he was talking about.

"You know the other night when you were throwing cheese and crackers around."

"Oh that. No, I just don't like you looking under my desk uninvited."

Amy got up abruptly and he quickly stepped back. She almost laughed. He actually looked intimidated by her. This was new. Maybe a brand new pair of shoes did improve one's self esteem. She might need a few more pairs. "I have rounds to do," she said, "I assume you have the same."

"I've been off for an hour."

"Then why are you still here?"

"I was hoping to see you."

She crinkled her brow. Hadn't she made it abundantly clear that she didn't want to have anything to do with him? "Why?"

Chad unrolled *The Oregonian* newspaper and held it up. It was folded over to the Art section. "Can I have your autograph?"

Amy zoomed in on the paper. There was a photo of Amy's car with the bike duct taped to the top. The caption underneath read: *Emerging Artist, Amy Stewart, Exhibits One of the Many Uses of Duct Tape.*

"What's the meaning of this?" Chad said.

"It was a joke," Amy said. "It got a little out of hand."

"I'll say," he said. "You have to make them retract this. You're a doctor. You can't have things like this tainting your reputation."

Amy wrinkled her nose at him. "Are you being serious?"

"You can blame it on that woman. She made you do it," Chad went on.

Amy was set to spew bile and hate all over his perfect cleft when her pager went off. She said huffily, "I gotta go." She snatched the newspaper out of his hands and strode out the door with her new tennis shoes squeaking on the linoleum. As she walked down the hallway, she opened the paper. She squeaked to a sudden stop. "Oh my God." Below the photo of her car was another photo. This one was of Jordan and Amy kissing.

She had just come out to the entire world. "What's my mother going to say?" she said aloud.

## Painted Whore

"Irma!" Jordan yelled. "What the hell?"

Edison laughed. Irma had sloshed her can of green paint and most of it splattered across Jordan's face. Jordan looked like a sad clown at the circus, crying green tears.

"I thought you Slavic people were more methodical than messy," Jordan said, looking up at Irma who was standing above her on a ladder. Irma was painting the second story while Jordan and Edison painted the first story.

"We are methodical in techniques of torture and interrogation. Messy elsewhere," Irma said. She was still dressed all in black and her hair was as lacquered and shellacked as an eight ball. She painted like Jackson Pollack, more dripping and splattering than brushing.

"Well, be careful, would you?" Jordan said grumpily. "You're getting more paint on me than on the house."

Irma held out her can to Jordan. "Retrieve more paint for Irma. Irma cannot paint if Irma have no paint. You see dilemma? Irma have no time for idle chat-chit."

"You mean chit-chat," Edison corrected.

"That is what Irma said," Irma retorted.

Jordan wiped her face, her hands, then her arms and shoulders on a rag. She handed Irma another gallon of paint and took the empty can from her. "Maybe you could aim it for the house this time."

"Irma work for free. You pay Irma, you get to be boss of Irma."

"She has a point," Edison said. "Oh my God, here comes the mail." Edison put down her brush and hurried around to the front yard, intercepting the mail carrier. Jordan watched in amazement as Edison smiled and chat-chitted with her. "Does she have a thing for the mail lady?" Jordan asked Irma.

Irma clucked her tongue. "Is absurd. Everyone knows civil servants have no heart. Edison makes fool of herself every day. Ask nonsense questions, talk about weather, price of stamps. Utter foolishness."

Jordan studied the mail lady. She was cute and she did have nice legs. Besides who was Irma to be talking about heart? The Tin Man had more heart than Irma.

Edison hopped from foot to foot and the mail lady didn't seem to find it odd. In fact, she seemed to be flirting back.

Jordan watched Irma watch Edison. If she didn't know better she would think Irma was actually jealous.

Several minutes later, Edison came flying back up the path to the house waving a rather elaborate piece of mail.

"What's that?" Jordan said, setting her brush down.

"It's addressed to you. I signed for it," Edison said. "Open it up."

Jordan took the envelope and studied the front and back.

"You think she's cute?" Edison said, gushing but trying to hide it. "She has great legs, huh?"

"If you like civil servants," Irma said, her voice dripping with something that sounded a lot like jealousy.

Jordan opened the envelope and peered inside. "It looks like an invitation."

Edison snatched it out of Jordan's hands and looked it over. "It *is* an invitation. From that new theater down on Hawthorne. There's going to be a short play, a comedy act and a poetry reading."

"They send invitation? What is so special they send invitation?" Irma said. She swung her arm in emphasis and nailed Mr. Pip with a glob of paint. He hissed at her before scurrying away.

"Oh, looky here," Edison spit. "Guess who's doing

the poetry reading?"

"Oh, no," Jordan said. She only knew one lesbian poet.

"Irma despises rhetorical questions. They serve no purpose," Irma said.

Edison glared at her. "Petronella, that's who." She looked back to Jordan. "We can't miss this. We have to go."

"Why would we want to do that?" Jordan said.

"We could extract revenge for the violation of your bike," Edison said. "A dish best served cold and all that. And I know just how to do it."

Irma sighed heavily. "Irma can imagine your plan. One brain, two lesbians." She slapped more paint around. Jordan and Edison moved back out of splatter range.

"Listen, Jordan. We take my remote control car and create havoc during the poetry reading."

"And how are we going to create this havoc?" Jordan said, pouring more paint in a tray.

"I haven't gotten that far, but you have to agree that my car is on the breaking edge. We have to test drive it. Keeping it hush-hush, of course. If the government finds out about my advanced technology..."

Irma interrupted, "Advanced piece of crap."

"You missed a spot," Edison snapped.

Jordan took her tray and brush around to the back of the house. She was hoping for some quiet time away from the others. Unfortunately, Edison followed her.

"What I'm saying is that my car led you to Amy, right? And I think it can rid you of Petronella. Just think of my newest invention as a good luck talisman."

Jordan rolled her eyes. "I think Petronella will get tired of her little game as soon as she finds a new girlfriend. That's how she works."

"Rubbish," Irma said, joining them in the back of the house. She wagged her brush at Jordan. Jordan dodged the flying paint spatters as Irma said, "Petronella is gorgeous, sexy, smart woman. She could have any person she choose. She choose to not have girlfriend because she is not done with you."

Edison spoke up, "You sound like you have a crush on Petronella."

Irma said, "Irma recognize beauty and brains when she see it."

Edison made a barfing sound.

"Maybe I should hook you two up," Jordan said to Irma. "You could divert Petronella's attention away from me."

"Yeah, right," Edison muttered. "That would never work."

"You are only jealous," Irma said to Edison. "You do not want to share your Irma."

"Your Irma?" Jordan couldn't believe her ears. "What are you talking about?"

Her question was met with silence. Irma and Edison painted furiously, both concentrating on their brush strokes.

"You two have slept together!" Jordan accused.

"It was an accident," Edison sputtered. "Completely unplanned."

"Yes, a most unfortunate accident," Irma said, slapping more paint than the brush could handle on the side of the house, splattering green globs everywhere.

"Unfortunate? You didn't seem to think it was unfortunate at the time," Edison snapped.

"Irma was drunk on juice of potato," Irma said.

"Where was I?" Jordan said. "Why didn't I know about this?"

"You were on your museum date with Amy," Edison said.

"Edison was depressed. Irma cheered her up," Irma said.

"How sweet of you," Jordan said.

Irma didn't hear the sarcasm in Jordan's voice. "Irma has hardened shell of a Soviet, yes, but under the armor Irma has beating heart of black wolf howling for mate."

"So you mated with Edison?" Jordan was still trying to process this. She had always operated under the assumption that they barely tolerated each other – and now she finds out they slept together. It was a lot to swallow.

"It was one time bedding," Irma said, dismissively.

"Were you all right…afterwards?" Jordan asked Edison who was avoiding her gaze.

"Well…" Edison muttered. She averted her eyes. "My you-know-where was a little you-know-what."

"Huh?"

"Please don't make me say it again."

Irma answered for her, "Edison had smagina. Irma cured her."

"She had what?" Jordan asked.

"Smagina," Irma said again. "Is word I create. Means small vagina. Two words smoosh together into one word. Small vagina. Smagina. Is funny, no?"

Nobody laughed. They all resumed painting. In silence. For a long time. Finally, Irma broke the silence. "Is like cold war."

Irma put down her brush and marched over to Edison. Edison froze. "You have nice vagina, Edison. Irma apologizes for remark. Is small and cozy vagina."

"Thanks, I guess," Edison muttered.

Irma continued, "The lining of vagina is stretchable. It is written that one vagina can stretch so far as to completely envelope the planet."

Edison shuddered. "Well, if I ever want to hug the world with my vagina, I'll let you know."

"Well, as touching as this scene is, I need more paint. I'll be right back." Jordan walked around the house to the front porch where the rest of the paint was stored. She walked up the steps and stopped.

She screamed.

Painted on the porch was one giant word: WHORE.

Someone had opened one of the many cans of paint stacked on the porch and painted the word in huge block letters centered directly in front of the door.

Irma and Edison came running. They skidded to a stop when they saw the painted word.

"Well, I wonder who did this?" Jordan said, pacing back and forth in front of the word. She considered herself a pacifist but right now she wanted to strangle Petronella.

"Perhaps is joke," Irma suggested. "Funny, no?"

"No!" Jordan and Edison yelled.

"Irma did not think so," Irma said.

"Nah, there's only one person who despises Jordan enough to do this," Edison said.

"I'm going to finish painting," Jordan said. She stomped up on the porch and grabbed the open paint can. She stalked down the steps and across the front yard.

"Do you think she's having a delayed reaction?" Edison asked Irma.

"It would seem so," Irma said.

They both eyed Jordan who was trudging back to the painting site. Suddenly, Jordan spun back around and said, "Remember what I said about the poetry reading and your revenge plan? Cancel that. I want to go."

Edison gave a little leap. "With my remote control car?"

"Definitely with the car," Jordan said.

"Will you help, too, Irma?" Edison said.

Irma smiled and rubbed her hands together. "Of course. Irma loves lesbian poetry."

## Amy's Big Coming Out

Amy was high. She didn't know if she was high on love or high on life, but whatever it was felt delicious. Jordan had called her last night and asked her out on another date. Amy said yes before even asking where they were going. Jordan told her they were going to a lesbian poetry reading and she thought it was going to be quite the spectacle. Amy didn't care if she was inviting her to the dump to shoot BB guns at rats, she would go anywhere with Jordan.

Today was her day off and she had bounced out of bed and gone shopping. She bought 47 different pair of panties with matching bras. That should have been her first clue that she was in love. Nothing says "I'm in love" like a woman buying new underwear.

On her way back from the mall, Amy slammed on her brakes when she saw a familiar pair of shoes sticking out of a dumpster. They were turquoise cowboy boots with pleather snakeskin uppers. She would have known those boots anywhere.

Amy pulled her car up next to the dumpster and honked the horn. The boots wiggled but didn't come out. Sighing dramatically, Amy got out of her car and approached the dumpster.

"Mom, it's me," Amy said. "Your daughter. Remember me?"

The boots wiggled in response.

"Can you please come out of the dumpster for a moment? I need to tell you something."

*To be continued...*

## Claire's Story

Long before she dove headfirst into dumpsters, Amy's mother, Claire, was a sorority girl dating a frat boy at an Ivy League college. They fell in love, graduated and married. Everyone thought them the perfect couple until Amy's father, Brent, discovered the two true loves of his life: Golf and Philandering. Amy often wondered if her father had always been a philanderer. Did he also cheat on her mother when they were in college? She liked to think that he'd been madly in love with her mother once and cared for her deeply before he turned into the Brent-the Fuck-o-rama Man.

The part that Amy despised the most was how her mother didn't do anything about it. Claire had to have known she was being cheated on. If Amy had figured it out, then surely Claire had. But instead of leaving him, Claire enabled him. She made excuses for him not showing up at Amy's seventh birthday party. She laughed over the telephone with other women and told jokes about being a golf widow. Amy swore that she would never be like her mother.

Then the unthinkable happened. Brent didn't come home one day. A week went by and Claire received divorce papers. Amy was helpless to do anything but watch her mother go off the deep end. Claire became a hippie artist who dumpster-dived to gather her art materials. She filled their house to overflowing with smelly objects rescued from dumpsters. Amy was embarrassed to bring friends home. Then the backyard filled up with junk that was welded together to form totem poles. And wind chimes. And windmills. And anything else imaginable.

Amy graduated high school and left home. She went to med school on her father's dime and didn't feel guilty about it.

She visited her mother occasionally. Two or three times a year they would get together at a local restaurant. (Amy never went to the junk house.) Claire called Amy occasionally and they would chat about Claire's art. Claire had become a locally famous avant-garde bohemian type artist whose art shows embodied buzzwords like "upcycle," "recycle," and "unicycle."

So when Amy saw her mother's trademark turquoise boots sticking out of the dumpster, she thought it was fate interceding. Now was the time to tell her mother she was in love with a woman. If she couldn't deal with it, that was her fault.

## Amy's Big Coming Out, Continued

"If you don't come out of there, I'm coming in," Amy said.

The boots wiggled again, but made no move to right themselves and come out.

"Okay, I lied," Amy said. "I'm not coming into that stinky dumpster. But I am going to tell you what I need to tell you and if you don't like it, then... well then you don't like it, that's all. So there. I'm a lesbian. At least I think I am. I mean, I'm pretty sure I am. I mean, I am. I'm in love with a woman. And we've kissed. Several times. And I liked it. I'm going to kiss her again. I'm going to kiss her as much as possible and I even bought new underwear. I hope you won't disown me or be embarrassed by me. It is my wish that you will accept Jordan – that's her name – I want you to accept Jordan as my significant other. That's all."

There was no answer from the dumpster.

"That's all I wanted to say."

Silence. No movement.

"The end."

Amy stared at the boots. They didn't move.

"You can respond now."

Nothing.

"Mom? Are you okay in there?"

Amy was gripped by a fear that her mother had suffocated under the heap of stinky, gooey dumpster stuff. She quickly mounted the side of the dumpster, yelling, "Don't worry! I'll save you!" and dove inside headfirst.

Amy pushed off the bottom of the dumpster with her feet and swam to the top. Her head broke above the surface of the trash and she gulped down fresh air. She was face to face with the turquoise boots. She grabbed them both and pulled with all her might.

The boots came away easily and the force of her pulling sent her reeling backwards. She plopped into a corner of the dumpster and stared at the boots in her hand.

"Hey, what's the idea?"

Amy looked up. An old woman stared back at her. The woman had only one tooth and her face was as wrinkled as a dirty dishrag. "Those're my boots!" the old woman yelled. She grabbed the boots out of Amy's hands, jumped overboard and scurried down the alley.

"Sorry, I thought you were somebody else! My bad!" Amy called after her.

## Amy's Real Coming Out

Amy stood on the front porch of her childhood home and rang the doorbell. She hadn't been home since the day she left for college. She nervously shifted from foot to foot. She was determined to really tell her mother and get this over with.

**Meet Claire Stewart.** Claire may have been fifty years old, but she looked more like forty. She was the summer of love personified – tie-dye, moccasins, beads and bangles. She always had a smell of incense or patchouli about her. When Claire opened the door and saw Amy she smiled and grabbed her in a hug. Claire was a big hugger.

"Amy! What a wonderful surprise!" She took a step back and her face darkened. "Nothing's the matter is it?"

"No," Amy said quickly. "I just wanted to… I was in the neighborhood, so I thought I'd drop by." Amy could kick herself. Where had her courage gone?

Claire pulled Amy into another big hug. Then she held Amy at arm's length and wrinkled her nose. "You're a little stinky, sweetheart."

"Um, yeah… Can I come in?"

Amy followed Claire through a spotlessly clean house and into a sparkling kitchen. Not one piece of junk anywhere. Wow. Amy was flabbergasted. "Where's all your dumpster stuff?"

Claire laughed. "I rented a storage unit to store all my art supplies. Coffee?"

"Sure. So, what made you decide to clean up the house? And what happened to your boots?"

"Well, it's a little embarrassing to tell the truth. One day I got a phone call from a Hollywood producer."

Amy raised her eyebrows.

"He wanted to know if he could interview me for

his TV show."

"Really? What show?"

"It's called *American Hoarders.*"

Amy laughed out loud before she could catch herself. She clasped her hand over her mouth, saying, "Sorry. That's not really funny."

Claire laughed along with Amy. "Yes, it is funny. It wasn't then, but it is now. Anyway, that gave me the impetus to clean up my life. And as for the boots, I threw them away, too."

"I like the place now, Mom. It looks and feels like a real home."

"Thank you, sweetie. Now what did you come to tell me?"

Amy didn't know where to begin, so she just opened her mouth and hoped for the best. "I came here with a purpose. A reason. I need to tell you something."

Claire put a cup of coffee in front of Amy and sat across the table. "Is this about you being a lesbian?"

Amy spit her sip of coffee across the tabletop. "How did you know?"

Claire smiled. "It was in the paper, dear, I think the whole city knows by now. And I have to say, I've never been prouder."

"You're proud that I'm a lesbian?"

"No, silly, I'm proud that you are creating art. I mean, the doctor thing is wonderful, but creating spontaneous art heals the soul. Your soul and the souls of others. I'm glad that you can not only heal bodies, but can heal souls."

"You're not freaked out that I'm going out with a woman?"

"God, no. To tell you the truth, I didn't care for that Chad fellow."

"Chad? How do you know about Chad?"

"He came over here one day and got some of your

old things."

"What things? When?"

"Nothing important, I don't think. Some old stuffed animals from your childhood, your yearbooks from school. Hasn't he told you yet? He was getting the things to give to you as a surprise. I hope I didn't ruin it."

"Did he say or do anything, you know, unusual?"

"Well, he did call me Mother. I thought that was strange."

Amy decided enough was enough. She was going to give Chad a strong talking-to. And get her things back.

Claire continued, "Anyway, I'm glad you got rid of him. Now tell me all about this young woman of yours. Does she love you? What does she do? Is she as pretty as she looks in the paper?"

Amy laughed at her mother's inquisitiveness and told her all about Jordan. About her fall from the window, how she stitched her up, their first kiss, everything.

"What do you have planned for the rest of the day?" Claire asked.

Uh oh, Amy thought, here it comes. She'll want me to go dumpster diving with her. "I don't know…" she stuttered.

"Well, I have the perfect thing. Why don't you go to the bathroom and freshen up some? Maybe brush the coffee grounds out of your hair?"

"Where are we going?"

"You'll see," Claire said. "Now go splash on some patchouli, baby, you really do smell over-ripe."

## A Big, Fat, Gay Wedding

Ten minutes later, Amy was wearing a tie-dyed dress of Claire's. She had so much patchouli splashed on that she smelled as though she'd just gotten back from a Grateful Dead concert. They both squeezed into the Smart car and Claire directed Amy to the posh side of town.

Amy chanced a question she had long wanted to know the answer to. "Did you love Daddy?"

"Oh, yes."

"Did he love you?"

"In his way," Claire said. "Take the Columbia exit. The house is in the Kenton District. I think he was in love with the idea of being in love but whenever our love became deeper and required a fuller commitment, he flitted off like a humming bird at a feeder. Now turn right on Denver."

Amy turned. She hoped she didn't inherit her father's genetics. The flitting part, anyway. She didn't want to be a hummingbird. She wanted to be a penguin. They mated for life.

"You can park right here."

Amy pulled over in front of an old yet beautifully restored Victorian house. Everything was perfect and very coordinated and looked like Martha Stewart lived here. Then it dawned on her. "Do gay men live here?"

"They do. It's their wedding we're doing the decorating for."

"And they're letting you?"

"Lillian is the decorator. I'm just her helper. C'mon, Lillian will be so happy to see you again." Claire opened her door then froze, looking back at Amy. "You don't have to come in. If you don't want to."

"Of course I want to," Amy said.

Claire's face lit up and Amy realized at that

moment that she'd been steering clear of her mother for a long time and it was hurting her. She hadn't meant to hurt her, but she had. She felt immensely guilty and resolved to spend more time with her mother from here on out.

Claire rang the doorbell that was shaped like a *fleur de lis*. It was brass and was polished recently, probably every day at ten sharp.

**Meet Desmond Quartermaine.** A perfectly turned out man with heavy brows and thick dark hair opened the door. In a voice that seemed on the verge of hyperventilating, he exclaimed, "Oh my God, Claire, you've got to help. It's a disaster!"

"Desmond, this is my daughter, Amy. She's a lesbian."

If Desmond was shocked by Claire's pronouncement he didn't show it. He barely nodded at her before grabbing Claire's arm, pulling her into the house and pleading, "It's a disaster, Claire, you have to help."

"Where's Lillian?" Claire inquired.

"She's in the pond." He fanned himself with his hand.

"Why is she in the pond?" Claire asked as Desmond lead them through the most perfect house Amy had ever seen.

"Because of the frogs. That's the disaster. It's like one of the seven plagues on Egypt. Frogs everywhere!"

They followed Desmond through the house at such a brisk pace that Amy only glimpsed flashes of divans, ottomans, book shelves lined with leather-bound copies of books, gilded table lamps, tasseled pillows, and lots of gold brocade.

When they stepped out the back door and into the yard there was a gazebo, a myriad of benches strategically placed, perfectly manicured hedges, and several gazing balls. And in the thick of it all was Lillian, wearing hip waders and standing in the middle of the pond with a net in her hands.

**Meet Lillian Drake**. Lillian made perfect look easy. She called everyone darling and blew air kisses. Even in hip waders, her lipstick wasn't smeared and her hair didn't look messy; it looked windblown. She was overweight, but bore the weight like it was a privilege and something to be admired.

Claire and Lillian had been best friends since their sorority days. They were an odd match, but inseparable. What Amy found so interesting with Lillian was that she supported her mother in whatever endeavor she took on, no questions asked.

"Amy!" Lillian said, putting the net down and slogging across the yard. "Darling, how are you?" She wrapped Amy in a warm embrace and air kissed both her cheeks. "I haven't seen you in ages. Come let me look at you." She looked Amy up and down. "You look more like your mother every day."

"Well, I am wearing her clothes," Amy said, trying hard not to feel self-conscious.

"Amy is a lesbian now," Claire said proudly like Amy had won the Nobel Prize.

Lillian's eyes widened. "Really, dear? That is *wunderbar*."

"Now about those frogs," Desmond tittered.

"No worries, I think I've gotten rid of them and their soon-to-be offspring," Lillian said.

"They were so disgusting," Desmond said, flapping his hand in front of his face. "Nature is so..."

Claire filled in, "Natural?"

"Disgusting," Desmond said.

Lillian whispered *sotto voce* to Amy, "It's the green sludge he doesn't like." Lillian sat on a bench and began to tug off the hip waders. She was having difficulty getting them off. It was like trying to peel a sausage. Amy took a boot and pulled. "Thank you, darling." Together they removed Lillian from the hip waders.

"Now, Desmond," Lillian said, taking his arm. "Why don't you make us some of that divine lemonade of yours and we'll take a break and regroup afterwards. That way, we can all catch our breath."

Desmond seemed delighted. "That's a marvelous idea." He lifted a small, discreet walkie-talkie to his mouth and commanded, "Bring a pitcher of lemonade and five glasses. Miss Lillian is parched from her frog killing spree." He turned back to Lillian and said, "You are my savior. You are my Rambo of the pond. The Terminator of frogs. Whatever would I do without you?"

"You would manage, I am sure, darling," Lillian said.

Desmond looked at his watch. "Oh no, the yo-yo'ers will be here soon." He put his hand to his forehead in a very theatrical swoon. "I wish Evan didn't have his heart set on the yo-yo'ers for entertainment. It's so tasteless. The cabaret thing I wanted at least had class."

"Desmond, we talked about this," Lillian soothed.

"I know. I know. It's his wedding too," Desmond said, pouting. "It's just so tawdry," he muttered as he walked toward the house.

"And cabaret dancers are so high class," Lillian muttered.

"So, this seems like a rather unusual wedding," Amy said.

A young woman came out holding a silver tray with a cut-glass pitcher of fresh lemonade and five glasses. "Is this where the sane people gather?" she asked.

**Meet Janice Cohen.** Janice was very pretty under the military buzz cut and facial piercings. She even had a nice body, if you could find it under the extra large sweatshirt and baggy gray chinos. Her aura screamed feminist, but her lingering gaze at Amy whispered lesbian.

Lillian looked relieved. "Oh darling, thank

goodness you're here. He's out of control again."

Janice set the platter down. "I know. He's hyperventilating all over the kitchen."

"But, I got all the frogs and the green stuff. The pond looks fine," Lillian said. "I mean it is a pond; it's going to have pond stuff."

"No, it's not that," Janice said, pouring lemonade all around. "Now, he's fighting with Evan about the yo-yo'ers." She handed Amy a glass of lemonade. "I don't think we've met. I'm Janice. Desmond's friend, but don't hold that against me."

"Oh, I'm sorry. Where are my manners," Lillian said. "This is Amy. She's a lesbian."

"It's nice to meet you. Why haven't I seen you out before?"

"Out?" Amy said.

"You know, in the clubs. Or events. Or potlucks," Janice said.

"She's a brand-new lesbian," Claire said. "A late bloomer."

"Fresh meat," Janice said.

"Huh?" Amy said, alarmed. She nervously gulped her lemonade.

"Have you been initiated yet?"

Amy slowly shook her head and took another gulp.

Janice leered and wagged her eyebrows. "Maybe I can initiate you, then. It doesn't hurt. Much. Well, it only hurts the first time. I need a new toaster oven anyway."

What was this woman talking about? Amy was befuddled. Befuddled? Was that really a word? Or was it confuddled? She was confuddled and befused.

Janice took her arm. "Are you okay? You looked like you were going to faint. I was only kidding. Lesbian humor. It was a joke."

"Oh," Amy said and forced a fake-sounding chuckle.

"So who's the girl?" Janice asked.

"Girl?"

"Yeah, what lucky woman rescued you from the bondage of heterosexuality?"

"Oh. Her name is Jordan March."

"You're dating Jordan March? *The* Jordan March?" Janice said.

Amy didn't know exactly how to take this. Did she mean to imply Amy wasn't good enough to date someone like Jordan March or that Jordan March was a bad person to date?

"Unless there's another Jordan March," Amy said, tentatively. She almost hoped there might be two of them and Amy got the good one, not the one this woman knew.

"She's tall, gorgeous, talented, witty, and lives in that crazy house in the old part of town where all the mansions are?" Janice said.

Lillian and Claire were conspicuously silent. Amy knew they loved getting the info without having to be the ones to extract it. She could feel their eyes on her.

"Yep, that's her."

"How'd you manage that? She never dates anyone, especially after the Ice Queen episode."

Lillian couldn't help herself. "Ice Queen?"

"She was Jordan's last girlfriend. Her name is Petronella and she's a professor at the University and she's a poet and she is the nastiest person I have ever met. She's having some big poetry-reading thing at the New Little Theatre tonight. I'm going."

"So am I," Amy said. "I mean, Jordan and I are going."

"Can straight people come, too?" Lillian asked.

"Sure," Janice said.

Lillian poked Claire in the ribs with her elbow. "Let's go crash the lesbian party. It sounds fun."

"Oh, Petronella's poetry isn't fun," Janice said.

"It's angry. You know how Rita Mae Brown's cat, Sneaky Pie Brown, started writing mystery novels? Well, Petronella is now writing poetry with her vagina. She's named it Vagina Woolf."

Claire clapped her hands. "That sounds wonderful! Maybe I can get some ideas for my sculptures."

Before Amy could object to her mother crashing her date, there was the sound of metal crashing against metal, and a high-pitched scream. The back door was thrown open and six muscular, oiled, naked men strutted into the back yard with their doodles dangling. They lined up in a chorus line, and began to yo-yo and kick step in perfect synchronization.

Claire and Lillian sat in rapt attention. Amy and Janice exchanged a confuddled look. "I think that's my cue to leave," Amy said.

## Dry Run

Jordan, Edison and Irma were in their backyard making last minute preparations for their attack on Petronella at her vagina's poetry reading. They had dubbed their revenge attack "Operation Meltdown."

"Three hours, ladies," Jordan said. "We have only have three hours to get this right."

"Don't sweat it," Edison said. "We'll be ready. Then her angry vagina will be a sorry vagina."

Irma chimed in, "Petronella does not own corner market on angry vagina. My vagina can beat up her vagina any day."

"That would make a great bumper sticker," Jordan said. Her vagina was pretty angry, too. It was angry with Petronella for leading her astray, making her believe she was the only vagina in the world that mattered, and then cheating on her with a younger vagina. Jordan, owner of said vagina, was pretty steamed also. All the throwing things, all the stalking, all the destruction of property, not to mention the graffiti on the porch which took a whole can of paint thinner to remove, had made Jordan mad enough to extract a fitting revenge.

And what was more fitting than giving the Ice Queen a taste of her own medicine?

Edison made a last-minute final adjustment to her remote control car. "Ready?" she asked.

Jordan nodded. Irma licked her lips in anticipation.

They were surrounded by cardboard cutouts of Petronella that Irma had created. Irma had Photoshopped pictures of Petronella's head and enlarged them so they would fit the cardboard cutouts. They'd placed these around the yard.

"You better be sure about this, Jordan. You could be starting a Hatfield and McCoy kind of thing," Edison

## More Than a Kiss

said, flipping the power switch on the car.

"You have icy shoes?" Irma taunted.

It took Edison a moment before she realized Irma meant 'cold feet.' "No, I'm not scared."

"You lie. You are turkey. Gobble gobble gobble. You are big turkey," Irma said. She pranced around the yard, gobbling and doing a weird turkey strut.

Jordan and Edison exchanged an amused look.

"You mean chicken. Cluck cluck cluck. And I am not chicken," Edison said. "I'm just concerned that this will start World War Lesbo. I want to make sure we all know that."

"This was your idea," Jordan said. "You're backing out now?"

"I'm not backing out," Edison said.

"Edison is big plump chicken," Irma said. She walked around the yard poking her neck out, flapping her arms up and down, and making clucking sounds.

"Stop that!" Edison said. "I'm not a plump chicken! I'm just making sure is all."

Irma stopped the chicken dance and squinted one eye. "Edison is right. In Mother Russia we give person one chance to fess clean."

Jordan rolled her eyes. "Do you think Petronella is really going to admit to everything?"

"Irma is master interrogator. Irma can make her talk. Here is best technique Irma learn from… never mind who, is not important. Irma hold rat by tail. Make it big, ugly, scary rat with pointy teeth. Rat is dead or alive, make no matter. Irma hold rat by tail and put in Petronella's face. Petronella is tied to chair. She sees rat and is scared like little girl. Irma shake rat in face, like so." She demonstrated with an imaginary rat in Edison's face. "Irma then say, 'Rat will eat your face if you do not confess.' You shake rat more. Make rat seem angry and hungry, see? This work many times for Irma in past."

After a long pause, Jordan said, "I like our idea better."

"Me, too," Edison said. "Though I will keep that in mind as a back-up plan."

"Fine with me," Irma said. "Irma have no rat anyway."

"Good to know," Edison said. "Okay, you guys ready for the dry run?"

"Rock and roll time," Jordan said.

"Who let the dogs out," Irma said, looking like a stern P.E. teacher.

"That makes absolutely no sense," Jordan said.

"To you, maybe. To Irma it is eye of the tiger," Irma said.

Edison donned her special glasses and grabbed the remote. Jordan and Irma took five steps back.

"It's show time, folks!" Edison said.

## Operation Meltdown, Phase One

What with all the hoopla about Operation Meltdown, Jordan had almost forgotten she had a date with Amy. That is until she saw Amy walk in the door of the theatre. Jordan inhaled sharply. Amy absolutely took her breath away. Normally, not being able to breathe was a bad thing. This time, however, it felt great.

Jordan rushed up to Amy's side and took her hand. She said in an avalanche of words, "You look great. I'm so glad you could make it. It's going to be exciting. You smell good."

Amy blushed. "Thanks. You're not so bad yourself."

Jordan glanced at two older women that were standing behind Amy. She escorted Amy away from the women, whispering in her ear, "Don't look now, but there are two dykes behind you. I think they're checking you out."

Amy turned to look, but Jordan whispered harshly, "Don't look! They'll know we're talking about them."

Amy snapped back to attention. Jordan oh-so-discreetly led Amy even further away. The two women followed close behind. Way too close. Jordan decided she had had enough. She couldn't tolerate stalking any more. She turned to the two women and with her hands on her hips, summoned her most authoritative voice. "Listen, you two. Back off. This is *my* date. She doesn't want anything to do with you, *Capice*? So you can take your little stalker eyes and your little stalker ears and go stalk someone else. *Capice*?" Jordan threw the Italian lingo in there twice. She wanted to make sure they knew she meant business. And maybe they would think she had some Mafia connections.

"Ooooh, I like you," one of the women said.

The other woman agreed, "So tough and strong. Like an Amazon warrior."

Jordan took a threatening step in closer to the women, intending to throw them out the front door, but Amy stopped her. "Jordan, I would like you to meet my mother, Claire, and her friend, Lillian."

Jordan blinked, then looked sheepishly at the ground. "Sorry. I just thought…"

"Oh, don't worry about it," Claire said.

"It was very chivalrous," Lillian agreed. "So, are you a lesbian, too?"

"Of course she's a lesbian. She's dating my daughter, isn't she?" Claire said.

Lillian shrugged. "You never know. I dated a lesbian once and didn't know it."

"How could you not know it?"

"It was dark and she had a mustache."

Claire nodded. "Did you ever see *Yentl*?"

"Oh, I would date Barbra in a heart beat," Lillian said.

Claire shook her head. "I don't know. Those fingernails are scary."

Jordan looked at Amy. She was still flabbergasted and didn't know what to say.

Amy apologized, "Sorry about this. I don't always take my mother on my dates. I just didn't know how to tell her no. I hope you don't mind."

"The more the merrier," Jordan said. "Anyway, I have my roommates with me. I hope that's cool."

The four of them walked through the double doors and into the small ninety-nine-seat auditorium. Claire and Lillian gasped at the same time. "Oh my!" Claire said. "Just look at all the lesbians!"

Lillian said, "When did lesbianism become so popular?"

"Where have all the lesbians been hiding?"

Amy butted in, "Um, Mom? Lillian? Do you all mind keep your voices down? Maybe not embarrassing me?"

Claire whispered, "Good idea. I don't want to get you kicked out of the lesbo club, dear." She then said to Lillian, "This is the first time she's shown an interest in any club. Even in high school she was a loner."

Jordan guided them to the last row of seats. Amy and Jordan sat. Claire and Lillian sat in the row directly in front of them.

Claire said, "Let's pretend to be lesbians together, Lillian. It will make us fit in."

"When in Rome," Lillian said. She then turned to Amy and Jordan and asked, "What do lesbians do at the theatre?"

"Hold hands," Jordan said.

Claire and Lillian held hands and turned back to the front.

"Sorry," Amy mouthed.

The lights began to lower and everybody crowded into the chairs.

## Operation Meltdown, Phase Two

Edison stumbled into the dark theatre and slid into the seat next to Jordan. Her sunglasses were on top of her head. She leaned over Jordan and said to Amy, "What's up, Doc?"

Jordan rolled her eyes. "How original, Ed."

"I know right? I always wanted to say that and now I can."

Amy laughed. "Okay, I'll let you say it, but only you."

"I feel special," Edison said.

"Soooo," Jordan said, putting as much meaning as possible into one little bitty word. "How's things?"

Edison nodded slowly and whispered, "Operation Meltdown is a-okay and ready to rock 'n roll. Irma is baby-sitting the... uh, baby."

Amy leaned across Jordan and said to Edison, "What's going on?"

"What makes you say that?" Edison asked much too innocently to be innocent.

"Code words and subterfuge," Amy said.

"You have highly developed observational skills," Edison said.

"I'm a doctor. I'm supposed to," Amy said. "Now, spill."

"She might have to be our new mastermind," Edison said.

"I concur," Jordan replied. She looked over at Amy dressed in loose organic hemp pants, a tie-dyed blouse with a plunging neckline, and her blue high-top sneakers. She was cute and loveable and sexy all wrapped up into one package.

"Do you really want to know what we have planned

or wait for the surprise? I think you'll like it as a surprise best, but we'll tell you if you want. I'll even give you a hint. It involves the Ice Queen and tires and paint," Edison said with an evil chuckle.

Claire and Lillian whipped their necks around and stared at Jordan. "Are you plotting revenge on your ex-girlfriend?" Claire asked.

Jordan was shocked into silence. Edison was not. "Hey, nobody likes eavesdroppers. So, turn your faces back around. And if you know what's good for you, you'll forget you ever heard that."

"That's Amy's mom and her lesbian, Lillian," Jordan explained.

"Oh," Edison said. "Sorry." She leaned over and said to Amy, "I didn't know your mom was a lesbian."

"Oh, goody," Claire said, "It's working. We're officially undercover, Lillian."

Amy shrugged. "I don't know what's going on anymore."

The house lights went out and the stage lights came up. Jordan took Amy's hand. Edison noticed and sighed. Irma slinked through the doors and sat in the chair beside Edison.

"All set?" Edison whispered.

"Of course is set," Irma said.

Edison nodded and looked at her watch. She punched a few elaborate buttons.

"Look it's a lesbian on stilts," Claire said, pointing to the stage. All six women sat up straighter in their seats and watched intently.

## Operation Meltdown, Phase Three

The lesbian on stilts was not funny. Her wandering around the stage telling jokes and stories was not funny. The stilts did involve some skill. Jordan knew this because she and Edison had used stilts to finish putting up the dry wall in the dining room. "It's not easy to walk on stilts," she whispered to Amy as if apologizing for the not-funny comedienne. The comic ended her performance with a joke about two vulvas, one Catholic and one Jewish, walking into a bar. Irma *hurrumphed* with disgust. Jordan was inclined to agree.

"Oh, she wasn't that bad," Amy said as the stilted lesbian exited the stage.

"I remember being like you - everything lesbian was bright and shiny," Edison said, "But you'll get over it. Believe me."

The next act was a short play called *Sweet Sufferings* and it was good, and not just because the previous act was so bad either. It was a clever little play about a lesbian on her deathbed. Not to be confused with lesbian bed death.

There wasn't a dry eye in house at the end of it. Jordan swore she heard Irma, the tough as nails Russian, sniffle back tears.

"Now, that was good," Lillian said.

"The Ice Queen is up next," Jordan whispered to Edison. "Start the timer."

"I know, I know," Edison said, furiously punching numbers into her watch.

The lights onstage changed from warm and inviting to bright and cold. A woman dressed in all black put a three-legged stool center stage. A spotlight popped on and pinpointed the stool. It grew quiet and expectant. Jordan knew from past experience that Petronella always had to make a grand entrance. She even did it when they were going to bed. Jordan would be about half asleep and no longer in the mood and Petronella would come into the room in a white negligee and lean against the door like some 1930's movie star. It was so overblown and fake that Jordan found it a major turn off.

After an interminable length of time with nothing happening onstage, Petronella made her entrance. She glided on from stage right, wearing an all white tuxedo with long tails. There was a collective inhalation of breath from the audience as Petronella took her place in the spotlight.

When is she going to start?" Edison hissed.

"What do you mean? This is her favorite part," Jordan replied.

Irma glanced at her watch. "Irma thinks she better step on her poetry before she is never late than better."

Jordan had no idea what the fuck Irma just said.

Petronella addressed the audience, "Tonight I'm going to read from my latest collection of award-winning poems, *La Furie Vagin*."

Lillian whispered to Claire, "Did she just say 'the furry vagina'?"

"Sshhh," Amy said.

Petronella continued, "The poems I have chosen for this evening center around a theme of the persecution, subjugation, instillation, fabrication, illumination and excommunication of the Great Female Spirit. They are poems of destruction and triumph, of creation and defeat, of sensuality and sadism."

"How uplifting," Jordan said, under her breath.

"This first poem is titled *Vagina Dentata*. Or *My Vagina Has Teeth*," Petronella said, solemnly.

Irma whispered, "Irma like this poem already."

Petronella stoically recited:

*Vagina Dentata*

*My vagina is angry*
*Since the dawn of time*
*Men have raped her*
*Men have beaten her*
*Men have bruised her soul*
*Then*
*My vagina grew pointy teeth*
*And this scared the men*
*Now men try to*
*Bind my vagina so she cannot walk*
*Make her wear high heels so she cannot run*
*Shave her so she will be shamed*
*Pierce her so she can be chained*
*Pay her only seventy percent of every dollar earned so she will be poor*
*Ah, but my angry vagina*
*Will not take it lying down*
*She gnashes her teeth like Hannibal Lector*
*Waiting to eat the penis with fava beans*
*...And a nice chianti*

Petronella dramatically bowed her head. The audience sat stunned and silent. Then Irma stood. She brought her hands together in one loud clap. Then another clap. And another. She shouted, "Brava! Brava!"

The rest of the audience surged to their feet and joined in the standing ovation, clapping and whistling.

"What are you doing?" Edison whispered while tugging on Irma's arm to make her sit back down.

"Irma is mesmerized." Irma looked at Jordan. "You did not tell Irma that she was so gifted."

Jordan said in her best imitation Russian accent, "Jordan did not know Irma would like."

Claire looked over her shoulder and smiled. "Makes me proud to have a vagina."

Edison lowered her sunglasses and discreetly pulled a remote control out of her jacket pocket.

## Operation Meltdown, Final Phase

As the audience quieted and took their seats, the theme song from *Jaws* blared from off stage right. Petronella looked offstage and made slashing motions across her neck. The music continued. Petronella looked out at the audience and put her finger up as if to say "Wait, I, the Ice Queen, Mistress of the Universe, will take care of this." She strode toward the offending music.

Petronella stopped.

She froze with eyes wide open, horror-struck.

She took a step backward.

Edison's remote control tanker car wheeled onstage. Edison had built another car like the prototype that had caused the Mr. Pip-falling-out-the-window accident. Only this car had a tank on its back. A tank filled with blue, red, green, and yellow paint. The paint nozzle was attached to a retractable arm that could be raised or lowered from the remote control that Edison was now pointing at the stage.

Petronella took another step backward.

The audience clapped, mistakenly thinking this was a part of the show.

The car braked. The paint nozzle raised and pointed at Petronella who was too confused to move.

Edison punched a button on the remote. Irma shrieked. She threw her body at Edison, shouting, "Do not shoot!"

But Irma was too late. The tiny car shot a stream of paint out of its nozzle. The red paint arced high in the air and splattered Petronella right in her angry vagina.

Jordan threw her body on top of Irma's body who was on top of Edison's body and they all three rolled around the floor. Edison's glasses flew off and her remote control skidded down the aisle and out of sight.

Chaos erupted. Petronella shrieked. The audience

screamed. Claire and Lillian stood on their chairs so they could see all the action. Amy covered her face.

The house lights flickered on and off like a strobe light.

Jordan climbed to her feet and chased after the remote. She ran from person to person as it was kicked around the audience like Charlie Chaplin's hat.

The car obeyed each command from the remote as it was kicked. The car shot paint left and right, up and down; red and blue and orange and yellow paint spewed from its nozzle, splattering Petronella and the audience. The car whizzed back and forth across the stage, in elaborate figure eights, gushing paint like a rabid, demon-possessed lawn sprinkler.

Petronella, now wearing a rainbow-colored tux and tails, picked up her stool and chased after the car, shouting Dutch obscenities.

The audience was a swirling mass of hysteria and color. The people bumped, banged and barged into each other, smearing the paint into one swirling mass of brown.

Petronella cornered the car against the proscenium arch and brought the stool down, hammering it, over and over and over, until the car was smashed to smithereens and nothing more than a giant rainbow puddle.

Once the car was demolished, the audience quieted down except for a few intermittent sobs. Everyone stared at the stage. Before them was a striking *tableaux vivant*: Petronella, legs spread, arms akimbo, *a la* Rambo Warrior, Victorious Vagina Woolf. The Ice Queen brought her hands up over her head in a victory gesture.

Claire and Lillian began clapping. The audience joined in, whooping and hollering their approval.

Petronella bowed deeply. The audience went wild, stamping their feet and chanting her name.

Jordan dejectedly walked back to Amy and collapsed in a chair. Edison fell into the chair next to her.

"Operation Meltdown failed," Jordan said. Amy sat down beside her and patted her shoulder sympathetically.

Irma sat next to Edison. "What the hell were you doing?" Edison said.

Irma gestured helplessly. "Irma does not know. Irma was overwhelmed by feelings here," she pointed to her heart, "and here," she pointed to her lap. "So sorry. Irma hear rousing poem and lose control."

Jordan stood and pointed a finger at Irma, saying, "You owe me. Big time."

Irma nodded. "Irma will make good. You will see."

Claire and Lillian joined the trio, grinning broadly. Lillian said, "So what do lesbians do for fun next?"

## Ambushed

Amy was humming an Indigo Girls tune as she entered the ER to start her shift. It was a damn fine day. The sun was shining. Mount Hood with its spectacular white cap seemed to substantiate the awesome beauty of nature. And Amy was on her third cup of coffee for the morning and flying high on caffeine and infatuation. She was certain she was falling in love for the first time in her life. None of her other relationships compared. Not that there were that many to compare to, but she knew she'd never felt like this before.

Chad snuck up behind her, wrapped his arms around her waist and whispered into her ear, "Good morning, my little love button."

Had Amy been taller, more muscular and trained in martial arts she would've kicked his ass right there. He'd be lying on the floor gasping and holding his nutsack as pain coursed throughout his entire body. As it was all she could do was wiggle away from him. "What the hell are you doing?" Amy said, disgustedly rubbing at the wet spot on her neck.

"I saw you come in," Chad said. "Whistling and smiling. Looking like a woman in love."

"So what if I am," Amy said.

"Maybe I am, too," Chad said with an icky smile. He reached out and stroked her cheek with one finger. Amy swatted his hand away like it was an annoying fly.

"I made lunch plans for us," Chad said. "I know how you love Italian."

"I have plans without you forever," Amy said. "And I'll be eating in the cafeteria today."

"I know," Chad replied, tapping his cleft with a forefinger. "I know."

Amy watched him saunter off down the hall,

wondering what that weird exchange meant. That was when she noticed his shoes. He was wearing pink Converse high-tops. She looked down at her own blue high-tops. That fucker! He was trying to do that thing where couples in love start dressing alike.

She turned to the two nurses at the nurses' station. "How long has he had those shoes?"

**Meet Veronica and Valerie.** Identical twin sisters. Beehive wearing, bubble gum popping, sisters. The only way to tell them apart was by their nametags.

"Since yesterday," Valerie said while Veronica blew a bubble.

"He says the pink makes him more manly because only real men can wear pink. It means they are secure in their manliness. Those were his exact words," Veronica said while Valerie blew a bubble.

"He told us that he hopes you two can bond over your joint love of high-tops," Valerie said.

Amy recoiled.

"It's disturbing, we know," they both said.

Usually Amy found their ability to speak simultaneously amusing or at least interesting. But today she found it annoying, more annoying than it should be because she was angry at Chad. Angry might be a poor word choice. She was livid.

Valerie and Veronica must have seen the smoke coming out her ears. They both said, "We can do something about those shoes."

"Oh, yeah. How?" Amy snapped, studying her day's roster.

"We can make those shoes disappear," Veronica said, snapping her gum for emphasis.

"Disappear?" Amy said. She felt like she was in an episode of the *Sopranos*.

"With this," Valerie said, pulling a bobby pin out of her piled high elaborate beehive hairdo.

Amy didn't get it. "You're going stab him with a bobby pin?"

They sighed simultaneously. "No," Valerie said.

"We are going to pick the lock on his locker and steal his shoes because he is an absolute fucker and we hate him," Veronica said.

Amy finally connected the dots. "Aha. You both slept with him too?"

They nodded.

"At the same time?" Amy asked. She quickly used her hand as an eraser on an imaginary chalkboard. "Erase that. Don't answer, I don't want to know."

"Let's just say he'll get what he deserves," Veronica said.

Valerie popped a bubble.

Amy smiled. She felt a strange symbiosis with the twins. "You'd do that for me?"

"No. Not just you. We'll do it for all the women of this hospital," Valerie said.

"You will be our mascot. The anti-Chad. We've named you Amy the Banana Slayer," Veronica said.

Amy didn't really want to be the Banana Slayer but if the twins could make the shoes disappear they could call her anything they liked. "What do I have to do?"

"Act like nothing happened," Veronica said.

"This conversation never happened," Valerie added.

Amy nodded. "What conversation?"

Valerie knitted her eyebrows. "This one. The one we just had."

Amy smiled and lightly punched her in the arm. "I know. I was pretending it never happened."

"Oh," Veronica said. "You're good."

"Really good," Valerie said. She handed Amy a manila folder, saying, "Mr. Bolster is back. He's in room three. It's his testicle again. If I were you I'd get that one over with first."

"Right," Amy said, and went to exam Mr. Bolster's man tackle. Again. He showed up at least once a week asking specifically for her. All the other doctors figured he had a crush on Amy, which was alarming because he was eighty-six and only had one testicle. There wasn't anything technically wrong with his testicle. He insisted it didn't fire properly. Amy tried and tried to explain that age did things to one's manhood equipment.

After the testicle debacle, Amy went on to set a broken finger, stitch two lacerations – one a two-year-old who ran into the corner of the wall while being chased by her brother, and another by a prep cook who was having an argument with his girlfriend while cutting up carrots julienne style.

She advised the cook to not text and chop as he could have lost his finger. At eleven forty-five things slowed down enough that Amy could actually catch her breath. She told the Veronica-Valerie duo that she was headed to grab a bite at the cafeteria. They nodded and went back to charting.

## That's Amore

In the cafeteria there was an ominous silence when Amy walked in. It was reminiscent of the banana-peel incident. She glanced around but saw nothing out of the ordinary until Jeremy took her by the arm.

"If you would just follow me this way, Madame," he said.

"What's going on?" she asked, stumbling along beside him. "What's this about?"

"You'll see," Jeremy answered.

She allowed herself to be led her to a table where Chad was sitting with his dimple on display. The cafeteria table was covered with a red-and-white checkered cloth. A lit candle sat in the middle along with a vase containing a single red rose.

She looked at Jeremy and tried to telepathically send him a thought message: *Help. Get me out of here.*

But Jeremy only smiled and gestured elegantly at the empty chair.

It occurred to Amy at this moment that she'd been leaving her roommates out of the loop. Jeremy hadn't a clue that Amy was in love with Jordan. She hadn't told Isabel either. She liked to think it was an oversight on her part but perhaps not. After coming out to her mother and being in the newspaper kissing another woman, Amy had figured it was now *de rigueur* that she was gay and everyone knew it. Wrong. It figured that the people closest to her were the ones she was going to have to spell it out for.

"Jeremy, what's going on here?"

"Only the biggest, baddest booty call ever. Chad is major courting you. The dude's got a bad case of the 'love me tenders.'" Jeremy said. He cocked his head and his Adam's apple twitched. He appeared to be moved.

Amy felt certain she was going puke. "Please tell me this isn't happening."

Chad stood, put his hand over his heart and began to sing in an off-key baritone about the moon and pizza pie and amore.

When he finished, Jeremy pulled out a chair for her to sit. Chad whipped the lid off a serving dish, exclaiming, "As the Italians say, *mangiare mangiare, amore*."

"Pizza," Jeremy said. Like she couldn't see that for herself. "How do you say pizza in Italian?"

"I think it's pizza," Chad answered.

"I am not doing this," Amy said.

"Just sit and we'll have a nice meal," Chad said, beginning to get nervous. The whole cafeteria watched - everyone painfully aware of a man pleading his case for the woman he loved.

Amy sat. But only because she didn't want to cause a big scene in the middle of the cafeteria.

"You can go now, Jeremy. Thanks," Amy said, giving him the I-will-deal-with-you-later look.

Jeremy fist-bumped Chad. "Good luck, dude."

Amy smiled at their audience who now went back to stuffing their mouths, trying not to look like they weren't engaged in group-stare.

Chad reached across the table and took her hand. In return, she grasped his pinky and bent it backwards. He squeaked.

"Listen to me you ignorant fuck," Amy said harshly, "if you ever pull a stunt like this again I will personally castrate you. You will have one less ball than Mr. Bolster. I don't want to have any sort of a relationship with you ever. Do you understand?"

Chad's red face bobbed up and down. Amy got up and slammed her chair back under the table. She turned to leave and that was when she saw Jordan. She was standing in the middle of the cafeteria watching the scene with

Chad. Confusion and hurt were etched across her face.

Amy grabbed Jordan's hand and dragged her out of the cafeteria. She threw open the first door she saw, a linen supply closet, and stepped inside. She turned on the light and faced Jordan.

Amy said, "Take me to lunch. I have to get out of here."

"That's why I dropped by. To apologize for the fiasco last night. For threatening to beat up your mother. For the lesbian on stilts not being funny. I wanted to make it up to you by taking you out to lunch. I should've called first. I wasn't stalking you. It probably looks like I was, but in reality I wasn't."

"Stop talking," Amy said.

"Why?"

"So I can kiss you."

Amy threw her arms around Jordan's neck and kissed her. And when an orderly opened the door, goggled at them a full minute before grabbing a stack of linens and then shutting the door, neither woman noticed.

## Nobel SurPrize

Back at The Original Dinerant, Jordan nibbled on a blue-corn tortilla chip. She had never seen anything so sensual, so intoxicating, so downright sexy as when Amy took a huge bite of her taco.

So far Jordan had refrained from asking anything further about that man in the hospital cafeteria. For one thing, she wasn't sure she wanted to know. On the other hand, it was going to bother her until she did. "So what was with that guy?" Jordan asked. She tried to make her voice sound light and carefree, however it came out sounding more like Alvin Chipmunk, "Somebody escaped from the psych ward?"

Amy reacted like Jordan had thrown a bucket of ice on her. "What guy? Oh, that guy. He… he… he… We went out for drinks one night. He can't take no for an answer," Amy said and shoved a blue chip in her mouth, signaling the end of the conversation.

Jordan dropped the subject. "How's your taco?"

Amy froze with her taco halfway to her mouth. "Uh oh."

Jordan froze with her tea glass halfway to her mouth. "Uh oh what?"

"Petronella is in the building," Amy whispered. "And she's coming this way."

Jordan's first instinct was to hide. It was too late to crawl under the table, so she did the next best thing. She draped her napkin over her head.

Two seconds later, she heard an icy voice say, "Hello, Jordan."

"Petronella," Jordan said back. Sighing, she took the napkin off her head.

Petronella looked down her nose at Amy and said, "I am sorry, but I do not know your name."

"We met once," Amy stammered. "Here, in fact. I mean in this restaurant. Not at this table. You were leaving. You probably don't remember me."

Recognition flashed across Petronella's face. "Oh yes, the girl with toilet paper stuck to her shoe."

"Yep. That was me." Amy chuckled nervously. "I don't have toilet paper on my shoe today."

Petronella leaned to see. "Indeed you do not. Good for you." Petronella's skinny neck swiveled back to Jordan. "I saw you at my poetry reading and…"

Jordan cut her off, "We came to see the show. You just happened to be there."

"Be that as it may. You observed what happened, am I correct?"

"Yes, I saw," Jordan said. "It was quite colorful."

Petronella ignored the obvious pun. "Did you see the reviews?" she inquired.

"If you mean those little ezine-online thingies, not really," Jordan said.

"And the City Pages and the Arts and Entertainment section," Petronella added.

"Yeah, whatever," Jordan said.

Petronella pulled out a chair and sat. "I need your help."

"First, what could you possibly want from me?" Jordan asked. "And secondly, why should I do anything for you?"

Petronella ignored the questions. Which was not unusual. If she didn't want to know about something, she ignored its existence. Just like she was ignoring Amy right at the moment. Petronella scooted her chair several inches closer to Jordan. "I need your little inventor friend… what is her name, Einstein?"

"Edison," Jordan corrected.

"Yes, of course. I need Edison to build me a machine."

## More Than a Kiss

"What kind of machine?" Jordan asked. She wondered if it was too much to hope for Petronella wanting a time machine to blast her back into the past. Or the future. Or anywhere but here.

"A machine like the one that attacked me last night."

Jordan paled. "Why?" She squirmed in her chair. Did Petronella know she was responsible for the paint-spraying incident? Was she playing some type of game, hoping to trap Jordan into admitting her culpability? Jordan looked to Amy for help. But Amy was nervously stuffing blue-corn tortilla chips in her mouth.

Petronella continued, "I tried to find the machine after the show. I was going to gather up the parts and see if Einstein could put them back together. But, unfortunately, the terrorists made off with it before I could."

"Terrorists?" Amy said through a mouth full of blue goo.

"Yes," Petronella said. She had the gleam of a zealot in her eyes.

"Terrorists for what?" Jordan said.

"There are certain people, Jordan, who wish to see me harmed."

"Really?" Jordan said, trying hard to appear appalled at such a thing. "Who would want that?" Besides me, she added inside her own head.

"People who dislike poetry," Petronella said like it was obvious. "Republican people, no doubt. But their little plan backfired."

"It did?" Amy chirped up.

Petronella did not look at her. "The audience loved the paint splattering. They thought it was part of the show. My reviews were fantastic. There is talk of short-listing me for the Nobel."

Amy choked on a chip. Petronella glared at her. Amy smiled weakly and thumped herself on the chest.

"Sorry. Wrong pipe."

Jordan smirked.

"So," Petronella continued, "I would like your little friend to build me another paint machine. I will go on tour with it. I will call it my Rainbow Tour."

"What a fantastic idea!" Jordan said. The thought of Petronella being on tour and out of her life was too good to be true. Wait, Jordan thought, what if it really is too good to be true? "For realsies?" she asked.

"Yes," Petronella said. "For realsies."

"When would you be leaving on this tour?"

"As soon as I get the paint machine."

"I'll call Einstein, I mean, Edison, today."

Petronella smiled and stood. "Contact me after you have talked to her. You know my number."

Jordan and Amy watched Petronella as she left. No sooner had the door closed behind her than Edison entered through the back door. She saw Jordan and hurried over to the table. Skipping hellos entirely, Edison panted, "Was she here?"

"Petronella?" Jordan asked.

Edison nodded, trying to catch her breath. "Who else? I've been following her, but I lost her about a mile back. I invented a motorized bicycle, you know, for the lazy cyclist so they wouldn't have to pedal up hills, but I think I ran out of gas. Do you know how heavy one of those bikes are when you have to pedal?" She wheezed a couple of times and sucked in a giant lungful of oxygen before continuing, "I lost her, but figured she was headed here."

"You just missed her," Jordan said.

"Motorized bicycles have already been invented," Amy said.

Edison sat in Petronella's vacant chair. "They have? Are you sure?"

"Yeah, pretty sure," Amy said.

Edison looked downcast. "Damn. All the good inventions are already taken."

Jordan leaned across the table until her nose was six inches from Edison's nose. "Guess what? Petronella wants you to invent a paint car just like the one that sprayed her."

Edison looked confused. "I invented the one that *did* spray her."

"She doesn't know that," Jordan said. "She wants to take it on tour. Build another one and Petronella will be out of my hair forever. Can you do it?"

"Of course," Edison said.

"If you build it, she will go," Amy said.

## Congress of Cow

Amy walked into the house and was immediately engulfed by the aroma of curry emanating from the kitchen. She followed her nose to the source, expecting to find Isabel. Instead, she found Jeremy stirring something in a saucepan and reading a book - both very unnatural things for him.

"You're cooking?" Amy said.

"Actually, I'm only babysitting. I have strict orders to not stop stirring."

Amy peered into the pot and saw something green and lumpy. She was no expert, but she knew enough to know that wasn't a good sign. "What is that?"

"It's Saag Paneer. Or will be when it's done," Jeremy said, not looking up from the book he was holding. He cocked his head and then turned the book upside down and squinted his eyes.

"It's what?" Amy said, taking the wooden spoon from him and giving the goop a good poke. It had the consistency of something found in a touch pool at the aquarium. She felt the urge to do it again, the way kids like to poke dead things with a stick.

"Saag Paneer is Indian for green slime. It's essentially cooked spinach with this Indian cheese stuff. The sauce is supposed to be thinner than this but he ran out of coconut milk. He went out to get it. He's making you dinner."

"He? He who?" Amy asked with a note of panic.

"Chad he, that's who. You know a man's in love when he starts cooking dinner."

"What!" Amy said, dropping the spoon and splattering green stuff everywhere.

"Seriously, the dude's got it bad for you. He was like so down about what happened at lunch that he took an express cooking class this afternoon to woo you back. The only class they had available was Indian cooking. Hence, the green slime."

"That's just great. I thought I could spend an evening alone with you and Isabel. I had something important to tell you both and…" her voice trailed off when she realized Jeremy was more interested in his book than in what she was saying. "What're you reading?"

"*The Kama Sutra*. Talk about a real eye-opener."

Amy looked over his shoulder at the drawing he had been studying. "That's not even humanly possible."

"Apparently, it is. Those bodies are drawn to scale. I think you just have to be really limber."

"Why do you even have this?" Amy made some deductions and she hoped she was wrong about all of them.

"It's not mine. It's Chad's. He bought it with the cookbook. He's boning up on some new positions to try out on you." He laughed. "Boning up. Get it?"

"Not funny. This is wrong on so many levels I don't know where to start," Amy said.

"No, I think the dude is right on target. His plan is to feed you and then fuck you like…" he shows her a picture in the book, "a congress of cow."

"That is so not going to happen."

"You prefer him to fuck you like a panda?"

"Jeremy, there is going to be no fucking – panda, cow or any other animal."

"He's going to be totally bummed out. What're you going to tell him?"

"Good question." She could call Jordan and have her call back with some fake emergency. Amy bit her lip. In theory that was a good plan but maybe the wrong person. Jordan was already skittish about Chad. Amy didn't want to make it any weirder. She thought some more. Her mother! She'd be perfect. Who can deny the call of a sick mother? And it would have the added benefit of not looking like she was rebuffing him because the rebuff strategy was backfiring. It was making Chad more ardent than ever.

"Do you think that Chad thinks I'm trying to play 'hard to get' and that's why he's trying so hard to get me?"

Jeremy stared back at her. "Could you put that in like man-speak?"

Men and women were not of the same species despite the claims of science, Amy had concluded. She tried again. "That's what you told me once. That he thinks I'm playing hard to get."

"Yes, and he likes it."

"So if I acted like I wanted him then would he go away?"

"No, he'd totally marry you."

"And then cheat on you the day after," Isabel said, entering the kitchen. She was carrying a bag of groceries with celery sticking out of the top and something moving in the bottom.

"What's in the bag?" Amy asked.

"A live lobster which I really need to get into some water," Isabel said, setting the bag down on the counter. She peered into the pot on the stove. She took the wooden spoon from Jeremy and poked the green, lumpy stuff. "What is this?"

"Saag Paneer," Jeremy said.

"It needs more coconut milk."

"Chad went to get it," Jeremy said.

Isabel ran water into the sink. She carefully extracted the lobster from the sack and dumped it into the water.

"What are you making for dinner?" Amy asked. "Lobster bisque?" Amy didn't know what lobster bisque was exactly, but it had to better than Chad's Pig Veneer or whatever it was Jeremy was stirring.

"No, the lobster is for the lobster race that's being

held at the Extreme Cook Off downtown in the Convention Center," Isabel said.

"Lobster race?" Amy asked. She did a double take when she saw Jeremy was now studying a diagram on cunnilingus. She made a mental note of the page number.

"The placement of your lobster in the race determines your place in the cook off. Obviously being in the top ten is best. Judges' palates get jaded and gastric problems start occurring so you want to get in early." She gestured at the lobster in the sink, saying, "I thought this guy looked pretty fast and he was hot-to-go getting out of the tank. Look at him trying to get out of the sink now." She grabbed a spatula and parried it at the lobster, like an errant knight defending a damsel. The lobster evaded Isabel's thrust, reached out with one deadly claw and snapped the spatula in half.

"Wowzer," Isabel said, surveying the decapitated spatula.

"Wowzer is right," Amy said. "Remind me not to get on his bad side."

Isabel threw the spatula in the trash. "I guess that's why they're usually sold with rubber-bands around their claws."

"So, after the race, are you going to eat him?" Amy asked. Jeremy was totally engrossed in the book and not stirring. She poked him with her elbow. "Keep stirring."

"Depends on if he wins or loses the race," Isabel said, looking down on him. "His performance will affect my life. If he places high I should reward him with life, don't you think?"

"You could take him to the beach and free him," Amy said.

The front door slammed, announcing the arrival of Chad with the coconut milk. Amy panicked. He was the last person she wanted to see. She was about to sneak out the door when Chad appeared, blocking her only exit.

"Hello, my little love button."

Amy gritted her teeth and looked at Isabel, sending her telepathic messages. Isabel caught on and came to her rescue by saying, "You better get that coconut milk in the Saag Paneer because it has the consistency of wallpaper glue."

Chad quickly began tearing the top of the container. "How much do you think?"

Isabel shrugged. "Don't know. Never made the stuff. I have a spastic colon."

Chad noticed Jeremy reading and snatched the book away from him. "No one was supposed to see that, you idiot."

"Hey, I needed entertainment. Stirring is boring."

Chad poured in a tiny bit of the coconut milk. Jeremy had to use both hands to stir the thick gunk. "Keep stirring," Chad ordered.

Isabel grabbed the carton of coconut milk out of Chad's hands, saying, "Let me help. You men are useless." She poured a little at a time into the pot while Jeremy continued stirring.

Chad leaned up against the counter next to the sink, affecting a pose that Amy supposed was calculated to look like a male model. He tossed Amy his famous wink. She didn't bother to catch it.

Chad changed poses, leaning on one arm, crossing his feet and pooching out his bottom lip. Amy supposed it was his sultry look.

"Where are your pink shoes?" Amy asked.

Chad's smile disappeared. "They were stolen. I couldn't believe it. Who would steal pink size 12 men's shoes?"

"A clown?" Isabel said.

Amy snickered.

Chad ignored the insult. "Do you know how hard it is to find a shoe like that?" he said, petulantly. "And now

## More Than a Kiss

I've got to do it again. But you should see all the adorable kid Converse shoes. You know for when we've got little ones," Chad said, raising his eyebrows up and down like Groucho Marx.

Amy might have decked him if what happened next hadn't happened.

Chad's face turned red and he screamed. He plucked his hand up off the counter by the sink. The lobster was dangling from his finger! The lobster had a death grip on his forefinger with one of its enormous claws. Chad jumped up and down, spun in a circle and then banged the lobster on the edge of the counter. The lobster sailed across the room, splashing into the pot of Saag Paneer.

Jeremy yelped and jumped back.

Isabel screamed, "Save him!"

Amy said, "I'll save him!" She rushed to Chad who was now spurting a stream of blood from his hand.

Isabel shook her head. "Not him! Save the lobster!" Isabel pushed Jeremy back and whacked the back of the pot. It turned over, emptying out the green lumpy stuff and one seriously dizzy lobster onto the floor. The lobster scurried away.

Jeremy put his hands over his ears, screaming, "Will somebody please turn off the alarm?"

"That's not an alarm. It's Chad screaming," Amy shouted. "The lobster bit off his finger!"

That seemed to be news to Chad. He looked down at his hand and, for the first time, saw that he was missing his index finger. He stopped screaming. His eyes rolled back into his head, his knees buckled and he crumpled to the floor.

"What kind of doctor faints?" Isabel said.

"One that just lost his finger," Amy said.

"He's bleeding an awful lot," Isabel said. This observation kicked Amy into gear. She grabbed a dishtowel and kitchen shears. She cut the towel into strips. "Snap, snap, you two," Amy said, gesturing to the floor, "find the finger. The lobster probably dropped it into that green goo." She tied the strips to Chad's hand, fashioning a tourniquet.

Jeremy and Isabel knelt on the floor, searching the globs of Saag Paneer with their bare hands. They looked like two kids making mud pies. *Green* mud pies.

"How do we know which lump is it?" Isabel asked.

"Just find a lump that looks like a finger," Amy said.

"They all look like decapitated fingers," Jeremy said.

Amy said, "Get them all, we'll sort it out later."

"I found it!" Isabel yelled triumphantly. She held the finger up for everyone to see.

Jeremy gently pinched the dismembered digit between his thumb and forefinger and dunked it in the sink of water, to rinse it off. "Isabel, get a baggie. Fill it with ice."

Isabel leaped up and got a baggie and ice. Jeremy dropped the finger inside. Isabel put her hands on her hips and looked at the kitchen floor. "Gross. It looks like Linda Blair was here."

Satisfied that the tourniquet was working, Amy turned her attention to waking Chad up. She slapped him across the face. He didn't move. She slapped him again, harder.

Chad's eyelids fluttered. He opened his eyes and smiled at Amy. "I knew it. I knew you cared."

She gave him one more slap just because she could.

## Indy 500

Isabel was driving her Jeep Cherokee with Jeremy riding shotgun. Amy sat in the back seat with Chad's passed-out head in her lap. Amy couldn't believe this was happening, although she had to admit that this was far more exciting than the evening Chad originally had planned.

Isabel had the accelerator mashed to the floor and weaved in and out of traffic with a steady hand. Jeremy and Amy held their breath each time Isabel cut in front of another car.

"Did anybody turn off the stove?" Isabel asked, not slowing through a yellow light.

"Shit," Jeremy said. He sat up straighter. "Did anybody catch the lobster?"

"Shit," said Isabel, taking the corner on two wheels.

"So we have an open gas flame and a killer lobster on the loose in our house?" Jeremy said. "Could this day get any more weird?"

"I'mmalesbian," Amy blurted. Wowzer. She didn't know that was going to pop out. The words were out of her mouth before the thought was even formed. Or maybe the thought had been formed for a long time and it escaped her head once her guard was down.

Isabel looked at Amy quizzically in the rear view mirror. Jeremy turned in his seat and looked her up and down before turning back around. Finally he said, "Well, that answers a lot of questions."

"It does? Like what?" Amy asked.

Jeremy shrugged. "Why you were kissing that hottie in the paper. Why you hate Chad."

Isabel laid on her horn and swerved around an old man walking his dog across a crosswalk. "Is it because of Chad?" Isabel asked. "Because that's a little extreme, isn't it? You don't have to change your sexual orientation just to make him go away."

"No," Amy said. "It's not because of Chad. And in my own defense, plenty of women hate Chad and they're not all lesbians."

"True, true," Jeremy said.

Isabel careened around a corner without touching the brakes. She gunned the engine up to the emergency room, leaving twin skid marks in front of the double doors.

"If this cooking thing doesn't work out, you might consider race car driving," Jeremy said.

"Yeah, who knew I had a natural talent?" Isabel said.

"I'll be right back, don't try to move him yourself," Jeremy said. He baled out of the Jeep and sprinted inside the emergency room to gather a gurney crew. After a moment, Veronica and Valerie ran outside. Amy opened her door and once the twins saw Chad passed out on Amy's lap, Valerie said, "This was a little over the top, wasn't it?"

Veronica continued, "Yeah. You didn't have to try and kill him."

"I didn't do this!" Amy protested. "A lobster did it."

"Well," Valerie said, "You get an A plus for creative excuses. I don't know if a jury will buy it, though."

"If I were you," Veronica said, "I would have cut off his penis. But a finger is good, too."

Amy handed Veronica the finger in the baggie, saying, "Just take this. Make sure it gets to wherever the rest of him is going."

Jeremy rolled a gurney up to the Jeep. It took two EMTs to load Chad onto the stretcher.

As they rolled the stretcher into the hospital, Chad awoke and started screaming. Amy, Isabel and Jeremy all watched Chad being wheeled away until they could no longer hear his screams.

"Do you think they'll be able to reattach it?" Isabel asked.

Jeremy shrugged. "Who knows? We might be calling him Dr. Stumpy from now on."

Isabel giggled. Jeremy joined in. Their laughter was infectious and soon Amy was laughing, too.

## Steve

Jeremy drove the Jeep back home. He had insisted on driving until Isabel's adrenaline rush had subsided. Halfway home, he pulled off onto a side street and into a strip mall. "I have to pick up a few things. It'll only take a minute." Jeremy got out of the jeep and walked into Uncle Miltie's Party Land.

"Is it someone's birthday tomorrow?" Isabel inquired.

"I don't think so," Amy said. "Maybe that's not a birthday party place. Uncle Miltie sounds like a perv. Maybe it's a sex shop."

"Yeah," Isabel giggled. "Maybe it's a sex shop for clowns." They both laughed and the tension of the past hour eased.

"So speaking of sex," Isabel said. "What's up with the lesbian thing?"

Amy took a deep breath. "You know how I've been hanging out with that woman Jordan, the one I met at work?"

"The pretty one? Yeah, Jeremy told me."

"We're sorta kinda dating now."

"I don't have a problem with it. Just tell her if she's not nice to you, she'll have to deal with me. I'll sic Steve on her."

"Who's Steve?"

"The lobster," Isabel said. "He needed to have a name before I could wrap my mind around what just happened. Besides, despite the Chad thing, I still need him for the race. I don't think I can handle picking up another one."

"We've got to find him first. We should use gloves to handle him," Amy said, thinking they didn't need to lose any more fingers tonight.

"Baseball gloves," Isabel said. At that moment, Jeremy opened the driver's door and handed a big sack over to Isabel. "Mission accomplished."

"What did you get?" Isabel said, peering inside the bag.

Jeremy smirked. "I couldn't resist. Check it out."

Isabel rooted around in the bag and pulled out several small plastic lobsters, an inflatable lobster, several hard plastic lobster true-to-scale models, light up lobster patio lights, a lobster cooking apron, a ceramic coffee mug with a lobster painted on the side and one peeking up from the bottom, lobster towels, a pair of lobster boxer shorts and even lobster socks.

"You are terrible," Isabel said.

"I know, right?"

"Jeremy, aren't you being a little harsh?" Amy said.

"And the banana thing wasn't? Look, he got a lot of mileage out of tormenting you. Dude gets what he gives. Picture it: tomorrow he wakes up and his entire room is lobsterfied. You gotta admit, it's funny."

Amy smiled. Maybe Chad did deserve a little retribution. Okay, *a lot* of retribution.

Jeremy started the car while Isabel repacked the bag. "He is an asshole," Isabel said.

"And it is funny," Amy added.

"He uses people, dudes included. All I'm saying is he needs to come down from Chad mountain," Jeremy said. "Doctor Stumpy is going to wake up tomorrow in lobster world." He hung a lobster shaped car deodorizer from his rear view mirror.

## Here, Lobster, Lobster!

Amy had barely walked through the front door before she heard Isabel yell, "Oh no!" Amy ran to the kitchen and got there only seconds before Jeremy. "What? What? What?" Amy said. "What is it?"

Isabel was standing in front of the stove, staring at it. There was nothing wrong that Amy could see. Even the burner was turned off. Isabel slowly turned to Jeremy and Amy, saying, "The Saag Paneer. It's gone."

"Gone?" Jeremy said. "It fell on the floor."

Isabel gestured to the floor. It was mostly clean except for a twin pair of green drag marks leading toward the dining room. She picked up the pot the Saag Paneer had been cooking in. There was nothing inside but a crusty green ring where it had once been.

"Steve ate it," Amy said, drawing the obvious conclusion.

"Who's Steve?" Jeremy asked.

"The lobster," Isabel said. "I named him Steve."

"You named a man-maiming, Indian-food-eating lobster Steve?" Jeremy asked.

"Mr. Claw was too obvious," Isabel said.

Jeremy nodded like it made absolute and complete sense.

"We need to find Steve," Isabel said. "Before the Saag Paneer kicks in and he goes really crazy."

"Yeah, no way I'm sleeping in this house with him on the loose," Amy said.

"If you find him, don't hurt him. I still need him for the race tomorrow," Isabel said.

"Okay, well, let's split up and check all the rooms," Amy said.

"Can lobsters live outside of water?" Jeremy asked. He was opening kitchen cupboards. "I mean, they keep them in that tank at the store, right?"

"They need water but as long as they keep moist they can live outside of a pool," Isabel said.

"Could he have gotten outside?" Amy opened the back door that led outside from the kitchen. She turned on the light. "Here lobster, lobster, lobster!"

"I'll go out and search," Jeremy said, pulling on oven mitts. He clicked his heels and saluted them. "If I'm not back in three days tell my mother I loved her," he said, soberly.

Isabel snickered.

"I'll start in my bedroom. You start in yours," Amy said. She opened the storage closet and grabbed a bucket and a Tupperware tub. She handed Isabel the bucket. "If you see him trap him under that."

Amy left Isabel and went to her room. She looked under the bed and had just opened the closet door when she heard Isabel's blood-curdling scream. She flew out of her room, crashing into Jeremy who was running down the hallway. Isabel screamed again.

Amy was the first to throw open the bathroom door and step inside. Jeremy skidded to a stop behind her. Isabel was standing on the bathroom counter with her pants bunched around her ankles and her panties up, but twisted. She was bug-eyed and pointing at the toilet.

Amy tiptoed over to the toilet and peered inside. Sure enough, Steve was in the bowl. He was trying to crawl out, but kept sliding on the porcelain. "He looks mad."

Isabel said, "I peed on him."

Jeremy burst out laughing and walked toward the toilet. Isabel flapped her arms, stopping him in his tracks. "Don't look at my pee!"

Jeremy jumped back. "I think we need to get him out of there, Isabel," he said.

Isabel nodded. "I know. But I don't want a man to

see my pee."

"So Amy can see your urine, but I can't? That's really weird, Isabel."

"It's just my thing, okay? I don't want you to see my pee."

"I'm a doctor, Isabel, I've seen lots of pee."

Isabel shook her head. "You're my friend. We're roommates. I read in a magazine once that if a man sees you urinate he'll never look at you the same way again."

"What way?" he asked.

"Just don't look at my pee!" she shouted on the verge of hysteria.

"Okay, okay," Jeremy said, backing up and not looking anywhere near the toilet.

"I have a plan," Amy said. "I think I can flush the toilet, the pee will disappear and then we can get Steve out."

"Won't that make him madder?" Isabel said, untwisting her panties and pulling up her pants. "He might get really violent the madder he gets."

"It'll just be like a wave crashing over him," Amy said. "He can pretend he's on the beach." She flushed the toilet. Steve bumped about and then settled, his antennae seeming to approve.

"You can look now," Isabel said to Jeremy.

"How about we put him in the tub," Amy said. She stopper-ed the tub and turned on the faucet, adjusting the temperature to what she believed Steve would find comfortable.

Jeremy studied Steve, being careful to keep his fingers out of claw range. "We have those BBQ tongs, right?"

"Yes," Isabel said. "I'll get them." She jumped off the counter and ran out of the room.

"Do you think she's all right?" Jeremy whispered after Isabel was gone.

"I think so. Although she'll never sit down again without looking," Amy said.

"I've never sat without looking after I saw that movie where alligators roamed the sewers of New York," Jeremy said.

Isabel ran back in with an enormous set of metal tongs. "These should work."

Isabel poked around in the toilet with the tongs. Steve thrashed. "Listen, you little shit. We have to get through tomorrow and then I'll set you free, so just settle down and I'll get you out of there. I'm sorry I peed on you but if you're going to hang around in a toilet bowl that's to be expected."

"She does know she's talking to a bug wearing an exoskeleton, right?" Jeremy said.

"Well, they did share an intimate moment," Amy replied.

"I'll say. He could've bitten off my vagina," Isabel said. She frowned. "I'd never get a date then."

"You're more than the sum of your parts," Jeremy said.

"That's very nice of you to say, Jeremy, but a girl that hasn't got a vagina stands no chance against one that does," Isabel said. She furrowed her brow, opened the tongs and clamped Steve around his midsection. "Ha! I got you." She dashed toward the tub with the flailing lobster dripping water everywhere and his antennae going wild. She dropped him in the tub with a big plop.

"Wow, awesome job," Amy said. They all watched Steve for a moment as he swam to and fro. "He looks happy, don't you think?"

"What do we do when we want to bathe?" Amy asked.

"Use the shower in my room," Isabel said. "I'll have him out of here tomorrow afternoon."

"Okay," Amy said.

"So, let's order a pizza and forget any of this happened. What do you say?" Isabel said, her face flushed from her triumph.

"Good idea," Jeremy and Amy said in unison.

Isabel was the last one to leave the bathroom. She flipped off the light and whispered in the dark, "Good night, Steve. Sleep tight."

"Don't let the crustaceans bite," Amy said from down the hallway.

"Ha ha," Isabel muttered. "Not funny."

## The Interrogation

All hell was breaking loose. Jordan had always thought that expression was nothing more than a silly cliché. Now she was changing her mind. As soon as she walked in the front door and heard the commotion (banging, muffled yelling, strange machine-like whirring noises) from upstairs in Edison's laboratory, Jordan knew all hell was indeed breaking loose.

Her brain shifted into rescue mode while her body went into survival mode. She didn't know whether to run to the noises or run away from the noises. In the end, brain and body compromised and she slowly crept upstairs to Edison's lab. She felt like the virgin in a horror movie. The virgin was always the last to die. If she heard any creepy music she was running back down the stairs.

Jordan put a hand on the lab door like she was testing the temperature within the room. She had seen that in a safety video once. If the door felt hot that meant there was a hellish backdraft waiting to jump out and crispy-fry her.

The door felt lukewarm. Jordan thought that meant she could open the door; that nothing hellacious was contained within the confines of the four walls on the other side of that wooden two-inch slab.

She was wrong.

What she saw took a bloated moment to register: Petronella, dressed all in white, was sitting in a straight-backed chair in the middle of the room. Her hands were tied behind her back. Her feet were tied at the ankles. And the scariest part? The entire room was covered in plastic wrap.

Every. Single. Thing. Covered. In. Plastic.

Jordan's brain balked, refusing to admit what her eyes were seeing. Then once it did register, she very nearly upchucked. She had unwittingly entered a murder den. Petronella was going to be slaughtered and the murderer didn't want blood to get all over everything.

Edison jumped out from behind the door with a big smile plastered on her face. "Good! You're here!"

Jordan opened her mouth, closed it, opened it again and stuttered, "What the fuckity fuck?"

Edison said, "You got here just in time for the interrogation."

Interrogation? Something clicked into place and Jordan's mind flashbacked to yesterday. Edison had led her to the garage, saying, "I have to show you something. Petronella has been up to her old tricks."

"You're talking about the slashed tires and the whore on the porch thing?" Jordan asked.

"Yes, among other things."

"Other things?" Jordan said.

Edison pointed to the corner of the garage. A stack of political signs, the kind politicians stick in front yards during elections, leaned against the wall. Jordan went over to look closer. They weren't political signs; they were Biblical signs.

"What the hell?" she said and began reading them. They were Bible verses, indictments against homosexuality of the "man shall not lie with man" variety.

"I came home the other night and the lawn was plastered with them. And, boy, GLAAD is mad. Their spokeswoman called and warned me that such bigotry will not be tolerated," Edison said.

"Wait a minute. They actually thought we were putting these in our yard on purpose?" Jordan asked.

"Yep."

"Did you explain that we're gay?" Jordan asked.

"I tried but the woman was ranting so much I couldn't get a word in edgewise. I took the signs down and stacked them in here."

"This is pretty low, even for Petronella."

"Duh, think about it. It's a perfect premise. She's trying to make us look bad in front of the whole neighborhood. Mrs. Wickersham from across the street flipped me the bird this morning. Even the cute letter-carrier snubbed me."

Jordan shook her head in disbelief. "Why didn't you tell me?"

"I made an executive decision not to tell you because you were so happy with Amy and I didn't want to ruin it. But that's not all."

"There's more?"

Edison pointed at a cardboard box. Jordan reached down to open it, but Edison stopped her, saying, "I wouldn't open that if I were you."

"Why, what is it?"

"Evidence."

Jordan wrinkled her nose. "It smells poop-ish."

"That's because it is poop-ish. Burned and charred dog poop to be precise. Someone set it on the porch, lit it on fire and rang the doorbell. Irma was not happy when she stomped it out."

Jordan's face darkened. "Petronella tried to light my house on fire."

"I think she just wanted you to get shit on your shoes."

"But she could've burned down the house."

"Yes, she could have. That's why I mean to put a stop to her evil and vandalistic trickery."

"If Petronella was doing all this why did she ask me to get you to invent the remote control paint car?" Jordan asked.

"Duh," Edison said. "To throw you off her scent."

That was yesterday. Today, Jordan was standing at the murder scene and what Edison said made sense. She had had no idea that Edison was meaning to kill Petronella.

She had thought Edison meant to give her the remote car and send her away on tour.

Jordan grabbed Edison by the shoulders and shook her none too gently. "You can't do this. You can't kill her. I don't want her blood on your hands."

"Kill?" Petronella gasped. She strained against the ropes tying her to the chair. "Kill!" she yelled. She bounced up and down, managing to make the chair hop. She hopped toward Jordan, begging, "Please, Jordan, do not kill me. I was not perfect. I know that now. But to kill me?"

"Nobody's killing anybody," Jordan said.

"You're going to wish you were dead, though," Edison snarled. With that, Edison put on her sunglasses and whipped a remote control out of her pocket. She aimed it Petronella.

Petronella blanched. "What are you doing? Is that a taser gun?"

"I vill ask you again," Edison said, using a fake German accent that sounded like it came straight out of *Hogan's Heroes*. "Did you or did you not put zee signs in zee yard?"

"Not!" Petronella said. "I have no idea what you are talking about!"

Edison pushed a button. From the corner of the room an engine buzzed. A remote control tanker rolled on four wheels up to Petronella. It was a duplicate of the one that caused the brouhaha at the poetry reading. A nozzle telescoped out and up. It rose, lowered, moved from right to left until it was in perfect alignment with Petronella.

Edison laughed and punched another button. Red paint shot out of the nozzle and splattered Petronella in the chest.

Petronella looked down at the red spot on her white shirt and yelped, "This is Armani, you idiot!"

Jordan was relieved that Edison was only

euphemistically killing Petronella. And the sight of the Ice Queen red-faced and blubbering sent Jordan into hysterics.

"This is not funny!" Petronella barked.

"Gimme that," Jordan said, taking the remote out of Edison's hands. "Don't hog all the fun."

"NO! Do not shoot!" Petronella pleaded.

Edison clasped her hands behind her back, paced back and forth and interrogated, "Then tell the truth, Petronella. Did you put the flaming dog poop on the porch?"

"I have no idea what you are talking about," Petronella said.

Jordan pushed a button.

Petronella gasped as a jet-stream of blue paint hit her full in the face. "Damn you!"

Jordan high-fived Edison. "She looks good in blue don't you think?"

"You're right. Her white hair really makes her blue teeth pop."

"Next question," Jordan said, poising her thumb over the yellow button. "Did you paint the word 'WHORE' on my porch?"

"You are demented and crazy," Petronella spit. This time the yellow paint splattered her crotch.

Edison giggled. "It looks like she tinkled her panties."

Petronella bounced in her chair toward Jordan. She was so mad she was frothing at the mouth. Or maybe that was just the blue paint bubbling out.

Jordan backed away from Petronella's hopping chair, using the remote to keep the tanker car between herself and Petronella. She fired another question, "Did you slash my bike tires?"

"No. No. No. No. No. No," Petronella enunciated with each bounce of her chair.

Jordan splattered her with green paint. Then topped

it off with a small splash of red. Petronella kept bouncing, kept advancing.

Jordan walked backwards. She aimed the remote and said, "Tell the truth Petronella. The paint will not stop until you admit to your crimes."

"I. Did. Not. Do. It." Bouncity bounce bounce.

Jordan hit the button labeled "rapid fire." Four streams of pulsating colors hit Petronella. It was like she was standing under a colorful waterfall. Petronella stopped bouncing. Soon, she was a rainbow collage of colors. She began to sob.

Jordan stopped firing.

Petronella hung her head, gasping for breath. "I give up," she said weakly between sobs. "I can take no more. I surrender."

Jordan handed the remote to Edison and said, "Admit it, Petronella. You are jealous of Amy."

"Yes," Petronella said. "Yes, I am jealous. Is that what you wanted to hear?" She looked up, her eyes meeting Jordan's. "Can you blame me? She has captured your attention. You are in love with her. I loved you once. But you never loved me back."

Jordan opened her mouth to disagree, but Petronella interrupted. "Oh, do not tell me you loved me, Jordan. I am a lot of things, but I am no fool. I would have given anything to have you look at me the way you look at her. All I ever wanted was your love." She looked away and sniffled. "To be loved," she said softly. "Alas, it is not to be. I shall perish, old and alone, wrinkled and shriveled. The Ice Queen will never be warmed by another's heart." She snuffled.

"Irma loves you," a voice said.

Jordan looked toward the door. It was Irma. Jordan had been so engrossed in Petronella's sob story, she hadn't noticed Irma come in.

"What do you know about love?" Petronella

sniffled.

"Irma knows a beautiful, talented woman when Irma sees one," Irma said as she slowly approached Petronella.

Petronella met Irma's gaze. If she wasn't mistaken, Jordan saw something in Petronella's eyes, something that burned from deep within, a desire that hadn't been there before, if ever. Irma, the woman in black, gazed longingly at Petronella, the woman in white. Well, she was usually all in white. Right now, she was covered in colors.

Petronella said, "You are a strong, sexy Russian woman. Why would you want me?"

Irma knelt before Petronella's chair and placed her hands on Petronella's knees. "Irma wants to make love to you. Irma wants to take care of you. Irma wants to love and protect you for all time. If you will have Irma?"

"Untie me," Petronella whispered hoarsely with desire coloring her cheeks. "Untie me and show me what it is to be loved so completely."

Jordan whispered to Edison, "I think that's our cue to leave."

Edison nodded and whispered back. "I just puked a little in my mouth."

Jordan and Edison quietly left the room and shut the door on the new lovers. "I think Petronella was telling the truth."

"Me, too," Edison said.

Jordan pulled the rubber ball out of her pocket and squeezed it. "So if Petronella didn't do all that stuff, who did?"

## Lezebel

Amy was on her way to Chad's room at the hospital. She knew he would be held hostage by pain medication, so what better time to confront him about his unwanted advances? "Unwanted advances" was the phrase Amy had substituted for what was really beginning to look like a severe case of stalking. She was starting to think that Chad wasn't only missing a finger, but was also missing a few of his marbles.

As Amy neared his room, she saw the twins, Veronica and Valerie, peering through the rectangular window of his door. They were snickering and talking in hushed tones. Unbeknownst to them, Amy peered over their shoulders and through the window. Chad's room was decorated entirely in lobster motif.

Jeremy had been good on his word. There were lobster lamps, nightlights, curtains, towels, blankets, throw rugs, and plastic/rubber lobsters everywhere. Chad was lying in bed, tossing and turning, intermittently moaning and whining as he slept. He was probably having a dream about giant lobsters chasing him. At least Amy hoped he was.

"I've never seen anyone with so little pain tolerance," Veronica whispered. "He acts like he's had major surgery."

"It's a finger not a pancreas," Valerie said.

"I never figured him for such a pansy," Amy said. Her already low opinion of Chad was dropping as rapidly as a runaway elevator.

The twins parted, allowing Amy into Chad's room. She walked up next to his bed. "Chad?"

He stopped whimpering and opened his eyes. They were red and swollen. "Amy," he breathed. "I knew you'd come."

"I love what you've done with the room," she said.

"God, how I've missed your sense of humor. I love the room. I know you did it to make me feel better – like making lemons out of lemonade." He smiled and patted the bed beside him with his good hand.

Ignoring the gesture, Amy picked up his other hand and checked the bandage.

Chad said, "Will you still love me now that I have a freakish hand?"

"It's a Mickey Mouse hand now," Amy said. "Cartoon characters only ever have three fingers. You ever notice that?"

Chad tried to smile, then gave up. "Was that supposed to make me feel better?"

Amy slid into doctor mode. "The surgeon did a great job. He says you should regain most of your mobility. Do you have any feeling?"

"I feel your love for me." He gazed at her with unfocused eyes. Amy realized he was completely and utterly looped.

"I meant do you have any tactile sensations in your finger," she said.

He made a clumsy grab for her. "Come here, I want to kiss you. I want to marry you. Amy, oh my beautiful Amy." He rolled toward her with outstretched arms. Amy took a step back and Chad wobbled on the edge of the bed. He teetered and then he tottered, caught in limbo between the safety of the bed and the danger of the hard floor. Instinctively, Amy reached out to save him from falling. But she was too late. Chad tottered too far, and fell, taking her down with him. She hit the floor first, cushioning his fall.

Lying prone of top of her, he looked into her eyes and said, "You little vixen. You couldn't even wait until I was released from the hospital."

"I think I'm getting sick," Amy said. This position

and Chad's breath in her face brought back some very unpleasant memories.

"I knew you wanted me," Chad said, nuzzling her neck.

"Get off of me." Amy struggled but she couldn't budge him.

Amy heard the door swing open. "Help me," she muttered.

Jeremy's face appeared over Chad's shoulder. "Whoa, get a room, you two."

"Hey, buddy," Chad said. "I told you I'd get the girl."

"Jeremy, please, get him off me," Amy said, still struggling to free herself.

"What happened?" Jeremy dead lifted Chad to his feet. Chad staggered and then went limp as a noodle. A very big noodle. Jeremy pushed him onto the bed.

Amy said, "He fell out of the bed. I tried to catch him."

"Next time just yell 'timber' and get out of the way," Jeremy said.

Chad grabbed Jeremy's hand, saying, "I love her, man. She's my everything. I love her so friggin' much. I love her hair. I love her eyes. I love her breasts."

"Whoaaaa there, big boy," Jeremy said, interrupting him before he could add any more parts to the list. "You're talking about my roommate, Dude."

"How much morphine did they give him?" Amy inquired.

Chad's head bounced to Amy. He smiled in surprise that she was still in the room. "Marry me, Amy. Marry me." He looked back to Jeremy, saying, "Be my best dude at our wedding?"

"Sure thing. I'm so there for you." Jeremy put the bed rails up. "It's beddie-bye time, Dude."

Amy leaned over the rail and took Chad by the chin.

She waited until his eyes focused, then said, "I can't marry you. I can't be with you. I can't be your girlfriend and I can't date you. I came in here to tell you that. Understand?"

"You're so funny," Chad said. "I love your sense of humor." Then he closed his eyes with a big smile still on his face.

Amy sighed and turned to Jeremy. "What am I going to do? Nothing works."

"He won't remember any of this," Jeremy said. "You'll have to try when he's not so medicated." He opened the door just as Jordan was opening the door. They collided, bouncing off each other.

"We have to stop running into each other like this," Jeremy said.

Jordan laughed. "Sorry. I was looking for Amy. A couple of twin nurses said she was in here."

"Ah, she's right here."

Amy stepped forward. "Jordan! Hi!"

"I love you! You're my little love button," the reawakened Chad yelled at her back.

Amy laughed nervously and pushed Jordan out of the room before she could get a good look at Chad, saying, "Don't pay any attention to that patient. He's so drugged up he doesn't know what he's saying."

As the three of them stepped into the hall, Chad yelled, "Don't leave. That woman is a Jezebel. She's a lesbian. She's a Lezebel!"

Jeremy quickly shut the door. He laughed and flapped his hand in Chad's direction. "Homeless dude. Crazy. Loco." He twirled his finger in little circles beside his temple. "Cuckoo."

"I'll say," Jordan said. She smiled at Amy, "So, I just dropped by to see if you want to do lunch?"

"Sure," Amy said.

Jordan looked at Jeremy. "You know, Jeremy, I'd

like it if you'd come too. I haven't really met any of Amy's friends yet."

Amy and Jeremy exchanged a look. Jeremy clasped his hands under his chin. "I promise to be good," he said, making puppy dog eyes.

Amy laughed. "Okay, but you're buying."

Jeremy rubbed his palms together. "Deal. But if I'm buying, we're going to this new place I've been scoping out."

"What's it called?" Jordan asked.

"P.C.'s," Jeremy said.

"Never heard of it," Jordan said.

"It stands for politically correct. It claims to have the smallest carbon footprint of any restaurant in the world. It's a gas." He paused then added, "Not literally a gas, you understand."

Amy looked uncertain. Jeremy and Jordan each took one of Amy's hands, and in unison said, "C'mon, it'll be fun."

## Zombie at the Restaurant

P.C.'s turned out to be housed in what was once a car dealership. The entire front of the restaurant was glass and there was plenty of parking. This was a bonus in a city with parking issues. Amy wondered if that wasn't the big draw to the place. They'd taken Jeremy's Buick Le Sabre, inherited from his grandmother. They'd popped Jordan's bike in the humongous trunk.

"I mean I love this car but I can hardly park it anywhere," Jeremy said, sighing with relief as they parked easily. "One of the bonuses of this restaurant. Miles and miles of parking. Who knew?"

"Yeah, but is the food any good?" Amy asked.

"We'll soon find out," Jeremy said. They all got out of the car. Jeremy lovingly patted the hood of the Buick.

Jordan said, "There are a lot of cars. The food must be pretty decent."

"There are a lot of BIG cars. Doesn't that sort of defeat the purpose? An organic restaurant that attracts gas guzzlers because it has a huge parking lot," Amy replied, as they walked to the restaurant which seemed to be a half a mile away from where they were parked.

"Not necessarily. If the food is all sustainable and does positive things for the environment then the carbon footprint with the car thing brings it to the level of a Burger King," Jordan said, as they passed into the slide glass doors. "It's kind of a wash."

"I like how you think," Jeremy said.

Jordan thought that the inside was exactly how you would expect a used car dealership turned restaurant to look – all chrome, glass and plastic. Jordan took one look at the booths and chairs and joked, "You know how many naugahydes had to die to make this place?"

Amy giggled and put her hand over her mouth like a little kid in church. Diners stopped chewing and scowled at them.

Jordan marveled about how everybody in the whole place was so solemn. Obviously, being P.C. was serious business. She set her face to serious mode and scowled back at the patrons. Amy giggled again, then snorted behind her hand.

"Sorry," Amy said. "That happens sometimes when I laugh."

"No snorting allowed," Jordan said. "Didn't you see the sign?"

Amy snorted again. Jeremy moved several feet away, trying to appear as if he didn't know them.

A hostess rustled up to Jeremy. She was wearing a plastic mini-dress that crinkled when she moved.

"Can we have one of those big booths?" Jeremy asked. "In the back? Far away from other diners?"

"Of course." The hostess grabbed three menus and said, "Follow me."

"With pleasure," Jeremy said, following her swinging hips and barely managing to keep his eyeballs in their sockets.

The hostess showed them to an oversized booth – the kind where seventeen people could sit comfortably and still have elbowroom. As Jordan scooted in, Amy asked the hostess, "What sort of a car dealership was this place?"

"Hummer," the hostess said. "The owners, Labia International, wanted to take the worst possible place and transform it." When she said the word transform, she waved her arms up and down her body in an imitation of Vanna White.

Amy said, "Excuse me. Did you just say Labia?"

"Yes. It's an acronym. It stands for Lesbians Against Brutality In Animals," the hostess explained.

"So then, this is a vegetarian restaurant?" Jordan

asked.

"Oh no," the hostess said. "Dead animal flesh is served as tasty entrees, but during the animal's life it is given a name and treated as part of a family. All our meat has died a natural death. The animal has not been brutally killed for its flesh to be devoured by consumers. Its life was not cut short during its prime, but it was allowed to live to a ripe old age."

"I see," Jordan said. "So, if I order a hamburger, it comes from a really old cow who died of old age."

"That's correct. Today's bovine was Sonja. She lived her life with the Johannson's of eastern Nebraska. She loved hay and sunny days and standing in the pond."

"I'll have a salad," Amy said.

"Would you care to hear the bio of our chicken, Florence?"

"No, thank you. But I do have one more question," Jordan said. "Is that a plarn dress you're wearing?"

"It is. Do you like it?" the hostess asked, evidently very impressed that Jordan knew what plarn was. "I crocheted it myself."

"I love it," Jordan said. Actually, she didn't love it at all. She thought it looked scratchy. And how would you clean it? You could wash it, but wouldn't it melt if you put it in the dryer? And if you hung it out to dry, there was the possibility of it molding. Jordan thought she would stick to cotton.

The hostess stuck her ample chest under Jeremy's nose. "Wanna touch it? It's softer than you'd think."

Jeremy was more than happy to oblige. He ran his palms up and down her front. Bliss was written all over his face. Amy stuck out a tentative finger to touch next. Jordan laughed and swatted Amy's hand away.

Jeremy was in complete and total lust. "Do you want to go out sometime?" he asked.

"Love to. Here's my card." The hostess pulled a

business card out of her plunging plarn neckline. It appeared to be made out of ordinary card stock.

How very un-P.C., Jordan thought.

The hostess rustled her way back to the front. "Wow, this place truly rocks," Jeremy said, studying his newly and unexpectedly given phone number.

"What is plarn exactly?" Amy asked.

"It's plastic bags cut into strips, knotted together into one long string and then crocheted or knitted together to form whatever you want," Jordan said.

"Do you have any plarn clothing?" Amy asked.

"No, nor do I intend on getting any," Jordan replied. "It's too loud for my taste. Just like those wind pants people wear. You can hear them coming a mile away."

Jeremy was checking out his silverware, which appeared to be fashioned out of cut up tin cans wrapped with duct taped handles. "How very dystopian," he said.

Jordan examined her fork. "It's like something Tina Turner would use in the Thunderdome."

"My mother would love this place," Amy said. "She upcycled before upcycled was even a word. How did you know about all that plarn stuff?"

"I downloaded this video from Norway. It was a knitting show where you watched people knit for nine hours. It was called Slow T.V. and it's a big hit with the Norwegians. They have other videos where you watch a fire being built and burn for twelve hours, a constipated dog doing circles for commercial breaks which are five minutes long, a three hundred and seventy eight hour documentary of looking out a train window. You get the idea," Jordan said.

Dumfounded, Jeremy and Amy stared at her until Amy asked the million-dollar question: "Why?"

"I don't think there is a reason. It just is. When I get stuck writing I watch these videos because they are so incredibly boring that it inspires me to do something. I watch for as long as I can stand it. Then I can work again because nothing I do can be as dull as that. I haven't had to watch since you came along. You truly are my muse."

Amy blushed.

Jordan turned to Jeremy and said, "You do realize that a woman who hands out business cards for dates might be a bit on the odd side, right?"

He nodded. "It says here she also sells Herbal Life supplements."

"I'd stay away from that if I were you," Jordan said.

"You'll have really icky stools," Amy added. "Remember when Veronica and Valerie got into that stuff?"

"Oh, yeah," Jeremy said. "It was like a full-on biohazard hit the place."

"The housekeeping staff threatened to go on strike if the twins continued to drop stink bombs," Amy said.

"The maintenance department was right behind them. Remember they kept clogging up the toilets," Jeremy added.

"I can't believe you're small-talking about stools. Is that what doctors do?" Jordan said.

The waitress, tall, blond and stacked, appeared at their table. She was wearing a maxi-dress made out of potato chip bags. "What can I get you to drink?"

"Are those potato chip bags?" Jordan asked.

"Yes, this dress is made from snack sized chip bags," the waitress said proudly. "My entire wardrobe is made from my neighbor's trash."

"Hmmm. If I did that with my neighbor's trash I'd be wearing a Budweiser can suit with Spam can earrings," Jordan said.

Amy laughed. "I'd be dressed in Lean Cuisine."

Jeremy got in on the joke. "If my neighbor orders one more pizza, I'll have a car."

The waitress frowned. "Are you making fun of

me?"

"Noooo," all three said at once.

The waitress seemed satisfied with that answer. She pulled out her order pad. "What can I get you to drink?"

"What is there?" Amy asked.

The waitress pointed to the menu with her pen. "The drinks are on the back."

Jordan flipped over her menu and studied the drink list.

Jeremy ordered first, citing the first thing on the list. "I'll have Horchata with lime."

"What is that?" Jordan asked.

"I don't know but it's fun to say," Jeremy said.

"What's this Tofurky?" Jordan asked.

The waitress said, "It's thanksgiving in a bottle. It smells and tastes like turkey and gravy, but it's really meatless. Made out of tofu."

"Liquid turkey and gravy," Jordan mused. "No, thanks. I'll have this Chari-tea instead."

Amy asked, "What's the Real Eel?"

"Just what it says," the waitress said.

"Okay, I'll have a Lemon-Aid."

"Good choice." The waitress and her potato bag dress crinkled away.

"If the drinks were that difficult, how is figuring out what to eat going to be?" Amy said.

"Good question," Jordan said. She pointed at the menu, "Do you want to split the deer penis appetizer? I've heard it's good for the libido."

Quicker than Samantha Stephens could wiggle her nose there was a flash of white and Petronella was sitting in their booth. "Stay away from anything with squirrel in the name," she said.

"Petronella? How did you… Where did you…" Jordan stammered. "What are you doing here?"

"I am here celebrating with Irma," Petronella said. She gestured to the other side of the room. Irma, sitting at a table, had a big smile on her face. She waved. Jordan limply waved back.

"What are you celebrating?" Amy asked cheerfully.

"Our anniversary," Petronella said.

Jordan said, "Your what?"

Petronella smiled. "We have been together for nineteen hours. We are deliciously happy. We are in love."

Jeremy piped in, "Sex is a mood enhancer. It raises your serotonin levels and causes you to think you're in love."

Petronella glared at him. "Men," she scoffed. "They know nothing of the heart. Only the penis."

"I beg your pardon. My penis is quite romantic," Jeremy said.

"As I was saying," Petronella said to Jordan, throwing Jeremy one last scalding look, "I want to thank you for introducing me to Irma. She is amazing. She has helped me realize my potential as a woman, a feminist, a poet, a teacher and now as a performance artist. She has made me realize how extraordinary I am."

"I had no idea that you didn't realize you were extraordinary," Jordan said.

"I didn't know my full potential until I was drowning in paint, on the edge of a nervous breakdown. Then along came Irma," Petronella said. She actually had glistening eyes.

Jordan handed her a napkin. Petronella dabbed at her happy tears.

"All this in only nineteen hours?" Amy said.

Jordan explained, "Nineteen hours in lesbian time is like three years in normal time. They've probably already moved in together."

Petronella nodded. "We adopted a kitten this

morning."

"Holy shit," Amy said.

"You don't like kittens?" Petronella said, aghast.

"It's not that. It's him." Amy pointed to the entrance just as Chad stumbled through the front door. "I have to hide before he sees me." Amy slipped under the table and hid in the first place she could find – under Petronella's skirt.

"Oh!" Petronella said.

"Sorry," Amy said, burrowing further between Petronella's thighs. "Pretend I'm not here."

Petronella giggled.

"Since when did you become a giggler?" Jordan said.

Chad lurched up to their table. He was wearing only his hospital gown, which was flapping open in the back. His hand was bandaged and tubes were sticking out of both arms. His hair was standing on end and he had a glazed, feral look in his eyes.

"Where is she? Where have you taken her?" Chad pointed a finger at Jeremy. Then he realized his bandage didn't allow for pointing. He lifted his other hand and pointed that finger. "Tell me what you've done with my Amy," he threatened.

"Dude, I don't know what you're talking about," Jeremy said. "You shouldn't be here. Your finger can't take the stress."

Chad leaned over the table and waved his bandaged hand around. "You know where she is!" Jordan, Petronella and Jeremy had to bob and weave to keep from getting bitch-slapped. Chad leaned closer, pushing his nose into Jordan's face. He slurred, "She's mine. Where have you taken her, you, you, Lezebel? I've warned you. Stay away from her. She's mine." He straightened up and thumped his chest like Tarzan, yelling, "Mine, mine, mine!"

## More Than a Kiss

"Who is this madman?" Petronella said, patting Amy's head to reassure her.

The waitress in the crinkly dress flew over with a man dressed in an Astroturf three-piece suit.

"Sir, you can't be in here," Astroturf said. He pulled Chad by the arm, trying to guide him toward the door.

Chad stumbled and jerked his arm away. "And why the hell not?" Chad spit. "I'm a customer. Customers are always right."

"You don't have any pants on and we have very firm rules about that," Astroturf said.

"She isn't wearing pants," Chad said, pointing at the waitress.

"Yes, sir, but her dress is covering her butt. Your dress, sir, does not," Astroturf said.

Chad looked over his left shoulder in an attempt to see his own butt. He spun in circles like a dog chasing his own tail. The spinning made him dizzy and he was flung out of his own orbit and onto the next table. Dishes and silverware and chairs clattered and crashed to the floor. Chad toppled on top of two diners and they all fell to the floor in one giant heap.

Jeremy said, "I think we should leave. Now."

"I agree," Petronella said.

"But how are we going to get Amy out of here without her being seen by him?" Jordan whispered conspiratorially.

"Yeah. How?" came Amy's muffled response.

"Under my skirt," Petronella said. "Amy, stay as low as you can, hold on to my thighs and walk with me. You two," she nodded to Jeremy and Jordan, "walk with me also. And act natural."

They began a slow, plodding march to the door. Petronella walked with her back arched, her legs splayed far apart and her skirt billowing out in front of her where

Amy's head bobbed up and down with each step. Jordan and Jeremy held on to Petronella's elbows steadying her.

"Make way," Jeremy said. "She's having her baby."

"Good cover," Jordan whispered. She said louder, "Watch out. Pregnant lady coming through."

More crashing sounded behind them as Chad got up and pinged off tables and diners like a pinball.

The waitress opened the front door for them. "Oh, I am so sorry about this. Please do come back when we don't have a Zombie on the premises," she said.

Amy laughed from under the skirt. Petronella thunked Amy on the head.

The waitress looked at Petronella's baby bump. "Did your baby just laugh?"

Petronella smiled and said, "My baby is very advanced."

At that moment, Petronella's white Mercedes skidded to a stop right in front of them. Irma smiled from behind the wheel. Jeremy opened the back door and Amy and Petronella jumped inside. No sooner had Petronella pulled her door shut than Irma mashed her foot to the gas and the car squealed out of the parking lot.

Jordan and Jeremy were left staring after the disappearing car.

After a heart-thudding turn onto the main road, Amy poked her head out from under Petronella's skirt. She crawled into the seat and peered out the back window. "But what about the others?" she said.

"No worries." Irma drove with one hand and dialed a cell phone with the other. After a moment, Irma said, "Agent Jordan, this is Black Bishop and Ice Queen. We have your package."

After a brief pause, Irma said, "Black Bishop will take care of package. Your mission, should you choose to accept it, is to lead Madman in Dress on wild chase of goose."

Another pause then, "Black Bishop signing off. Over and out."

Amy stared wide-eyed at Irma. "Who are you?"

Irma winked at Amy in the rearview mirror. "Irma is Black Bishop, a sleeper agent for Mother Russia. Do not worry. You are in good hands."

Petronella stared adoringly at Irma. She whispered to Amy out the side of her mouth, "Isn't she thrilling?"

## Martini Time

Amy sat in a chaise lounge with a wet towel draped over her forehead. She felt damaged, seriously damaged – like she might need some therapy time damaged.

"I am so sorry that happened to you," Jordan said as Amy's head screamed in pain. "No one should ever be subjected to that. The CIA should be informed of that torture method. It could crack any terrorist inside of thirty minutes."

They were out in the backyard of Jordan's house. Jordan had made Amy sit in the lawn furniture outside rather than risk letting her see the inside of the unfinished house.

After being rescued from P.C.'s, Petronella had taken Amy to her house and locked her in the study. She then proceeded to read aloud every poem she had ever written. Irma was overjoyed. Amy, not so much. Three hours later, Irma delivered Amy back to Jordan's house. Amy, her thirst for poetry forever sated, vowed to never go near another poem. Dr. Seuss included.

"Why didn't you just grab the key and run?" Edison said, bringing Amy a lemon-lime martini. Amy had never had a martini. She'd never had the need for a stiff drink until now. Of course, she'd never been locked in a room with an egomaniacal poet either.

Amy pulled the cold compress from her forehead, sipped her martini, and put the cold compress back on her head. "Because Petronella had put the key in her underpants for safekeeping. You also might be interested to know, her panties have kittens and puppies on them. I spent some time under her skirt, remember," Amy said.

"When did Petronella start wearing skirts?" Edison said.

"A better question is: when did she start wearing

underwear," Jordan said.

"Let me explain because I know all about it," Amy said, sitting up and taking another sip of the martini. It was starting to help. "She said skirts address her more feminine nature and she is practicing wearing them so she can whip them off during the performance to reveal her vinyl pant suit."

Edison and Jordan let that soak in.

"And," Amy continued, "The puppies and kittens remind her that it's okay to be weak and vulnerable. It's all a part of the cycle of life. Or something like that."

"Were her teeth still blue?" Edison asked.

"They did have a bluish tinge to them, now that you mention it," Amy said with an involuntary shiver.

Jordan took a sip of Amy's martini. She didn't normally drink martinis, but it was dawning on her that Amy was at her house, well, sitting in the backyard, and this wasn't how she'd imagined Amy seeing her house for the first time. She'd wanted the house to be finished and ready to showcase, not in this state of disrepair. She was afraid that Amy would equate the chaos of the house with the inside of Jordan. She wouldn't be far off either, Jordan mused as she drained the martini.

"Edison, maybe you should make Amy another martini," Jordan said handing over the empty glass.

"I'll make you one, too."

"I don't drink martinis," Jordan said.

"Okaaaaay," Edison said, tromping back up to the house.

Jordan's stomach rumbled. She was starving and had to eat soon. Maybe she could fix Amy dinner and light some candles and Amy wouldn't be able to see what the house looked like in the candlelight. It might even be romantic.

Edison returned with two martinis. She handed them both to Amy. "Just in case you need another one."

She cocked her head in Jordan's direction.

"Thank you. I'm feeling a little better. I think the vodka is making the buzzing noise in my head go away," Amy said.

Edison sat in a nearby lawn chair. Jordan looked at Edison and tried to communicate something with her eyes. Edison shook her head like she didn't understand. Jordan used her head to gesture toward the house. Edison raised her eyebrows in a questioning expression. Amy watched the entire exchange.

"What are you two doing?" Amy asked.

Jordan stuttered, "Uh… Oh, Edison, aren't you going to be late?"

"Late?" Edison said. "For what?"

"You know… that thing."

"Thing?"

"Yes, that *thing*," Jordan said forcefully. "That thing you do every week at this exact same time."

Finally, it dawned on Edison that Jordan wanted her to leave. "Oh! *That* thing." Edison rose to her feet. "I better hurry. Bye, Amy."

"Are you sure you have to rush off?" Amy said.

"Well," Edison wavered, starting to sit back down. "I could maybe stay for…"

Jordan quickly interrupted, "No, you can't stay, you have to go. You know how they get when you're late."

Edison hopped back up. "Right. They get really…"

"Mad," Jordan filled in.

"Sad," Edison said at the same time.

"I mean sad," Jordan said.

"Mad," Edison said at the same time. "Sad *and* mad." As an afterthought, she threw in, "And glad."

"Please don't rhyme anymore. I've had all the rhyming I can take for one day," Amy said while massaging her temples.

Edison laughed nervously and took several steps backwards. "So, goodbye!" She turned and trotted off toward the house, leaving Jordan and Amy alone.

Jordan chuckled and said, "Edison is brilliant, but sometimes a little dense."

"You really care for her, though," Amy said. "And she cares for you."

"Yeah," Jordan said. "I'm pretty lucky to have her for a friend."

"Jeremy and Isabel are the closest friends I've ever had. Med school was so competitive that it was dangerous to get too close to anybody." She sipped her martini.

"How about at work?" Jordan said. She sipped Amy's other martini.

"We're all friendly, but not friends, you know? There's still some climbing to do if you want to be head of a department or position yourself to get into a cushy clinic. So people don't let each other get too close."

"Are you still climbing?" Jordan wasn't sure how Amy felt about her career. What if having a girlfriend jeopardized her plans?

Amy responded, "The only other place I would consider working is Urgent Care. I like hands-on. I'm not interested in becoming the next director of Human Services and Surgery. I leave that to people like Chad. Even Jeremy just wants to help people. That's why we can be friends. He wants to eventually go overseas and do that Third World thing. I couldn't take the food."

Jordan's smile widened. She leaned in and kissed Amy lightly on the lips. "So having a girlfriend isn't going to mess up your life plan?"

"No, silly."

Jordan made her monumental decision. If Amy was willing to share her life with Jordan then a remodeled house that was stuck in the nightmare stage shouldn't stop her. "Would you like to come inside? If you promise to ignore the shambles of remodeling, I promise to not blindfold you. I can make us something to eat."

At the mention of eating, Amy's stomach growled loudly. She giggled. "I think that was a definite yes."

"Okay," Jordan said, draining the last of the martini. "Just remember the house is a work in progress."

"Aren't we all," Amy said.

## Pizza Sauce

Once inside the house Amy was truly awed. The grand central staircase, albeit, in need of refinishing, spoke of women in long, flowing dresses descending to be embraced in their lovers' arms only to be carried back up the stairs in a fit of unbridled passion. The stained glass windows on the first landing were still intact and the light that filtered through made the front hall look enchanting.

"This is the most beautiful home I've ever seen," Amy said reverently.

"That's the living room," Jordan said and pointed in its general direction. "Dining room is over there," she pointed again. "The second floor has four bedrooms. One is Irma's unless she's moved into Petronella's already. And the other is Edison's. Two unoccupied. The third floor is Edison's laboratory and we won't talk about that and the attic is my studio with a bed. Someday, I'll have a master suite."

"I'm only going to let you get away with cutting the tour short because I'm starving," Amy said.

"The kitchen is this way," Jordan said.

The once grand kitchen looked like a post-earthquake scene from a 1970's disaster movie. Amy half-expected Charlton Heston to jump out of the pantry, with a torn and blood splattered shirt, and yell, "Ladies first!" while tossing them out of the burning building.

Amy looked at the bright side. "It's like starting out with a clean slate. This kitchen can become anything you desire."

Jordan liked Amy's optimism. "The stove still functions. We just have to keep to simple fare. I thought we'd have pizza. Of course, pizza isn't the only thing I can cook, you know," Jordan said, opening a box and taking out a frozen pepperoni pizza.

Amy was amazed that Jordan could find her way to the stove much less use it. The cabinets were on the floor, the counters were nothing but makeshift plywood on sawhorses and the stove was shoehorned half inside the pantry, making fully opening its door an impossibility. No wonder she was only cooking a pizza, it was the only thing she could slide in the oven. And even to accomplish that she had to hold the pizza vertically and insert it like a coin into a vending machine.

"Oh?" Amy said. "Are you a good cook? Because I have to be honest, I'm horrible. I even burn Ramen noodles."

"Frozen pizza is my specialty," Jordan said, wiping her hands on a dishrag. "But hot dogs are my culinary masterpiece."

Amy laughed.

Jordan said with an ultra-solemn expression, "I'm serious, why are you laughing? I can make hot dogs dozens of ways. Boiled, baked, fried, charred, sliced, diced, on a stick, deep-fried, battered..."

"Okay, okay, I get the picture."

"I'm like the Forrest Gump of hot dogs."

Amy said, "I wasn't laughing at your culinary skills. I'm laughing at your nose."

"My nose?"

Amy hooked one finger into the collar of Jordan's shirt and tugged her closer. "Uh huh. You have a tiny bit of pizza sauce on the end of your nose."

"Are you flirting with me?" Jordan said, tugging Amy's hips closer to her own.

"No," Amy said. "This is flirting with you." She stood on her toes and lightly kissed Jordan. The kiss heated up and Jordan pressed into Amy, backing her into the fridge, which was sitting in the middle of the floor.

"Oomph," Amy said, conking her head against the fridge.

Jordan laughed.

Amy rubbed the back of her head. "Oh, you think it's funny?" she asked.

"I'm not laughing at that," Jordan said. "I'm laughing because now *you* have pizza sauce on the tip of your nose."

Amy chuckled and reached up to wipe it off, but Jordan caught her hand. "Let me get it." She kissed the end of Amy's nose, stepped back and licked her lips. "Hmm, I think it needs more garlic."

Amy stepped in to kiss Jordan again, but tripped over a stack of pots and pans on the floor. The pans crashed against the wall and Amy stumbled backwards into the far wall. She laughed, brushed herself off and took one step toward Jordan. She slipped on a cooking sheet, which acted like a skateboard, and sent her hurtling into Jordan's arms.

Jordan laughed. "Maybe we ought to sit down. It's safer that way."

"Ya think?" Amy said. She looked around the floor for any banana peels. She didn't think she could live down another trip to the emergency room. "Who keeps their cookware on the floor?"

"People without functioning cabinets," Jordan said.

Jordan found two chairs stacked behind the cabinets and placed them in the middle of the room facing each other. Amy sat as Jordan peeked into the stove and pronounced, "Won't be long now. It's almost done."

Jordan sat in the other chair and pulled her little rubber ball out of her pocket and squeezed it.

Amy said, "You've been practicing?"

Jordan nodded. "I can almost squeeze it the whole way now. And it's a good stress reliever, too."

Amy looked closer at the ball. She pointed at a blob of paint on the side of it. "What's that?"

Jordan smiled and held the ball up for Amy to see.

"Edison painted a nipple on it. She thought it might inspire me to squeeze it."

Amy laughed. "She's very creative."

"To say the least. Now if she'd just learn to finish a project." Mr. Pip came by and rubbed on Jordan's leg. She scratched his butt and he purred loudly.

"Can I ask you a question?" Amy said.

"Sure."

"How can you tell the difference between a friend and a girlfriend?"

"Well," Jordan replied, "If I squeeze their boob and it feels like squeezing this rubber ball, then I know they're just a friend."

Amy laughed.

"I call it the titty test."

"I suppose this is the part where I'm supposed to let you squeeze mine?"

"Well, if you insist," Jordan said. She leaned forward in her chair and kissed Amy. As the kiss deepened, Jordan slipped to her knees between Amy's legs. Amy wrapped her arms around Jordan and placed her hands under the back of her shirt.

Jordan let go of the rubber ball and it bounced across the floor. Neither one noticed.

Jordan moved her lips to Amy's neck, nibbling down her shoulder.

Amy shivered.

"You okay?" Jordan whispered in her ear.

"Better than okay," Amy said.

Amy wrapped her fingers around Jordan's neck and pulled her lips to hers. She sucked on Jordan's bottom lip and felt her body responding to Jordan in a way she had never experienced before. It was like her body had a mind of its own.

Jordan nibbled Amy's neck. "You have a little sauce on your neck," she said, nibbling down further and further.

Amy shivered.

"Whoops, there's some on your collarbone, too."

Amy moaned as Jordan licked and bit her collarbone.

Jordan breathed, "Wait. There's more sauce. Let me get it." She lifted Amy's shirt and nipped and licked, opening her bra clasp, and letting her mouth and tongue roam over the softness of her breasts. She teased a nipple with her tongue and when Amy moaned, she sucked the hard nipple into her mouth.

Amy wrapped her legs around Jordan's waist and arched her back. She felt as if every nerve, every fiber of her being was on fire.

"There's a fire," somebody said.

"There sure is," Amy mumbled.

"Fire!" the voice screamed.

Amy's eyes popped open. Fire? Where?

Edison stood in the doorway with the yellow titty ball in her hand. She was staring at the cloud of black smoke rolling out of the stove. "The oven is on fire!"

Jordan jumped to her feet just as tiny blue and orange flames shot out of the burners on top of the stove. Mr. Pip howled, arched his back, hissed and leapt up on the top of the cabinets. Jordan danced from foot to foot and flapped her arms, saying "Fire, fire, fire, fire." At first Amy thought she was trying to shoo away the smoke, but then she realized Jordan was over-excited and hopping around because she didn't know what to do.

At that moment, the smoke alarm went off. The shrill sound made talking an impossibility. Edison ran toward the stove, grabbed a hot pad off the top of the fridge, put it on and tried to open the oven door. She could only open the door a couple of inches. Thick black smoke billowed out. Edison coughed and waved the hot pad in front of her face.

Amy pulled her shirt down, ran to the stove and turned it off.

Jordan hopped to the sink and turned the cold water on full blast. She pulled the spray nozzle out and aimed it across the room at the burning stove. The water arced high in the air and came down directly on top of Edison's head.

Edison yelped, dropped the oven mitt and dove away from the stream of water, still hacking from the smoke.

Jordan threw down the nozzle and kneeled before one of the cabinets. She opened one of the doors and looked inside. She was yelling, but Amy couldn't hear what she was saying over the alarm. Jordan threw open another cabinet door and tossed boxes and cans out into the middle of the room. She opened the third cabinet, rummaged around inside and pulled out a fire extinguisher.

Jordan ran toward the stove, aimed the fire extinguisher nozzle in front of her. She slipped on the hot pad Edison had dropped on the floor. Her feet went up in the air and her butt slammed down on the linoleum. The spray of the fire extinguisher shot straight up like a fountain.

Amy ran to help Jordan. She slipped on the white gunk shooting out of the fire extinguisher and crashed to the floor next to Jordan. Edison rolled to her feet, crossed to Jordan and yanked the fire extinguisher out of her hands. She aimed the nozzle at the stove.

Unfortunately, the smoke was so thick she couldn't see where the stove was so she played it safe and sprayed the entire kitchen. The flames disappeared, but black smoke still oozed out of every possible crack of the oven.

Amy got to her feet slowly, slipping and sliding. She turned around in time to see Jordan with a chair raised above her head. She was aiming it at the smoke alarm that was hanging on the wall over the doorway. She whacked at the smoke alarm with the chair's legs. She succeeded in putting three holes in the wall without touching the smoke alarm once.

Amy grabbed the chair out of Jordan's hands. She put the chair on the floor, climbed on the seat and yanked the alarm off the wall. Jordan grabbed the alarm out of her hands and tossed it into the sink.

Edison aimed the sprayer at it and doused it with water. The alarm squealed, squeaked, bleated, belched, then died.

Silence.

Amy coughed.

Jordan threw open the window above the sink.

Edison turned off the water and marched out of the kitchen without saying a word.

"I don't think she's happy," Jordan said.

Amy and Jordan faced each other. They were both smeared with white goop and smelled like burnt pizza.

"Well," Amy said, "That was fun."

"What now?"

"Maybe we should go to my house."

"Do you have any hot dogs?"

Amy smiled. "Better. I have a bathtub."

## Bubble Bath

Half an hour later, Amy and Jordan were in the bathroom at Amy's house. Jordan was naked, in the tub and up to her neck in bubbles. Amy was wrapped in a towel and sitting on the edge of the tub with her back to Jordan. Amy was having second thoughts about this bubble bath idea. Well, her body wasn't having second thoughts. Her body was rip-raring to go. Her brain was worried. Her brain kept saying things like "What if she finds me unattractive? She's seen dozens of women naked, what if she thinks your butt is too big? What if she thinks your boobs are too small? What if you start to make love to her and you're doing it all wrong?"

"Aren't you getting in?" Jordan asked.

"To tell you the truth, I'm a little nervous," Amy said. "I've never done this before."

"You've never taken a bath?" Jordan teased.

"Not with a naked lesbian," Amy said.

Jordan laughed. "Put on your doctor personae. You see naked women all the time, right?"

"I'm not worried about looking at you. I'm scared about you looking at me."

"How about if I promise not to look at you?"

"Can I turn out the lights?"

"Okay. If that's the only way you'll get in the tub with me."

Amy crossed to the light switch and turned it off. The room plunged into darkness. She shyly let her towel drop to the floor. She slipped into the tub, facing Jordan and sighed with contentment as the hot water engulfed her.

"See? Taking a bath with a naked lesbian isn't all that scary, is it?"

"I could get used to it," Amy whispered.

Jordan took Amy's ankles and stretched her legs out

on top of hers. Amy rested the back of her head against the tub and relaxed as Jordan rubbed her feet. She'd never had anybody rub her feet before. It felt wonderful. Funny how Jordan rubbing her foot felt more sexual than Chad putting his hands all over her body. Did that mean she had always been a lesbian and didn't know it? Did it mean she was in love with Jordan? Or was it just lust? And why did she have to ask so many questions all the time? Why couldn't she let go and feel? Just *feel?*

"What're you thinking about?" Jordan asked.

"How good it feels, you rubbing my foot," Amy answered.

"Just wait until I get full use of both my hands."

Amy slid down further into the tub. Jordan switched to rubbing the other foot. "Can I ask you a personal question?" Amy asked.

"Sure."

"Have you been a lesbian your whole life?"

"Not yet."

Amy laughed. "You know what I meant."

Jordan continued, "Yeah, pretty much. I tried to date a boy in high school but it didn't work out."

"Why, what happened?"

"I kept kissing his sister."

Amy laughed. "So me being naked and feeling like making love is all right even if I haven't been a lesbian before?"

"Oh, it's seriously all right. But I have to ask you a question," Jordan said.

"Okay."

Jordan ran her hand up Amy's thigh. Amy shuddered. Jordan said, "That crazy guy at the restaurant. He was the one in the hospital room, right?"

"Yeah," Amy said, not liking where this was leading.

"He's not a homeless man, is he? He knew you."

"Yes. He knows me. His name is Chad Dorring. He's a doctor at the hospital." The water suddenly felt very cold to Amy. She shivered, but this time not in a good way.

"What is he to you? Is he your boyfriend?"

"No," Amy protested. "He's not."

"Because, if he is…" Jordan continued.

"He's not, I promise," Amy said. "I don't want to talk about him anymore, okay?"

There was a lengthy pause then Jordan said, "All right. Now where were we?"

"Right about here, I think." Amy leaned in to kiss Jordan. She ended up with a mouthful of bubbles and sputtered.

"What was that?" Jordan asked.

"I was trying to kiss you."

"Oh. Well, you stuck your face in my armpit."

They laughed. Jordan said, "You sure you don't want a little light? Just a tiny bit?"

"I know what." Amy crawled out of the tub, saying, "Wait right here. I'll go get some candles."

Jordan heard the door click open and closed. She sank back into the warm water and let her thoughts drift. Of course when she took the bridle off, her thoughts roamed toward the physical. She imagined Amy by candlelight. Amy naked. Amy's lips. Amy's lips kissing her. Amy's breasts. Amy's breasts sudsy and wet. Amy's stomach. Amy's thighs.

The door opened. "Cover up, I'm coming in."

"What?" Jordan squeaked.

The woman's voice said, "Sorry, but I can't wait. I just have to pee real quick. I'll be in and out."

Jordan held her breath and hoped this intruder was Amy's roommate. Maybe if she kept quiet she would hurry and pee and go away.

Jordan heard shoes squeak across the bathroom

## More Than a Kiss

floor, the sound of a zipper and then somebody peeing in the toilet. "Sorry, Amy, but I had to go. I don't want to interrupt your Zen bath or anything, but I thought I ought to warn you about something."

This peeing person thought she was Amy! Now Jordan was really at a loss. She didn't know what to do. If she told whoever it was that she wasn't Amy, she would have to explain what she was doing in the tub. And she didn't think Isabel, if it were Isabel, would appreciate a stranger in her bathtub – especially when she had her pants down around her ankles. So, she kept her mouth shut.

The woman continued, "The word is that Chad is going to ask you to marry him. Tonight. He's on his way over. He told Jeremy that he bought you a ring. Jeremy tried to call you, but you're not answering your phone, so he called me. He said it was huge! The ring, I mean. Chad told Jeremy you were playing hard to get. Said you were dating somebody else just to get him to man up and buy a ring. So, he did. Can you believe it?"

No, Jordan could not believe it. But it all made sense. It made sense in an icky kind of way. Amy was playing her just to get this Chad guy.

The toilet flushed. Which was a good thing because it covered the noise of Jordan's heart splintering into about a million fucking pieces.

There was a timid tap at the door and Amy's voice from the other side said, "Jordan? I couldn't find any candles. So get ready, here I come in the flesh and nothing else. Let there be light!"

The overhead light came on.

Amy stood naked in the doorway with a hand on the light switch. Isabel's pants were around her ankles. Jordan was naked in the tub.

They looked at each other.

Amy said to Isabel, "What're you doing in here?"

Isabel said, "Peeing. What're you doing naked?

And if you're over there who is that in the bathtub?"

They looked at Jordan.

Jordan rose, grabbed a towel from the floor and wrapped it around herself. She found her voice and said, "I'll tell you who I am. I'm obviously the other woman. The woman who doesn't know when she's being played for a fool." She headed for the door.

"Wait," Amy said, grabbing a towel and wrapping it around herself, too. "What're you talking about?"

"Game's over," Jordan said. "I'm out of here." She marched out of the bathroom.

Amy stayed glued to the floor, unable to comprehend what just happened. She heard the front door open and close. "What happened?" Amy said to Isabel. "I just went to get candles. What happened?"

Isabel grimaced. "I think I may have accidentally told her Chad was coming over to propose to you."

## Jordan Runs

As soon as she cleared the front door, Jordan sprinted around the side of the house and into the backyard. She was wearing only a towel and wasn't eager for the entire neighborhood to see her business. She cut through the backyard and stumbled down the alley. Less of a chance for somebody to see her and call her the cops. She could just see the headline now: *Children's Author Wearing Birthday Suit Runs from Lesbian Lover.* Or maybe it would be a headline straight from Chad's mouth: *Lezebel!*

"Ouch!" She was way too tender-footed to be running around barefoot. Why hadn't she thought to grab her clothes? Or at least her shoes. She tucked the towel tightly around herself and gritted her teeth against the stabs of gravel in her feet.

"Jordan!"

That was Amy's voice. Oh well, let her yell. Let her scream her fool head off. Jordan didn't care.

That wasn't quite true. She did care. But she didn't want to care. So she was going to pretend not to care in the hopes that eventually she really wouldn't care. That had always worked every other time she had gotten her heart smashed, stomped on and handed back to her.

"Jordan, stop!"

Jordan broke into a run. She ran as fast as she could, given the circumstances. She ran until she couldn't hear Amy's voice calling for her and the only thing in her head was the sound of her own blood pumping hard between her ears. Unfortunately, she couldn't outrun her thoughts. They came at her full force and would not be put off.

Was that all she was to Amy? A way to make her boyfriend jealous? Jordan was her girl-toy until Mister

Man bucked up with a big old fat diamond ring, so he could whisk Amy away to Happily Ever After Land. But why did Amy want to sleep with her? She answered her own question – because straight girls do that sometimes. Lord knows, Jordan had run into more than a few of those in her dating days. There should be a rule: One should not experiment with another's heart. It should be printed on T-shirts and bumper stickers as a reminder.

Jordan darted across a street without looking. A car's headlights blinded her for an instant, and just like the proverbial deer, she blinked and froze. The car screeched its brakes and the driver laid on the horn. Jordan regained her senses and leaped out of the way, but she was too late. The car slammed into her.

Jordan rolled over the hood of the car. She landed on her feet, thank God; nothing seemed broken. There was going to be a big bruise on her hip tomorrow and she had stubbed her toe, but that appeared to be the extent of the damage.

Jordan briefly wondered if she had tried to kill herself. Maybe her subconscious was trying to put her smashed heart out of its misery.

The car door opened. "Jordan, is that you?"

Jordan spun around, expecting to see Amy, actually hoping that it was Amy so she could give her a piece of her mind – so she could scream "Why did you do this thing to my heart? I may be a lesbian but I still have feelings just like everyone else. Can't you see I love you?"

But it wasn't Amy after all.

"Petronella?" Jordan said. "How did you find me?"

"I did not find you, Jordan. I was simply driving my car and you found *me*."

"Are you stalking me?"

"I would've thought after that paint episode you'd finally believe me. I am not stalking nor have I ever stalked you. I am no Kinsey Milhone, but it would appear that the crazy man in the hospital gown is a better stalking candidate than I."

Jordan felt like an overloaded fuse box. But instead of a switch shutting off, sparks flew everywhere and exploded. "I don't care!" Jordan yelled. "You're all the same. You take and take and take, then throw me away! I was nothing to you and I was nothing to her either!"

"Jordan, calm down," Petronella said softly. "You are obviously upset. And wet. And walking the streets with nothing but a towel to cover your nakedness."

Jordan wiped at her eyes. She hiccupped. "Yeah, well, tell me something I don't know."

Petronella said, "Without footwear your feet will be cut and bruised."

"Again, I'm aware of that."

Petronella walked around to the passenger side of her white Mercedes and opened the door. She stood patiently like the footman who escorted Cinderella to the ball. When Jordan didn't move, Petronella asked, "Would you care for a ride?"

Jordan thought about it.

Petronella waited for an answer.

Jordan didn't have to think too long. The decision was an easy one. It was over five miles to her house and she didn't have a phone on her and she was mostly naked.

Jordan shivered. "You'll take me straight home?" She was fearful that Petronella would hog-tie her and read all her poetry for the second time in one day. She didn't think even Petronella was capable of that but who knew?

"Of course," Petronella said with a smile. "Where else would I take you? It is not like you are dressed for an evening at the theatre." She laughed.

Jordan nodded and climbed into the passenger seat. Petronella closed her door and climbed behind the wheel. She turned on the heat, put the car in gear and drove.

Jordan peered through the dark interior of the car at

Petronella's profile. Her every feature was angular and harsh. It was like her face had been cut out of cardstock with an Exacto knife. Had she really found her attractive once? Had she really loved this woman? Or was she simply in love with the idea of Petronella being in love with her? Was that how Amy felt about her – that she loved the idea of having someone hang on her every word, kiss her soft lips, and want to take her to bed? And why was she asking so many questions?

And now Petronella was saving her despite being interrogated and paint-balled. Whoever was in charge of the universe was certainly strange. Petronella pulled her car into the driveway of Jordan's house. She put the car in park, but left the engine running.

Jordan reached for her door handle. "Thank you, Petronella. I owe you one."

"Jordan?" Petronella gripped the steering wheel with both hands and stared straight ahead. She said, "You were wrong. You meant a lot to me. I loved you. I did a lot of things wrong in our relationship. I know that now. But…" She turned to look at Jordan. "I thought you should know that. That you were loved."

Jordan couldn't speak past the lump in her throat. She nodded. She opened the door and got out. She leaned back inside and said. "Sorry for the paint thing. I hope the dentist can whiten your teeth."

Petronella smiled. "Ha, that was one time I should've kept my mouth shut. Goodbye, Jordan."

Jordan shut the door and watched as Petronella drove away. It crossed her mind that Petronella had said goodbye and not good night. She traipsed across the lawn and to the front door. She rang the bell.

Edison opened the door and stared. "Oh my God, what happened to you?"

Edison's voice sounded so caring, so genuine, it was all Jordan needed to burst into tears. Edison pulled her into the house and shut the door. She held her in her arms while she sobbed.

After a few moments, Jordan's sobs quieted to whimpers.

"What happened?" Edison asked as she patted her back and wiped away her tears.

"Everything happened," Jordan said. "Everything."

## The Marriage Proposal

Amy, wrapped in a towel, was sitting on the toilet. She held her head in her hands and made soft little whimpering noises like a seasick chipmunk. Isabel hoisted herself up on the cabinet and stared at Amy.

"Don't stare at me. I can feel you staring."

"Amy, look at me."

Amy peeked between her fingers at Isabel.

Isabel said, "I'm sorry. You have to know I didn't mean to upset Jordan."

"I know, I know," Amy said, burying her face in her hands. "This whole girl thing is so hard. Guys are easier. A lot easier."

"You just think that because you didn't care about the guys."

"Yeah. You're probably right."

Isabel picked at a piece of imaginary lint on her pants and said, "You know, I did it with a girl once."

"You did?" Amy straightened and became all ears. "When? Where? Who?"

Isabel waved her hand like it was nothing. "Oh, back in college. Some softball player had the hots for me. She plied me with peppermint schnapps and we got friendly in my room."

"What was it like?"

"Kinda fun," Isabel said with a shrug. "Except she wanted a relationship and I didn't."

"I want a relationship. With Jordan," Amy said mournfully.

"We can fix it. I can explain to Jordan that you despise Chad and I was only warning you. It's the truth, she has to believe it."

"What if she doesn't? I wasn't exactly forthcoming about Chad when he came to the restaurant. I should have told her he was crazy and that we went out once. Now it looks like I was trying to cover up my relationship with him. That I was using her to get him."

The doorbell rang. Amy and Isabel both looked toward the ding-donging. "That'll be Chad. You want me to get rid of him for you?" Isabel asked.

Amy shook her head. "No. I better do it or he'll never stop. Can you let him in while I get dressed?"

"Sure," Isabel said. She hopped off the counter and was turning to the door when it flew open. There was a loud crunch as the doorknob punched through the wall behind it.

Chad stood in the doorway, snorting like a bull. He pawed the ground with one foot and looked from Amy to Isabel and back to Amy again. He looked psychotic with his eyes rolling around in his head and he was still wearing the filthy hospital gown. His hair was even more rat's-nest-y and there was a pungent odor surrounding him.

"What are you doing?" Amy finally asked, wrapping her towel around her tighter. She felt at a distinct disadvantage standing naked with only a towel separating herself and her dignity.

"Where is she?" Chad snorted, looking around wildly.

"What?" Amy asked. "Who?" she also asked even though she was pretty sure she knew who he was talking about.

Isabel put her hands on her hips and lifted her chin in the air. "Do you mind? We were having a private conversation and then you just burst in and break the wall? Why the hell did you ring the doorbell if you're just going to barge in anyway?"

"Do *you* mind?" Chad echoed her like they were grade school again. "I would like to have a private conversation with my fiancée. And I rang the doorbell because it was the polite thing to do."

"Fiancee?" Amy said.

"Can you give us a moment, please?" Chad said.

Isabel looked to Amy. Amy nodded.

Isabel poked one finger into Chad's chest and said, "One minute and that's it. I got my eye on you, Bub. You mess with Amy and I'll go Sweeny Todd all over your ass."

"Sweeney Todd?" Chad asked. He lurched and slurred. "Who's she? Another lesbo?"

Isabel continued, "You so much as look at her cross-eyed and Chad will be the other white meat."

"What's that mean?" he said, backing into the hallway.

Isabel squinted in her most menacing manner and poked him a few more times, saying, "Chad. It's what's for dinner."

"Huh?" he said, more confused than ever. He put his hand on the doorframe to steady himself.

Isabel backed down the hallway, pointing two fingers to her eyes then pointing the two fingers at Chad in the universal "I'm watching you" signal.

Chad stumbled back into the bathroom. Amy took a step back and tightened the towel around her body again.

Chad dramatically dropped to one knee and bowed his head as if he were waiting to be knighted by a king. He lifted one hand into the air. There was a diamond ring glittering in the palm of his hand. He looked up at her from under his eyebrows and smiled.

Amy almost laughed at the absurdity of it all. "How on earth did you get that? In your condition, I wouldn't think anyone would sell you a diamond."

"I've had it. I bought it a long time ago so I'd be ready when the girl of my dreams came along. Besides it was marked down during a going out of business sale. See, I'm fish-oily responsible too."

"Fish-Oily?"

"Fiscally. I meant fiscally." Chad blinked away

actual, honest-to-God tears. "Will you marry me?" he whispered. "Will you become Mrs. Chad Dorring?"

Amy stared wide-eyed. Her brain simply wasn't processing this turn of events.

"I've wanted you all along, you know," he said. "And I can tell you want me, too. No matter what they're saying about you."

"Who? What're they saying?" she asked.

"That you're a dyke. But don't worry. I told everyone you weren't."

Amy stared at Chad's face. That shit-eating grin. That simple dimple. That toothy smile that blinged even brighter than the diamond ring in his outstretched palm. Something deep inside her broke open. She had never been too great at math, but she could add two and two. The stalker was Chad. It finally made sense. Jordan's stalker was Chad, not Petronella. How stupid could she be? "How stupid do you think I am?" she said.

Chad blinked. "Excuse me?"

"You slashed Jordan's bike tires. You put Bible signs in her yard. You put poop on her porch and lit it on fire. You come into my house, uninvited, and make green goopy stuff and get your finger snapped off by a lobster. You interrupt a perfectly romantic evening between me and my date. And all you can say is 'marry me?'"

"I love you?" he said more like a question.

"You don't know the meaning of love. You have never loved anybody but yourself, Chad Dorring. And I think you are a despicable pile of dog doody and I wouldn't stomp you out if you were on fire. Now move out of my way."

Chad rose to his feet and stretched out both of his arms, blocking the doorway. "You're not going after her."

"Get out of my way."

Chad stood his ground. He cleared his throat then said, "It's either me or her."

Amy couldn't believe her ears. Was this sicko really offering her a Sophie's Choice moment? Without further delay, Amy said simply, "Her."

"You'll regret saying that," Chad sputtered.

A tiny drop of Chad's spittle hit her in the face. She wiped it away with the back of her hand. Amy had a notoriously long fuse. But once it blew, it was worse than an atom bomb. She wadded up her fist and did something she had wanted to do ever since she first laid eyes on Chad. She socked him right square in the butt-chin.

Chad's eyes rolled back in his head and he slumped to the floor. Amy stepped over his body and ran for the front door.

## Amy Runs

Amy ran out the front door, thinking about the movie *The Graduate*. She felt like she was Dustin Hoffman's character, Benjamin Braddock. Not the Benjamin that slept with an older woman at the beginning of the movie. She felt like the Benjamin that ran after Elaine and pounded on the glass at the church and grabbed the bride and rode off into the sunset by bus at the end of the movie. However, Benjamin had been wearing shoes. He had on pants. All Amy had on was a towel. She only ran as far as the corner when she stopped. She turned and began to limp back home.

A car pulled up alongside her. Great, Amy thought, just frickin' frackin' great. This was exactly what she didn't need. She kept her eyes straight ahead. She didn't want to give the driver any more ideas.

"Hop in," the driver said.

Amy looked over at the car. Isabel was behind the wheel of her Jeep, motioning for her to get in.

"What're you doing?" Amy said.

"Are we going to go get the woman you love or not?"

Amy smiled and hopped in the car. Isabel gestured to a gym bag in the back seat. "My workout clothes are in that bag. They're clean. Put them on."

"Thank you," Amy said. "I'll name my first born after you."

"I hope it's not a boy," Isabel said, "Or he'll get beat up a lot at school."

Amy opened the gym bag and pulled on a pair of baggy gray sweatpants and a T-shirt. Isabel threw the car into D, saying, "Let's do this thing." She peeled off down the street.

Amy looked out the back window. "You're not

going to believe this," she said, "but Chad is running after us."

"This whole thing about you being with a woman has sent him into hyper-drive," Isabel said.

Isabel took the next corner without slowing down, leaving Chad standing in the middle of the street waving the wedding ring up in the air. It caught the light from the street lamp and flashed. He resembled a deranged Statue of Liberty.

As they drove across town, Amy got cold feet. "What am I going to say to Jordan? I mean we almost had sex and then my not-boyfriend comes over and proposes to me. Think how that must look to her."

Isabel snapped her fingers like she just had an "eureka" idea. "I know! You'll tell her the truth."

"What, that I got drunk and slept with him once and now he's got this idea in his head that we're going to get married."

"Don't forget the banana peel part," Isabel added.

"Thanks for reminding me," Amy said, plucking Isabel's phone out of her purse.

"What are you doing?" Isabel said.

"I should try and call her first. Maybe she doesn't want to see me yet."

"You're not chickening out are you?"

"No, I'm evaluating. I need to know what I'm up against. I mean how would you feel if this just happened to you?"

Isabel considered it. "Well, I'd be pretty mad because I'd feel like I'd been played."

"It looks like that doesn't it?"

Isabel raised her eyebrows. "Kinda," she admitted.

"So I don't think going over there while she's angry is such a good idea."

"Okay, I think you're right on this one. You should call her and see what the temperature is."

Amy poised one finger over the phone's keypad. "If she asks me to explain, what do I say?"

"Duh. That Chad is a stalking madman and you're not getting married."

Amy took a deep breath and called. It went right to voice mail like she knew it would. She hung up.

"Text her instead. She won't be able to *not* look at it," Isabel said. "It's a scientific fact."

"Okay. But what do I say?"

"That Chad is a stalking madman and you're not getting married."

Amy quickly typed that in.

Only five seconds passed before she got a return text. It read, "Fuck you."

"I think she's mad."

"Ya think? Ask if you can see her," Isabel said.

"We need to talk. Can I see you?" Amy typed.

The return, "Still fuck you."

"This isn't good," Amy said.

"What now?"

"Take me to her house. Benjamin didn't get Elaine by giving up."

"Who's Benjamin? Who's Elaine?"

"Can't you drive any faster?"

Isabel laughed gleefully and put the pedal to the metal.

## Blue Amy II

Isabel and Amy pulled up in front of Jordan's house a mere two minutes and seventeen seconds later. The entire house was dark. That meant Jordan was either gone, asleep, sitting in the dark, or pretending to be gone or asleep. "She's gone," Amy said with a groan. "She must have sensed I was on my way and left."

"Nah, I bet she's in there hiding from you," Isabel said. "That's what I'd do." She opened the car door, got out, and peeked back inside at Amy. "C'mon, let's go pound on the door until she gets sick of us and opens it."

"You're going with me?"

"Of course. Jordan has her homies, you're going to need yours."

"What do you mean?" Amy said.

"You need a back-up. I'll be your muscle."

Amy figured her cause was already lost if all the muscle she could round up came in the form of Isabel. Knowing she didn't have anything else to lose, she got out of the car and followed Isabel.

Isabel marched up to the front door on the balls of her toes like a professional wrestler who was ready to throw the competition in a headlock. In direct contrast, Amy slunk to the front door like a dog with its tail tucked between its legs.

Isabel pressed the doorbell. It played the first few notes of the "Banana Boat Song." It made her think of that scene in *Beetlejuice* where the people at the dining table danced and sang the "Banana Boat Song." That scene never failed to make her laugh. Amy suddenly realized she was smiling. She quickly replaced the smile with a frown. What would Jordan think if she opened the door and saw her with a big smile on her face?

The door opened. It wasn't Jordan. It was Edison.

"Hi, Edison, it's me," Amy said in a little voice.

Edison frowned at Isabel, then looked disapprovingly at Amy. "You have some nerve."

"Where is Jordan?" Amy asked. "I need to see her."

"She is at an undisclosed location that is not in this house," Edison said, as if she were repeating what she'd been told. "And she doesn't want to see you."

"It's not what you think, Edison, I swear," Amy said.

"It's really not," Isabel said.

"Who's the cute chick?" Edison asked Amy. "You not satisfied with humiliating Jordan with a guy? You have to rub her nose in another woman?"

"Rubbing her nose in another woman" brought up all kinds of images Amy didn't want in her head at the moment, but she thought it prudent not to remark on the poor choice of words. "This is Isabel. She's my muscle," Amy replied.

"You really think I'm cute?" Isabel asked, batting her eyes.

Amy didn't realize women still batted their eyes. She had thought that move went out the same time as the word 'coquette.'

Edison looked her up and down. "Another time, another place, maybe. You sure don't look like anybody's muscle."

"I could surprise you," Isabel said.

"Oh yeah?" Edison cocked an eyebrow at Isabel. "Give me your best shot."

Amy couldn't tell if they were flirting with each other or getting ready to beat each other up. She also didn't know which scenario she preferred. "Can we get back to my dilemma, please?"

Edison tore her eyes away from Isabel and looked at Amy.

"Thank you," Amy said. She summoned up her inner Bette Davis and said, "I am now going to come in your house. I am going to search the entire house. I am going to find Jordan and tell her my side of the story. This is going to happen with or without your consent. So you might as well step aside and make this easy on yourself."

Edison squinted one eye at Amy. "You really mean it, don't you?"

"I do."

Edison opened the door wider and gestured for them to enter. "Then be my guest."

Ten minutes later, Amy had searched every room in the house except Jordan's study. She saved that room for last. She walked in and turned on the light. What she saw froze her to the spot. Isabel bumped into her back.

"Whoa," Isabel said, looking at the far wall. "Is that what I think it is?"

Amy was stunned. There was a huge, blue portrait of her face painted on the wall. She was no expert on art, true, but even she had to admit that what the portrait lacked in variety of color, it made up for in feeling.

"It's me," Amy said.

Edison entered the room and looked at the painting. "She painted that the day you stitched her up. She had it bad for you, right from the start. I tried to tell her that you would end up hurting her. It's the first time I ever wished I was wrong."

Amy turned to Edison. "I didn't mean to hurt her. It wasn't even my fault."

"Yeah, right. Next thing you're going to tell me you were the victim in all this?"

"That's right," Isabel said forcefully, stepping toe to toe with Edison. "Why don't you hear what she has to say before you go making judgments?"

Edison opened her mouth to say something, then thought better of it and closed her mouth. She looked at the wall, studying Amy's blue likeness. "Okay. I'll hear what she has to say." She stepped around Isabel and looked at Amy. "Tell me your side of the story."

"That man is... his name is Chad. He's a doctor at the hospital. Chad is... living in Chad-World. We went out once," Amy said. "Only once."

Edison put her hands on her hips and said, "Why do I get the feeling there's more to the story?"

Amy sighed. She might as well come clean. "There is more." She sat down on the couch and said, "I got really drunk. I had sex with him. He threw the condom on the floor. I got up to go to the bathroom, slipped on it and knocked myself unconscious. He took me to the emergency room and to save face I told them I slipped on a banana peel. It turned into this big joke at the hospital. They all called me Banana Amy. I've hated Chad ever since. However, my hatred has turned into a personal challenge for him. He won't leave me alone."

Edison broke into loud guffaws. She slapped her leg and chortled, "Banana Amy? For real?"

It wasn't the reaction Amy had expected at all. Appalled and disgusted, yes. Laughing and mirthful, no.

Edison dropped onto the couch beside her, wheezing from laughter. "A banana peel? That's the best you could come up with?" She laughed herself out while Amy and Isabel only stared at her. Finally, Edison collected herself and wiped her eyes with the corner of her T-shirt. "Okay, well, so how did you end up being engaged to the guy?"

"Are you sure I can't talk to Jordan? This is so embarrassing. I don't want to do it twice," Amy said.

"Really and truly, she's not here. Irma whisked her off to some KGB safe house so she could get away from you and get her head screwed back on straight. Tell me the rest of the story."

Amy told her about the romantic pizza lunch, the

lobster, the stalking, everything."

"Really, he had his finger bit off by a lobster?" Edison said.

Amy and Isabel nodded their heads in unison.

"You expect Jordan to believe all that?" Edison said.

Isabel said, "It's the truth!"

Amy buried her face in her hands, hiccupped three times then began to sob. Isabel pulled her into her arms, held her tightly and patted her back like she was burping a baby. "There, there," she cooed. Isabel shot Edison a look that said, "Now look what you've done."

Amy blubbered through her tears and Isabel's bosom, "Chad's a creep and I hate him. And now the love of my life thinks I'm a liar and a philanderer."

"Philanderer wasn't the exact word she used," Edison said.

Amy sobbed louder.

"Do something," Isabel mouthed silently to Edison.

"Okay, okay," Edison said, rising to her feet and pacing. "We can fix this."

"We can?" Amy whined, looking over Isabel's shoulder. "How?"

Edison stopped pacing, ran her thumbnail along her lower lip and looked thoughtful. "We need to do some reconnaissance. Are you up for it?"

"Like in a spy movie?" Isabel asked excitedly.

"Exactly," Edison said.

"Like in a *James Bond* spy movie?" Isabel asked with her eyes glowing brighter.

"Exactly like that," Edison said. "I get to be James Bond, of course."

"And I'll be Pussy Galore," Isabel said, jumping to her feet.

Amy dried her tears and looked from one woman to the other. There was something happening between Edison and Isabel that much was evident. It was like an electrical charge was shooting from their eyes and fingertips to the other's eyes and fingertips. Well, okay, that sounded too science-fiction-y. It was more like an unseen magnetic force was pulling them toward each other.

Amy definitely felt like the third wheel in their James Bond movie. "Who do I get to be?" she said softly.

"Oh, you're Mrs. Moneypenny," Isabel said.

Amy frowned. She had hoped she would get to be Octopussy.

"What are we going to recon?" Isabel asked Edison.

"Our suspect. Chad, of course. If we can find proof of Amy's story, we'll present it to Jordan and she'll have to believe her." Edison rubbed her palms together. It was obvious she lived for moments such as these. "Come up to my lab. I need to gather up my gear and you all need some black clothes."

"We're going on a spy mission, we're going on a spy mission," Isabel chanted in a singsong voice, skipping out the door behind Edison.

"Some muscle you are," Amy muttered under her breath. She slowly followed behind them, shaking her head. She'd never seen Isabel quite so animated. Is that what love looked like? If so, it was pretty ridiculous.

## The Corndog

Edison led Amy and Isabel up to her lab on the third floor. As they entered the space, Amy knew why Jordan hadn't wanted her to see it. It was a mélange of every science fiction movie she had ever seen – makeshift tables, tubes, wires, computer motherboards, tools, and diagrams taped to the walls. There was even a rolling chalkboard with algorithms scrawled all over it. It was, without a doubt, the lair of a mad scientist.

"Watch where you walk," Edison advised, high-stepping over one of several electrical cords snaking across the floor.

"What is this place?" Isabel asked, obviously impressed.

"My lab. I'm an inventor, you know. That's why they call me Edison."

"What's your real name?" Isabel asked.

Edison stopped rummaging through boxes and looked at her. "You'll laugh."

"No, I won't."

Edison said softly, "Alma."

"Hmmm…" Isabel intoned. "Edison fits you better."

"I know, right." Edison turned and went back to rummaging.

Amy took that opportunity to swat Isabel in the arm. Isabel mouthed silently, "Why'd you do that?" Amy mouthed back, "Are you flirting with her?" Isabel shrugged and mouthed, "What's it to you?" Amy rolled her eyes.

"Now where did I put those binoculars?" Edison asked herself.

Isabel picked her way around the room, staring at objects, tilting her head this way and that, oohing and ahhing. Suddenly, she stopped, her mouth dropped open and she pointed a finger at a set of cylindrical objects displayed on a shelf. "Is that a Corndog?" she gasped.

Edison turned. "Sure is," she said proudly.

"Oh my God," Isabel intoned. She took her time looking at the rest of the objects. "And that's a Plunger! And a Muffin Mucker!"

"I invented those," Edison said, puffing out her chest.

"You're kidding me," Isabel said. She was obviously in awe. Or maybe in lust. Either way, her face was red and her breath came in excited pants.

Amy interrupted, "Are those what I think they are?"

Isabel nodded. "They're only the best dildos in the entire history of dildos."

"Wow," Amy said because she wasn't sure how a person was supposed to respond to such news. "The only time I've ever seen a dildo up close and personal was when I interned in the emergency room and had to remove it from a man's anal cavity when his sphincter muscles seized up."

"How'd you get it out?" Edison asked, ever curious about such things.

"I tickled him," Amy said. "He laughed and it shot out his butt."

"Genius," Edison said.

"Thank you."

"Okay," Edison said, clapping her hands in a "let's get back to work" manner. She looked at Amy, "What kind of building does Chad live in? Is it a house, apartment, condo? Is it on the first floor or second floor and does it have an alley or parking lot or both?"

"He lives in second story apartment building and there's a small parking lot and an alley. I think."

"You think?"

"I was drunk and then unconscious, remember?"

"Okay," Edison said. She pulled stuff out and tossed it on the bed, saying, "I'll need this and this and this..."

"What can I do?" Isabel asked.

"Go look in those tubs over there and find some black clothes that fit the both of you. I have all sizes and there should be a spray bottle of Febreeze to freshen them up a bit," Edison said, as she rooted around in one of the plastic bins located on a shelving unit filled with tons of other plastic bins.

Amy and Isabel dug through the tubs. Amy felt like her mother dumpster diving. Maybe this was how she got her start.

The tubs held not only black clothing but theatrical props as well. There were beards and hats and sunglasses and a Sarah Palin mask that scared her so bad when she pulled it out that she almost screamed.

They found a black cape for Amy and a black hoodie and commando pants for Isabel. Amy tried on the cape, spinning and whooshing it through the air. It made her feel like Lord Byron going on a romantic mission to clear her name and reclaim her lover. And when she held it over her head it made her feel invisible like Harry Potter when he was in sneaky-pants mode.

Edison popped up from her desk with a remote control helicopter to which she was attaching what appeared to be a set of binoculars with duct tape.

"What is that?" Amy said.

"It's my remote recording binoculars with aerial capabilities."

"That's what I thought it was," Isabel said smugly.

Amy rolled her eyes at Isabel. Does flirting have no limits? "I don't get it," Amy said. "Are you going to fly the toy helicopter to spy on him like through a window or something?"

"Bingo!" Edison said. "And if that doesn't work we

can always break in."

"What!" Amy said, recoiling.

"Only as a last resort," Edison assured her.

"I don't really understand what we're looking for," Amy said.

"We want to know how Chad ticks. He's got psycho-stalker written all over him. Let's check out his digs and see what we can find. We get some proof that he's a wacko and Jordan will believe your story. Because without any proof she's still going to think you played her no matter what you say," Edison said.

Amy groaned. She knew Edison was right.

"Okay, put your big girl panties on and let's get a move on," Edison said.

They loaded the helicopter with its attached binocular load and a scope thing and a box of sci-fi whatnots, as Amy thought of them, and an enormous toolbox into Edison's VW bug. Amy rode in the back seat because Isabel had called shotgun. "Why don't we put some of this in the trunk?" Amy asked as she sat on something hard, rubbery and pokey. It turned out that sitting on it wasn't near as much fun as it sounded.

"Trunk's full."

Amy figured as much.

"Okay what's his address?" Edison said.

Amy wasn't exactly sure. "I know it was on the corner of Pine Street and another tree name street."

Edison and Isabel stared at her like she was a hopeless excuse for a spy. Which of course, she was. Amy shrugged apologetically. "All trees look alike to me."

Edison harrumphed and then pulled out a super small computer looking thing. "What's his full name?"

Amy did know that at least. "Chad Earl Dorring."

Edison and Isabel made yucky faces. Edison plugged the name in and immediately was rewarded with a phone number. Amy didn't know if it was his or not.

"You really don't hang out with this guy do you?" Edison said.

"I already told you that."

"Has he ever called you?"

"About a zillion times."

Edison held out her hand and did the 'gimme' motion. Amy handed over her cell phone.

Edison found his number easily and punched it into her little computer. It beeped back an address on Pine Street.

"I could've just called the hospital and asked one of the twins," Amy said.

"No, we don't want to leave any sort of evidence trail," Edison said. She started the car and burned rubber out of the driveway and onto the street. Isabel looked delighted at Edison's driving technique. They really are soul mates, Amy thought.

♦

## Mission Chad

They pulled up to a two-story apartment house that, according to the mailboxes, contained eight units. Edison pulled into the parking lot where three other cars were parked. "Are any of these cars his?" she asked.

Amy did remember his car but only because he talked about it all the time. He had even named the car like it was his firstborn. He would say, "I took Beemer up to Mt. Hood," or "I took Beemer to the coast," or "I took Beemer downtown but I didn't want to park it anywhere in case it got scratched." Ugh, Amy hated Beemer. She told Edison, "All I know is that it's black and it has the shiny gold hub-cabs. He named it Beemer."

"Ah, well it's not here. And Beemer is slang for a BMW which is a German car and very uber-yuppie and they're called rims not hubcaps," Edison explained. She glanced over at Amy. "When we get this all cleared up I'm going to insist Jordan take you out more. Where have you been living? In a cave?"

"Med school mostly," Amy said.

"It sounds like you were in prison," Edison said. She studied the building. "Do you remember the apartment number?"

Amy looked out the window. "Nope."

"I'll be right back," Edison said, getting out of the car.

"Where are you going?" Isabel asked.

"To read the names on the mail boxes."

"Be careful," Isabel said like she was saying her last goodbye to a soldier headed off to war.

"This will just take a minute and don't play with any of my stuff." She chucked Isabel under the chin and strode away.

Once they were alone, Amy asked the question that

had been burning at her brain for the past half hour. "How did you know all about the Corndog and the Plunger?"

"Hey," Isabel said, shrugging, "Girls just want to have fun."

"You're really into her, aren't you?"

Isabel stared dreamily in Edison's direction. "I can't help it. Just look at her."

Amy looked. All she saw was a girl who could have been the anthropomorphic version of Thelma from *Scooby Doo*. Without the skirt and knee socks. "Different strokes," she thought.

Edison jogged back to the car and got in. "Apartment number six." She pressed a hidden button on the dash. There was a whirring sound as a previously hidden moon roof slowly slid open.

"Ooooh," Isabel intoned like she was watching the Bat Cave open.

"Okay, now had me that scope," Edison said to Amy.

Among the jumble of mechanical items, Amy had no clue what was a scope and what wasn't.

"That long tube looking thing," Edison prompted.

Amy handed it to her. Edison aimed it toward the moon roof and telescoped out until it rose over twenty feet high. She adjusted the swivel head back and forth with knobs until the scope's line of sight was looking directly into Chad's apartment. Peering through the end with one eye squinted, Edison said, "Lights are off. Nobody appears to be home."

Amy resisted saying, "You could've just knocked on the door and found out that much."

Edison reeled in the scope and stored it. "Now for step two."

Edison hopped out of the car, quickly picked up a chunk of broken concrete, took aim and heaved it at the window. Glass shattered inward. Edison jumped back into the car, yelling, "Duck!" They all three crouched down out of sight below the car windows.

"I can't believe you did that," Amy whispered like somebody could overhear. "You committed a crime. That's breaking and entering."

"Technically we haven't entered." Edison said.

"It's only breaking," Isabel said and giggled. Edison giggled along with her.

Edison peeked over the dash. "All clear." She sat up. "Next step."

"There's another step?" Amy said.

"Of course. Why do you think we brought the helicopter?" Edison said.

"You're not serious," Amy said.

"You're going to fly it into Chad's apartment?" Isabel said like an excited little kid.

"Bingo."

That word was beginning to make Amy nervous.

"Is that even possible?" Isabel said.

"With the right equipment and skills it is," Edison said. "And I happen to have plenty of both."

Edison got out of the car, opened the passenger back door and gently extracted the helicopter. She placed it on the hood of the car with its nose pointed toward the apartment building.

Next, Edison got back in the car and pulled a remote control out of her pocket. It looked as innocuous as a PlayStation remote control, except it had a small screen attached to it. Edison punched a big red button on the remote. The helicopter buzzed to life. The blades began to spin, faster and faster, until it lifted into the air. Using a thumb toggle to guide the helicopter and the viewing screen to see where it was going, Edison guided the helicopter to the broken window. It hovered a moment before the window and then easily slipped inside the apartment.

Edison punched another button on the remote and a

red light came on. "We're in and recording," she said.

Amy looked over Edison's shoulder and peered at the screen. "Why does it look green like that?"

"Night vision scope because all the lights are off," Edison answered.

Amy stared at the green screen, but couldn't make out anything other than big dark shapes she took to be furniture. "I can't see much," she said.

"I can enhance it when we get back home. I just need the initial information. Okay, one more loop then we're out of here."

Edison made a last swoop around the apartment and then with the finesse of a heart surgeon maneuvered the helicopter out of the window and landed it back of the roof of the car. The entire procedure took less than five minutes.

"Wow, that was impressive," Isabel said. She leaned back in her seat and fanned her face. She was flushed and a sheen of sweat had formed on her upper lip and forehead. Amy recognized the symptoms. Isabel was either pre-heart attack or post-orgasmic. Amy hoped it was the latter.

Edison quickly stowed the helicopter. When she got back in the car, she leaned over and whispered something in Isabel's ear. Amy would have thought nothing of it except that Isabel nervously looked at Amy then sat stiffly in her seat facing forward.

"What's going on?" Amy said. "What did she whisper to you?

"Oh, you know…" Isabel said. "Sweet nothings."

Edison started the car and backed out of the lot.

"She did not," Amy said. "She saw something in there you're hiding from me."

Neither Isabel nor Edison said a word. "So what did you see?" Amy asked. "Did you see something important, anything that will absolve me in Jordan's eyes?"

Edison drove in silence. Her jaw clenched and unclenched.

Amy wrung her hands. "Edison?" she said, "Did you see something bad? Something you're afraid will upset me?"

"Let's just say I think that Isabel and I should preview the tape first."

"Why?"

"Let's just say there is an unusual theme going on and I'd like Isabel's take on it. Will you trust us to do what's best for you?"

Amy looked out the window. It had started to drizzle and the streetlights looked blurry. Wasn't there a saying, "April showers bring May flowers?" Well, it was almost June. It had no right to be raining. It was like the weather was mocking her dilemma. Feeling blue? I will make it rain for you. She pondered her predicament. "How bad is so bad you don't want me to see it?"

More silence, then, "Will you please let me do it my way?"

Amy started to argue then hesitated. Did she really want to know what a creepy guy Chad was? Did she really want to examine the psyche of a man she'd gone to bed with and find out that he was truly a nut-job? Did love do this to him or was he already crazy? Did love make an otherwise sane person crazy? Maybe she should steer clear of the whole thing? What was she going to do if Jordan did dump her? Was she going to go all wacko-stalker-psycho on her?

They drove in silence. They went through three green lights and still there was more silence. Amy couldn't contain herself any longer. "How bad was it? Bad like there's small animals crucified on his bedposts bad?" Amy asked.

"No. Not that bad," Edison said, brightly.

"That's good to know," Amy said. Of course, a

moment later she realized it was both good and bad. It was good in the sense that Chad hadn't resorted to mutilating and sacrificing small animals. It was bad in the sense that he might not have hit bottom yet. His mutilating days could still be in front of him. "Yippee," Amy thought, tiredly. "Yip-fuckin-eee."

## Shrine Amy

Edison led Amy and Isabel back to the third floor lab. They were very quiet – too quiet, Amy thought. Edison hooked up her video and began to download it to her computer. Amy and Isabel watched quietly. When the download was complete, Edison glanced over at Isabel. "You need to take her to the other room while I work on this."

Amy stood her ground. "No. I have a right to see it. It's about me."

"In a few minutes," Edison said. Isabel took her by the wrist arm and half led, half-dragged her into the next room. "Sit," she said, and pushed her into a tattered Barcalounger complete with cup holder that had been duct-taped to one arm. "Don't move. Try to relax. Okay?"

"Okay."

Isabel patted her on the head and left, shutting the door behind her. Amy sat on tenterhooks. She didn't know what tenterhooks were exactly but they sounded uncomfortable and she certainly was that.

A few moments later, the door squeaked open and she almost jumped out of her skin. She breathed a sigh of relief when she saw it was only Mr. Pip. He lazily looked her over as he sauntered by.

"You started all this. I hope you realize that," Amy said.

Mr. Pip swished his tail and gave her a good look at his ass as he left the room by another door.

"Yeah, yeah, yeah, same to you," Amy said.

Isabel stood in the open doorway. "Who are you talking to?"

"Mr. Pip."

Isabel looked concerned. She spoke in a voice Amy had heard people use on crazy or old people. "Who's Mr.

Pip? Your imaginary friend?"

"No. He's the cat."

Isabel looked around the room. When she didn't see a cat, she smiled and patted Amy on the arm. "Is he an imaginary cat?"

"Don't be silly," Amy said. "He was here. And then he wasn't."

"Like the Cheshire Cat?"

"For God's sake," Amy said, rising and walking toward the door. "I'm going to get a look at this video."

Isabel grabbed Amy's shoulder, stopping her. "I don't think you should see it."

"What is on that thing? What has he done? Is it creepy? Should I be afraid?" Amy felt frantic and sick to her stomach. What were they hiding from her?

Isabel took a deep breath. "He has a lot of pictures of you."

Amy digested this. "That's not so weird."

"And by a lot, I mean hundreds."

"Hundreds of pictures of me?"

Isabel nodded. "Afraid so."

"My mother doesn't even have hundreds of pictures of me." Amy couldn't imagine where he'd gotten the photos. She sucked in her breath. What if he'd taken pictures of her while she was conked out. "Please tell they weren't naked ones."

"No."

"Okay, well then it isn't that bad. I want to see the video."

"Sweetie," Isabel said. "It's kind of creepy. You might want to let it go. The video is more than enough to convince Jordan that Chad is the stalker and that you weren't planning to marry him."

"I want to see it." Amy marched into Edison's lab. She walked straight up to Edison who sat hunched over the computer keyboard and said, "Show me."

Edison looked at Isabel. Isabel nodded, saying, "Show her."

Edison clicked a few keys and the video feed started.

Amy thought she was prepared to see the video. She thought she would see an Amy shrine. Maybe a few photos thumb-tacked to the walls. Nothing could have prepared her to see every wall, every table, every surface completely papered with her face. Wallpaper, pillows, throw blankets were all decorated with collages of her smiling face. It was worse than the Duck Dynasty line of interior decorating.

Once she got her breath back, she said, "How could he have gotten so many pictures of me?" She pointed at a picture that showed her and Jordan getting in her Smart car. "Did he hire someone to watch me?"

"From what I can ascertain these look like they were taken at work functions," Edison said, pointing to a cake in the break room in one of the photos. "And these are more I'm-a-creepy-stalker-following-you pictures."

"He was following me this whole time?"

"Apparently. And here he is taking pics of his handiwork. The signs in the yard. Irma stomping the flaming dog doody. Here're several of Jordan's slashed bike tires. And there's a whole bunch of you two making out."

Isabel put her arm around Amy's shoulder. "We'll put a restraining order on him and send HR at the hospital an anonymous tip with accompanying video. That should get him to leave you alone."

"I don't want him to just leave me alone. I want him gone," Amy said through gritted teeth. She felt violated. Somebody had been watching her in her most private intimate moments. She felt vulnerable and scared. She underscored what she felt with one word. "Gone."

"Understood," Edison said. "Do you think you'll be

safe at home tonight?"

Isabel said, "I texted Jeremy. He said Chad is gone from the premises and he's changing the locks on the doors right now. We'll take turns keeping watch. We'll be safe."

Edison and Isabel talked in hushed tones as they walked to Isabel's car.

Amy was so stunned by what she'd seen that her mind didn't seem able to process everything. She felt as if she were walking upstream against a strong current.

Edison opened Isabel's door for her. Isabel got behind the wheel, started the car and powered down her window.

"I'll see you tomorrow," Edison said.

"I can't wait," Isabel whispered breathlessly.

Amy got in the passenger seat and looked up at the house at Jordan's dark window. "This will all be over with by tomorrow," she said out loud. But even she could hear the doubt in her own voice.

## Elvis Has Left the Building

Amy didn't hear from Jordan the next day. Or the day after that. She had checked her phone for missed calls or texts approximately one hundred and seventy-eight times. She had called Edison at least twenty times each day. Edison reassured her that she was still trying to track Jordan and Irma down. But like Edison said, "If Irma wants to go off the grid, there was no way she'd be found."

Amy was exhausted. Worrying burned up a lot of energy. She barely slept. She worked like she was sleepwalking and drank coffee like a fish. She hadn't seen Chad since he proposed. He was off work until his hand healed. That was the only good news. However, Amy still couldn't help but look over her shoulder all the time. She felt like she was being watched everywhere she went. She even checked the women's restroom for peepholes before she allowed herself to sit on the toilet.

Veronica, twinless at the moment, rapped lightly on Amy's door. Amy looked up and smiled. "Come on in."

Veronica glanced down the hall then back at Amy. "Oh, crap, I'm too late." She jumped inside the office and slammed the door behind her. "Doesn't this thing lock?" she said, fiddling with the door.

"No. I put in a maintenance request but no one has showed up yet."

"Oh, holy hell!" Veronica grabbed a chair and wedged it against the door just under the knob. She tested it. "Hey, that really does work." She appeared surprised and excited that it did.

"What's going on? Why did you lock us in here?"

"I'm not locking us in. I'm locking him out."

"Him? Him?" Amy asked excitedly. "Him as in Chad him?"

"Yes. Chad is here. He's coming," Veronica ran to the window. "We need an exit strategy." She shoved up on the window. It didn't budge.

"Those windows don't open," Amy said. "They're sealed shut in a feeble attempt to lower the suicide rate among doctors."

There was a pounding on the door. Amy looked at the door and back to Veronica. "Shit," she mouthed. "Shit, shit, shit."

Veronica looked around frantically. The doorknob rattled. "Amy. Are you in there?" Chad's voice called. "Let me in, I need to talk to you."

"HR just got through telling him he has to leave you alone. I guess it didn't make an impression," Veronica whispered.

"They got the anonymously sent disc?"

Veronica nodded. "He's been in there talking to them and the hospital administrator, Haroldson. And when the Big H gets involved you know it's serious."

"I can hear you," Chad called out in a singsong voice. Then he pounded on the door with both fists. The chair wobbled from the force of his blows. Veronica steadied the chair, holding it firmly under the doorknob.

Amy wished she'd never seen *The Shining*. This was way too much like the "Here's Johnny" moment. She felt like she was going to throw up.

Chad bellowed, "Damnit Amy, I just want to talk. It's not what you think. It's not what *they* think. This is love. True love! No one understands how much I love you and they're trying to take you away from me." He pounded the door and it shook on its hinges.

Veronica looked up at the ceiling. "I've got it. Get up on the desk."

"Why?"

Veronica snapped her fingers at Amy. "Just do it. Now!"

"Amy! I fucking love you!" Chad screamed.

Amy quickly climbed up on her desk. She could

brush the ceiling with her fingertips, but that was all. Veronica plucked several thick medical volumes from Amy's bookshelves and stacked them on the desk. "Climb up on these."

"Am I going up there?" Amy said, pointing to the ceiling.

"That's right. Push the panel aside. Hoist yourself up. Put the panel back and lay flat on the joist. He'll never know you're there."

"AAAAAAmmmmmmyyyyyy!"

Chad's out-of-control scream sent Amy upwards. She scrambled up and into the ceiling as Chad's voice turned soft and pleading. "Let me in. Amy, please, I love you so much. I understand the mercurial nature of your sexuality and we can work through it. I want us to be together and have little Chaddites and Amyites and live in the suburbs and have barbeques." His fingernails scratched at the door.

Amy slid the panel back into place, disappearing from view.

"Elvis has left the building," Veronica said loudly.

"Elvis? Who's Elvis?" Chad hollered. "Is he vying for Amy's affection?"

Veronica moved the chair. She flattened herself against a wall and said, "Help me, Chad. The door handle is jammed or something."

"What?"

"This is Amy. Use your brute strength to rescue me," Veronica said. "Throw your body against the door! I'm locked in here and suffocating! Help me!"

There was a moment of silence. Then the door burst open and Chad flew into the room, headfirst. He tripped over the chair and sprawled facedown across Amy's desk. Veronica quickly pulled a syringe out of her pocket, took the cap off with her teeth and poked Chad in the butt with the needle.

He went out like a light.

"Okay, Amy, you can come out now," she said.

Amy slid back the panel and dropped down to the edge of the desk, then hopped to the floor. She was covered in a white residue and felt like the Pillsbury Dough boy. She hoped it was dust and not some chemical agent that would deform her children and give her cancer by the ripe old age of forty-five.

Veronica held the syringe like it was a smoking pistol.

Amy gazed at the snoring Chad. "What did you give him?"

"A shot of Propofol with a little Midazolam thrown in. He won't remember a thing."

## Bug, Bug, Who's Got the Bug?

Veronica pulled Chad's cell phone out of his back pocket. His butt muscles twitched reflexively.

"What're you doing?" Amy asked. "You're not going to steal his wallet, are you?"

"I'm just looking at his phone. Aha!" Veronica smiled triumphantly and showed Amy the screen on his phone. "It's a GPS tracking device, see?"

"What's that pulsating red dot?"

"That's you," Veronica said. "He has you bugged so he can follow you."

"Oh my God," Amy breathed. "That's how he always knew where I was."

"We have to find out where he planted the bugs. Then we can turn him loose back into the wild."

Amy shuddered. "Do you think he planted a bug on me, like inside one of my body cavities while I was unconscious from slipping on the, you know?"

Veronica raised an eyebrow. "Eww, I hope not. I'll search a lot of places, but that's not one of them. Let's see your purse, your jacket and anything else that you always carry with you."

Exactly seven minutes later they had found a tiny silver bullet-shaped device in Amy's purse, one in her kit bag and one neatly inserted behind the calendar in her DayTimer. "What on earth is he thinking? I didn't know these things even existed and I'm covered in them," Amy said.

"Come on, there's certainly one in your car," Veronica said. "We need to go check it out."

"What do we do with him?" Amy said, pointing at Chad's twitching buttocks.

"Don't worry about it. He'll be out a while."

They slunk out of her office. Amy didn't know

why they were the ones slinking around. None of this was her fault. Chad was the crazy person. "What exactly do you think is wrong with him?" Amy asked, as they rode the elevator to the parking garage.

"I really don't know. He must have always been a little off his rocker and this thing with you has sent him over the edge. Maybe no one has ever turned him down or maybe it's this girl-on-girl thing you have going on."

"You know about Jordan and me?"

"Honey, most of the hospital knows. All the boys are jealous and all the girls think you have great taste in women."

They exited the elevator and walked directly to Amy's Smart car. "Where do we look?" she asked.

"Usually, in the movies they're hidden under the car because in most cases the perps can't get in the car."

"Perps?"

"The bad guys. You don't watch TV much, do you?"

"Nope." Amy leaned down and looked under her car. It was so low to the ground that it was hard to get a good look at anything. Its low clearance had been a beef with some of the car's reviewers but since Amy was short she hadn't much cared and she didn't go in the mountain wilds so it didn't seem an issue. Unless of course, your crazy-ass-one-night-stand person put trackers everywhere. "I can't see anything. Should I crawl underneath?" She was wearing dark blue scrubs so perhaps parking lot dirt wouldn't show, but then she'd be unsanitary and would have to change anyway.

"I think so," Veronica said. "I'd do it but I might get stuck." She pointed to her breasts.

"We wouldn't want to have to call 911," Amy agreed. "They'd probably think I ran over a large-breasted woman."

Amy laid down flat on her back and looked at the

short space she was supposed to crawl under. She'd heard once that mice could squeeze themselves flat in order to crawl under doors. "Think like a mouse, think like a mouse," she thought as she scooted under the bumper. She managed to jimmy herself under the car, but once under she couldn't see a damn thing. It figured Chad wouldn't just stick it under the doorframe or under the tail pipe, no, he'd go as far under as he could and then the fucker would put it by all the other mechanical stuff. "Crap, I can't tell what's what. I don't want to mess up my car."

"What're you doing here?" she heard Veronica ask.

When Amy turned her head she saw a pair of shoes standing on the other side of the car next to Veronica's shoes. Big shoes. Big men's shoes. She bumped her head. "Ouch! Please, tell me that's not Chad."

"It's not Chad. It's me," Jeremy said. He squatted and peered under the car at her. "Why are you under your car?"

Veronica answered for her. "She's looking for a GPS tracker. Chad had her wired with three others. We're trying to find the one he put on her car."

Amy shimmied back out from under her car. Jeremy extended a hand and helped her to her feet. "Where's Chad now?" he asked

Amy tried to brush herself off, but managed only to smear the oil and dirt around.

"He's in her office," Veronica said. "I had to tranq him. Like how they do when a gorilla escapes from the zoo."

"The dude is seriously going to get fired at this rate," Jeremy said. He walked a circle around the car, looking it over. He kneeled down and peeked under the car. He rose back up, stood perfectly still, closed his eyes and held his palms out toward the car. He looked like he was meditating.

Veronica and Amy exchanged a look. Amy

shrugged.

Jeremy muttered, "If I were a crazy man, where would I put a tracking device?" Suddenly, his eyes popped open. He reached down and ran his fingers behind the license plate. He grinned and pulled out a small silver bullet-shaped tracking device with black electrical tape crisscrossed over it. "Got it! Now, where's his car?" He looked around and spotted The Beemer. "I'll put it on his car and then you can track him."

"Don't we need one of those GPS tracker thingies?" Amy asked.

"I'll download the app to your phone," Jeremy said. "That way he can never sneak up on you again."

"The man is seriously deranged," Veronica said.

Jeremy agreed. "He should be put in a loony bin."

"Great idea!" Veronica said. As Jeremy stuck the tracker under The Beemer's plate, Veronica dialed her phone.

"Hey, Sis," Veronica said into her phone. "Listen, there's a package in Dr. Stewart's office. Can you fill out a 2XC – 49R, put Dr. Jeremy Blevins name on it and give it to Salvatore? He can transport the package to its proper destination. Uh huh. Call me when it's done, okay?" She hung up and grinned at Amy.

"What's a 2XC-49R?" Amy asked.

"It's a Psych Evaluation Request Form," Veronica said. Chad will be in a rubber room before he even wakes up."

"That is totally brilliant. I've got friends over there that will keep an eye on him," Jeremy said.

"Why does that not surprise me?" Veronica said.

Jeremy continued, "They'll take good care of him." He winked.

Veronica looked Jeremy up and down. She must have liked what she saw because she looped one arm through his as they made their way back to the hospital.

"So, tell me, do you like twins?"

"Love them," Jeremy said.

"Well, isn't this your lucky day," Veronica said.

Amy shook her head. It seemed like everyone around her was falling in love. Or at least lust. She dialed her cell phone again. When Edison picked up, she said, "Me again. Have you found her yet?"

## Welcome to Las Vegas

Jordan was jumping up and down on the hotel room bed and chanting, "She loves me! She loves me!" The very expensive pillow top mattress of the MGM Grand had quite the bounce factor. And the louder Jordan yelled, the higher she soared.

Irma had spirited Jordan away from Portland and Amy. Jordan went willingly. What better place to get over a broken heart than the land of showgirls, glittery lights, and cheap buffets? Irma also brought Petronella. It was their honeymoon. They had, after all, been together for one whole week.

Irma and Petronella heard the commotion and ran into Jordan's room from their adjoining room. They got there just in time to see Jordan wave a letter at them and bounce so high that the top of her head came in contact with the spinning blades of the ceiling fan and...

*This part has been censored due to its graphic and bloody nature.*

*Five minutes later:*

"Did you learn nothing from the story of Victor Morrow and the helicopter during the filming of *Twilight Zone: The Movie?*" Petronella said. She was sitting on the bed, holding Jordan in her lap while Irma pressed an expensive hotel bath sheet to Jordan's head in an effort to staunch the bleeding.

"Victor who?" Jordan asked.

"It was a cautionary tale of the eighties," Petronella said.

"Is my head still attached?" Jordan asked.

"Mostly," Petronalla said.

"Will I live? Be truthful."

"Probably," Petronella said. "Do you mind telling us why you were jumping up and down on your bed?"

"I got a letter from Edison. She sent it FedEx," Jordan said, pointing to a bloody, crumpled piece of paper lying on the floor. Irma retrieved the paper and examined it.

"Edison says Amy loves me. And the whole Chad thing was a mistake. He's stalking her. She says there is definitive proof of both things." Jordan sat up, but the movement made her so dizzy that she plopped back down. "We need to go back. I need to go back to Amy," Jordan said in a tangled rush of words. Then she fainted.

Irma pushed Petronella aside. She grabbed Jordan by the neck of her shirt, pulled her into an upright position then slapped her on both cheeks.

Jordan's eyes fluttered open. "Ouch. Why'd you slap me?"

"Do not sleep," Irma said. "Or Irma will slap you again."

Jordan rubbed first one cheek, then the other. "Did you have to hit me so hard?"

"Yes, Irma did it for your own good," Irma said. She turned to Petronella, saying, "Call the room service. Ask them to bring up something that is good for stopping the flow of blood. We must wrap her head and get her to hospital."

"My head hurts," Jordan said. She was seeing two of everything and her speech was slurred. "Did I drink? Am I drunk? Do I have a hangover?"

Petronella picked up the phone and dialed one.

Irma said, "Jordan, you sit here. Irma has to make arrangements. Irma will be right back." She ran into her room.

Unseen by Petronella, Jordan slipped off the bed and to the floor. She crawled over to the mini-fridge. She opened the door and took out all the bottles of booze. "Such bittle lottles," she said. "I need a little dair of the hog," she slurred to herself. She opened one bottle and downed its contents. When she realized she still had a headache, she downed another. And another.

    Meanwhile, Petronella spoke into the phone, "Room service? This is room 629. We need something to staunch blood flow." There was a long pause. "Um... do you have a box of sanitary napkins? You do?! That would be great. Um... Do you have the nighttime ones? Okay, make sure they have wings. And hurry, okay? Goodbye." She hung up and turned around.

    Jordan was sitting before the fridge with a dozen empty little liquor bottles in her lap.

    "What are you doing?" Petronella screamed.

    Jordan looked at her, tried to focus her eyes and grinned. "My hangover is going away." She squinted at Petronella. "Cheers to the both of you!" She held the last bottle before her eyes and said, "Upsy daisy." She downed it.

    "Irma!" Petronella yelled. "We have problem in here!"

## The Garbage Man

Amy yelped into her cell phone, "You did?! She did? You did? She did?" She was so excited she hopped up and down. "Oh, Edison, I love you! I mean, you know, not that way. But I do love you, I do, I do, I do!"

Amy hung up. She was elated that Edison had found Jordan. She didn't care if she was in a hotel in Las Vegas. All that mattered was that Jordan said she was coming home to be with her. She was on her way back.

By the time Amy got to her office, she found Veronica, Valerie, Jeremy and a big, muscled-up man standing around Chad's limp body. Amy studied the muscle man. He had a flat nose that looked like it had been flattened by a snow shovel. He had big ears, shiny black hair and was missing some important teeth. "Who are you?" she asked.

"The less you know, the better," he said in a voice reminiscent of Marlon Brando.

Amy looked alarmed.

"He's the garbage man," Valerie said.

Veronica laughed. "He's here to pick up the garbage."

With that, the muscle man bent, picked up Chad and flipped him over his shoulder like he was nothing more than a bag of flour. He walked off down the hallway whistling the tune to *The Godfather*.

"I thought you were just sending Chad in for a psych evaluation," Amy said.

Veronica and Valerie shrugged simultaneously.

Veronica said, "All I do is fill out the forms. They go out the door…"

"And never come back," Valerie said.

## **Going Home**

"I think you need several stitches," Petronella said, pulling the sanitary napkin away from Jordan's head. Blood leaked out. She quickly replaced the old napkin with a fresh one. "Yes, definitely stitches."

"I have to see Amy. She can fix me up," Jordan slurred.

Irma said, "I have a plane waiting for us. It will take us back to Portland. From there I have a limo waiting. It will get us to the hospital where Amy works."

"Yippee!" Jordan yelled, jumping to her feet. The sudden movement made her woozy. "Oh my," she said. Her eyes rolled back in her head and she flopped onto the bed, unconscious.

Irma grabbed Jordan and threw her over her shoulder. She turned to Petronella. "You will be okay? You will follow us in car?"

Petronella nodded. "I will be back in your arms in no time."

Irma grinned slyly. "Irma loves Petronella."

"And Petronella loves Irma," Petronella said. She grabbed Irma and kissed her passionately.

Jordan's eyes opened. From over Irma's shoulder she said, "Do you two mind? I'm bleeding up here."

## Edison and Isabel

"Oh my God," Isabel moaned. She was sprawled under the covers of Edison's bed with the Corndog in her hands and between her thighs. It had taken them approximately twenty-three hours to go from meeting each other to rolling around in bed. This was not a lesbian record.

"Right there?" Edison asked.

"A little to the left."

Edison was sitting on the edge of the bed with her back to Isabel. She was wearing her camera sunglasses. She held a remote control in her hands. She moved the thumb toggle to the left.

"Oh my God!" Isabel shrieked in ecstasy.

"How's that? Good?" Edison asked.

"Better than good," Isabel panted. "Better than…Oh my God. You're a genius."

Edison beamed.

## Leaving On a Jet Plane

Ten minutes later, Irma and Jordan were sitting in a private jet, flying over the skies of Nevada. Jordan was slumped in her seat with her chin on her chest. Irma slapped her.

"Ow!"

"No sleeping."

"You Russians are mean," Jordan said.

"It is our way," Irma said. "We protect our soft hearts with armor."

"Whatever," Jordan said. "How much longer until I get to see Amy?"

"Not long."

"How did you get this jet on such short notice? Who's is it?"

Irma smiled and shook her head. "The less you know, the better."

Jordan felt the top of her head. It was sticky and oozy. "I think I need to change my sanitary napkin."

Just as Irma predicted, not much later the jet was landing at a private airport on the outskirts of Portland.

Jordan sat up straight in her seat. "How do I look?"

Irma's eyes roamed over Jordan. From the bloody sanitary napkin on her head to the blood spattered shorts she wore. "You look like you need medical attention."

Jordan was delighted. "Perfect, Amy will know that I need her. So, I really look injured then?"

"Yes, you have that sufficiently covered. Now, let's go."

Victor, the big bearded pilot, opened the plane door as soon as the ground crew wheeled the stairs over. "Thank you so much," Jordan said, trying to shake his hand. She missed it several times. It seemed her eye-hand coordination was still off kilter.

He grasped her in a bear hug. "May your love save you. Go in peace," he gave her a hearty pat on the back and Jordan weaved from side to side.

"Victor, can you get her down the stairs?" Irma asked as she poked her head out the door and ascertained the difficulty for someone with impaired motor skills.

"This little twig of a girl? Ha!" He lifted her up and over his shoulder and before Jordan had time to process what had happened she was in the back of another limo. Victor held the door open for Irma.

Irma smiled at him. "Victor, you shouldn't have." She kissed him on both cheeks.

"Victor is here should you ever change sides," he said, kissing her hand.

Irma was all business when she got in the limo. "Take us to University Hospital quickly before she leaks all her fluids out," she told the driver.

He was a thin, reedy looking man. In a deep voice he said, "Yes, comrade."

Jordan watched as the lights of Portland danced across the glass of the limo. She was glad to be home. If she could've hugged the whole city she would have. "My homeland," she whispered, leaning her head against the window. She closed her eyes. She was so happy.

Irma pulled her upright and slapped her. "No sleeping."

"Ow," Jordan muttered.

"We are almost there. How do you feel?" Irma gave her the once over. "Never mind, you look awful. Irma swears on Babushka's grave if you die Irma will haunt you forever."

"But you have to die before you can haunt someone, silly," Jordan said.

"Your little doctor will kill Irma," Irma said. "Irma will be dead."

"Don't worry. Amy will just kill you a little bit."

Irma shook her head and swore under her breath. Jordan didn't know exactly what she said, but it sounded like she said something about a mother and a moose and a compromising position.

The limo pulled into the emergency room entrance at University Hospital. Jordan grabbed Irma's arm. "I only want Amy. No one else. Please."

"Yes, I know. Irma will make sure of that."

## The Happy Ending

Amy sat beside Jordan's bed, holding her hand. Jordan had several tubes in her arms and her head was bandaged so thickly it looked like she was wearing a white turban. After a moment, Jordan's eyes flickered open. She saw Amy and smiled.

"I must be in heaven. There's an angel sitting beside me," she said.

Amy laughed. "Did you just now make that up?"

"Yeah," Jordan said. "Did you like it or was it too corny?"

"A little thick on the syrupy side, but I still liked it."

There was a long pause as they gazed at each other. Jordan was the first to look away.

"I'm sorry," they both said at the same time.

"What?" they both said again at the same time.

They laughed.

"You go first," Jordan said.

"Okay," Amy said. "You have sixteen stitches in your head. You lost quite a bit of blood. I had to shave part of your head, so you'll have a nice bald spot for a while. Other than that, you're in good shape and Chad was a mistake and I should have told you about him but I didn't want to lose you and he was psycho and we don't have to worry about him anymore."

Jordan asked, "My turn?"

Amy nodded and braced herself. She was expecting the worst. She knew she didn't deserve the love of this beautiful and talented woman. Still... she hoped.

Jordan took a deep breath, "I was scared. That's why I ran. The whole Chad thing was an excuse to run. Deep down I knew you loved me and not him."

Amy raised her eyes to Jordan's. They were glistening with happy tears.

Jordan continued, "Remember the last time I was here and you sewed me up?"

"How could I forget?"

"I told you something about how babies survive falling out windows. Remember that?"

Amy nodded. "You said the babies weren't scared. They didn't know fear. So they bounced. It was the bouncing that saved them."

"That's right," Jordan said. "So, I figure I'm going to do the same thing. I'm going to fall and relax and…"

"Bounce," Amy finished for her.

"Yeah," Jordan said. "I'm not going to be scared. I'm going to let myself fall."

Amy reached over to Jordan's nightstand and picked up a book. She held it out to Jordan along with a pen. "Do you mind signing this for me?"

"This is my book," Jordan said. "I mean it's not mine, it's yours obviously, but I wrote it."

"You never finished autographing it," Amy said. "I was hoping you could do that now."

"Gladly." Jordan took the pen and the book. She opened it to the title page and wrote: *Amy, What are you doing the rest of your life? Jordan.*

Amy read it and smiled. "I think I have plans," she said.

"You do?"

"If you'll have me."

Jordan crooked her finger at Amy and motioned for her to draw nearer. Once Amy was close enough, Jordan leaned forward and kissed her.

The sound of applause broke their kiss. Stunned, they looked toward the door. Crowded in the doorway were a smiling Claire and Lillian.

Behind them an old woman plodded down the hallway pushing her IV stand. She stopped and looked into the room to see what they were applauding.

"That's my daughter," Claire said proudly. "She's a lesbian."

"And she's in love," Lillian added.

## The End

If you enjoyed this book, we'd really appreciate it if you'd tell your friends – including those you haven't met – by blogging, posting an online review, or otherwise spreading the word. Thanks!

Layce and Saxon


Sign up for our email list! Be the first to know about new releases, discounts and giveaways!


## About the Authors

Layce Gardner has been writing for over half her life. She has written umpteen plays, a slew of movies and a whole gob of books and short stories.


Saxon Bennett has written fifteen or sixteen or maybe seventeen books (she lost count) and is the winner of a bunch of awards.


Saxon and Layce are happily married. To each other.

You can learn more about the authors by visiting their websites at Laycegardner.com and Saxonbennett.wordpress.com

You can check out Layce's other books at her Amazon author page.

Check out Saxon's books at her Amazon author page.